Also by Lauren Morrill:

Better Than the Best Plan

of a

CH

LO

STO

IT'S
KIND
of a
CHEESY
LOVE
STORY

LAUREN MORRILL

FARRAR, STRAUS, GIROUX
New York

Farrar Straus Giroux Books for Young Readers
An imprint of Macmillan Publishing Group, LLC
120 Broadway, New York, NY 10271

Printed in the United States of America
Designed by Cassie Gonzales
First edition, 2021

10 9 8 7 6 5 4 3 2 1

fiercereads.com

Library of Congress Control Number: 2020910169

ISBN 978-0-374-30621-2

Our books may be purchased in bulk for promotional, educational,
or business use. Please contact your local bookseller or the Macmillan
Corporate and Premium Sales Department at (800) 221-7945
ext. 5442 or by email at MacmillanSpecialMarkets@macmillan.com.

For Jackson Pearce
YOU'RE Hot 'N Crusty

IT'S
KIND
of a
CHEESY
LOVE
STORY

When the moon hits your eye like a big pizza pie
That's . . . a mess

—(not quite) Dean Martin

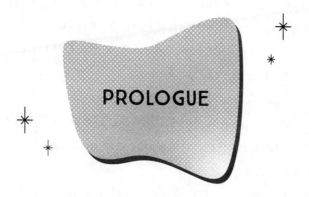

PROLOGUE

I was born on the bathroom floor of Hot 'N Crusty Pizza.

My mother, not realizing that those stomach pains she'd been feeling for the last several hours were, you know, *labor*, decided that she was craving a slice with pineapple and green olives and just *had* to have it. I wish I could blame that abominable combination on pregnancy hormones, but it's still her order to this day.

She made it exactly three steps into the restaurant before she gripped my father's arm like she was on the first hill of a roller coaster and told him that she no longer wanted pizza, she wanted this baby *out*. When my mother tells this story (and she tells it *a lot*), she leaves out the string of colorful expletives she let loose. But when Mom's not there, Dad likes to fill in the gaps.

Anyway, once they realized that their first child was about to come rip roaring into the world in a locally owned pizza parlor, my dad quickly dragged my mother to the bathroom.

"I don't know, it seemed like the place to go when your wife's about to give birth" is all he'll say by way of explanation, even though public restrooms don't exactly scream sterile.

A pimply-faced employee named Jordan was the first person to spring into action, yanking one of the red-and-white-checked tablecloths off a booth and sprinting after my parents, spreading it out on the floor. My mother lay down, and I—along with a metric ton of goo—made my appearance into the world. It all happened very quickly, which is how a teenage pizza cook ended up serving as midwife. The ambulance didn't even arrive for another fifteen minutes, because no one thought to call 911 until I was already screaming from the floor of the accessible stall.

When I finally arrived at the hospital, seven pounds, six ounces and smelling of garlic, there was already a TV camera waiting for me. Apparently, news of the incident had been picked up on a police scanner, so a plucky blond local reporter by the name of Molly Landau had yanked her cameraman into the news van and raced to Brook Park Memorial Hospital.

My parents used to pull out the DVD of the very first news spot at least once a year, but these days we can just search for it on YouTube. In it you can see me all red and squishy and asleep on my mom's chest. Mom is wearing a hospital gown, looking pretty good for someone who just gave birth with no medical professionals in attendance. But I'm clad in a brand-new onesie that reads I'M HOT 'N CRUSTY. Del DiMarco, the owner of the pizza parlor, apparently had a flash of inspiration and raced down to a local print shop to have the thing made. After its TV debut, he started making all his employees wear T-shirts with the phrase emblazoned across the front.

Sorry, guys.

The short spot features my father, mother, and Jordan the pizza midwife describing the miracle of life while standing an arm's length away from an automatic flushing toilet. It became quite the sensation. I was mentioned on national morning talk shows. I was the feel-good story on several cable news channels, breaking up the endless discussion of wars and political scandals. I was even featured in *People* magazine.

Because not only did my story have a happy ending,

Del had also generously gifted me with free pizza for life and a guaranteed job upon my sixteenth birthday. What a lucky girl I was!

It was my first taste of fame.

But unfortunately not my last.

CHAPTER ONE

I'm sitting in front of an extra large pepperoni pizza. There's a flickering tea light in the middle of it floating on a little lake of red grease. I'm supposed to make a wish.

All around me are people singing "Happy Birthday" with varying levels of enthusiasm. To my right is my dad, still wearing his Brook Park Middle School staff polo shirt, warbling away on the high harmonies—a joke he never ceases to find hilarious. On my left is my mom, who is devoting everything she has to maintaining her smile. She's still not over my tenth birthday, when the photographer caught her midsneeze. Del, a barrel-chested white man whose every bodily cell screams "I.

AM. ITALIAN," is standing behind me. His voice is booming like an Italian opera singer's as he leads his staff, a beleaguered and disinterested group of cashiers, busers, and kitchen crew.

Hot 'N Crusty is dark, with deep wood paneling and a chocolate-brown tiled floor that is always sticky, even though I see someone dragging a mop across it almost every night. Faux stained-glass light fixtures swing from chains mounted over each table, casting a crimson glow across the dining room. There are only a few windows, so it feels especially cave-like unless they catch the sun just right. The walls are painted a deep red that makes the whole place look half like a pizza parlor, half like a bordello, and the decor can most closely be described as "Italian Travel Book Vomits on Walls." Curling, yellowed posters of the Leaning Tower of Pisa, the Trevi Fountain, and the Vatican decorate the walls. There's even a signed, framed photo of Pope John Paul II by the bathrooms, but I'm almost positive that the handwriting is Del's. I also sincerely doubt PJP said, "Love the garlic knots!"

The tables are all covered in red-and-white-checked tablecloths that are fraying with age, each old enough to have been the very tablecloth upon which I was born lo these sixteen years ago. But at least I have the comfort of knowing it's definitely not, because that particular tablecloth—or a four-by-four cutting of it, cleaned, *thank god*—is framed on the wall with newspaper and magazine clippings heralding the story of my birth.

That particular collage marks the start of my very own personal hall of fame right there on the wall of Hot 'N Crusty. You know how your parents will frame every one of your school pictures and display them climbing up the wall of their staircase or lined up down their hall? And if you walk past at a brisk enough sprint, or take the stairs three at a time, those photos almost become a flip book animation of your entire life? Yeah, I have that, only instead of school pictures there are fifteen years' worth of photos of me parked in front of a flaming pizza. And it's in public for the whole world to see, which is super great. In some of the early ones, I'm crying, as babies often do. Later on, in elementary school, there's a crowd of class-mates surrounding me. But as I get older and into middle school, the group dwindles. My best friend, Natalie, is in almost all of them, her white blond hair lighting up the images like a halo. You can see my unfortunate experi-ment with bangs in the sixth grade, and my even more unfortunate experiment with winged eyeliner in eighth. My braces appear and disappear, and staff members come and go in the background. But in every one, my smiling parents flank me, and Del gazes down proudly over my shoulder like he's my godfather (a title he was probably lobbying for before discovering my parents aren't at all religious).

I glance up and see Larry across the table, his enormous camera poised and ready for the big moment. He's the only photographer left at our local paper, which now only publishes three times a week and once on Sunday, but he's been there since they published twice a day (as he likes to tell us *a lot*).

The song reaches a crescendo. Larry's about to snap the photo to mark my sixteenth birthday, a photo that will soon join all the rest and run in the Sunday paper. I cross my fingers that between now and then whoever spray-painted blobby penises all over the courthouse downtown strikes again so I can avoid making the front page. I almost wish for it, but at the last second, decide to stick with my original wish, the same one I've made since my thirteenth birthday.

"Happy birthday, dear Beck . . . ," the crowd sings. "Happy birthday to *youuuuuuuuu*."

There's a smatter of anemic applause and a shuffling of feet as the employees start to abandon their posts. My dad whistles and cheers as my mom leans in and whispers, "We love you so much, Beck." I close my eyes tight, lean forward, and just before I blow out that sad little tea light, I send my wish out into the universe.

Next year I want to eat somewhere else.

"I hope you didn't wish for a car," Dad says, reaching for a third slice of pizza.

"Just unfettered access to a sweet 2005 Toyota Corolla with questionable air-conditioning," I reply. I nibble on another piece of the crust, the cheesy part congealing on the plate in front of me.

"Well, whaddya know, wishes do come true!" Dad replies.

"We're going on Saturday morning, right?" I ask. I've been practicing three-point turns and parallel parking for weeks in preparation for my driver's test. I may not be getting a car, but I'm *definitely* getting a license.

"We'll get there right when it opens, so the examiners will still be in good moods," he says. "I was thinking maybe we could bring doughnuts, too. You know, grease the wheel."

"You have that little faith in me?"

"Beck, I love you and think you can do anything you put your mind to," he says, ruffling my hair like he used to when I was little. "But my Toyota still has a streak of yellow paint on it from where you hit the book return box at the library."

"That was months ago," I grumble. I pat my hair into submission, thinking back to one of my first lessons on the open road, when Dad decided we'd return some library books with me at the wheel. I learned a lot that day about how far those side-view mirrors actually stick out. But I haven't hit anything since, unless you count the curb while trying to parallel park (a skill I definitely won't need in suburban Brook Park, home of expansive strip mall parking lots). I wouldn't say I'm an expert driver, but children and stray cats don't need to run from my headlights.

"It's too bad Natalie couldn't make it," Mom says out of nowhere, and I don't say anything, because the truth is I didn't invite her. I knew she had dance class with Tamsin and Cora. And Natalie definitely would have skipped to celebrate with me, but I didn't want it to be a thing with the other girls. We're still sort of a new friend group, along with Tamsin's twin brother and his dude friends. Any chance to avoid reminding them that I'm the Hot 'N Crusty Bathroom Baby is one I'll take. In a small town, it's easy to get pegged with an identity early, and mine started as early as they come. Kids were throwing pizza puns at me on the playground before they even knew what puns *were*. And "Hot 'N Crusty Bathroom Baby" is way too delicious a phrase for kids to ignore. I wish I could say we grew out of it, but no one grows out of anything in a small town. I'll be the bathroom baby for as long as I live here, which hopefully won't be that much longer. I've spent the last few years trying to distance myself from the whole thing, and I've been marginally successful. Sure, it reappears every year on my birthday when the local news revisits the story with the latest birthday photo, but it dies down pretty quickly after that. And in two years I'll be off to college, where I'll be celebrating my birthday by studying in the library or dancing on a table at a frat house. Whatever I'm doing, there will be no pizza involved.

"We're celebrating this weekend," I tell Mom by way of explanation. Tamsin decided last week that she wanted to plan a "birthday extravaganza" (her words) for Saturday night. And I'm more than happy to go along, even though the idea of an "extravaganza" in my honor makes me break out in cold sweats.

"Who'll be there?" I can hear in Mom's voice that she's trying not to pry, but is also absolutely dying to know.

I begin ticking off names on my fingers. "Natalie, Tamsin, Cora, Tamsin's twin brother Colin, Cora's boyfriend Eli, and their friend Mac." I hope my cheeks aren't turning red, because my insides are positively on *fire* at the thought of going anywhere with Mac MacArthur. I still can't believe it's a thing that happens on a regular basis.

"That sounds fun," Mom says, trailing off. The *dot dot dot* is practically floating above her head as she works hard to poke at her salad. She wants to know more, but isn't going to ask. That's what makes her a good mom. But I'm not going to tell her, which is probably what makes me a terrible daughter. I know she's still sort of weirded out that my group of friends has boys in it now, and boys who she doesn't know at that. I know that she hates that I don't tell her everything anymore, but I don't want to talk to her about how I've had an intense crush on Mac for so long that I can't even remember how it feels to like someone else. I don't want to tell her that Tamsin scares me a little, or how worried I am that Natalie is only still my best friend out of habit. I know exactly what she'd say.

The thing is, my mom is great at pep talks. In the pep talk Olympics, she'd win a gold medal every time. If she wrote a book of pep talks, it would be an instant *New York Times* bestseller. She's the *American Idol* of pep talks. And in this case, she'd tell me to be myself and that my real friends will stick by me. She'd tell me that anybody who doesn't get me isn't a real friend. And let's be real, she might also give me another deeply uncomfortable talk about sexual health. But I don't want to hear any of that (especially not another lecture about STDs and condom use, because *ick*). The truth is, *I* don't get me. I don't exactly know who I am, not even a little bit.

And I don't know if my mom has a pep talk for that.

I just know that I like who I am when I'm with Natalie, Tamsin, and Cora. I like hanging out with the guys from the baseball team and going to football games and attempting to follow Tamsin's choreography to whatever song is blasting out of her phone. I want *that* girl to be me, the girl who can potentially get through the day without a barrage of pizza puns.

Mom neatly stacks her plate, silverware, and napkin for the buser. Then she sighs and leans back in her chair. "I can't believe it was sixteen years ago that I walked in here for pizza and walked out with you."

"Actually, I think you were rolled out, dear," Dad says with a wink.

And now comes the family birthday tradition I actually *like*. Because even though my birth story is weird and has branded me for life, it *is* pretty great. Or maybe it's just that my parents are really good at telling it. At this point, the annual recitation on the anniversary of my birth is practically a vaudeville routine. My mom romanticizes it, and Dad chimes in with the more vivid details. They have their lines down pat; I could recite it by heart. There's always plenty of laughing, and in the end I'm reminded how freaking lucky I am to have these two nerds as my parents. It's why I go along with our annual pizza party, with the photos and the newspaper and the wall of shame, the whole bit. It makes them *so* happy. And so I smile for the camera every year, even though on the inside I'm cringing so hard I worry I'll pull a muscle.

As busers clear our plates and Dad counts out cash (dinner may be free, but Dad always tips well), Del appears at the end of our table. He puts his hands on his hips, his feet shoulder distance apart like Superman, and surveys our table with a wide smile that manages to escape from beneath his heavy mustache.

"Another great year for the Brix family, eh?" he asks in his booming voice. He reaches for a stray paper napkin on the floor, shoving it in his pocket. Hot 'N Crusty may be a little, well, hot and crusty, but Del is still fastidious about the place. It's his pride and joy. "Oh, and Beck, I've got some paperwork for you to fill out, so stop by the register on your way out. We can talk about your first day. We're so excited to have you on the team!" He claps his hands like a Little League coach, and then he's gone, scurrying off to help a waitress who's seconds away from dumping an entire tray of soda onto the lap of an elderly diner.

I glance around the table, but my parents are busy stacking the rest of the plates and gathering their things.

"Um, why does he think I'm taking the job?" I ask.

"You're not?" Mom asks.

"No. I'm not," I reply. We had this conversation a few weeks ago, when my parents reminded me of Del's gift. It's a nice offer, but that's all it is . . . an offer. One I have absolutely no plans to take. But my parents are suddenly *very* quiet. Dad keeps rifling through his wallet like he's got a winning lottery ticket in there, and Mom is staring at her phone even though she doesn't have a single fun app on there.

"You *do* need a job, Beck," Dad says as he finally shoves his wallet into his back pocket.

"Yeah, but not *this* job. We talked about this."

"But then you didn't find anything, so when I called to make the reservation for tonight and Del asked if you were still interested . . . ," Mom says, then bites her lower lip. She knows she's screwed up. Mom is usually really good about letting me handle things, but apparently *this* is where she slips up. By telling Del I'll work at Hot 'N Crusty. My worst nightmare.

"You told him *yes*? Without asking me?"

"No. I told him you were still available. But you know how enthusiastic Del can be," Mom says. And boy do I. "I'm sure you can still tell him no."

I don't *want* to tell him no, though. I just want to pretend this isn't a thing at all. Mom's right, Del *is* enthusiastic. And telling him I don't want the job is going to be like sticking a pin in one of those Macy's Parade balloons, watching the air slowly leak out until it's just a pile of bummer wreaking havoc on a major city.

"You can work wherever you want, Beck. But you need a job. And this seems like a pretty good one," Mom says gently, glancing up at my dad. Something tells me *they've* already had this conversation.

"As food service goes, you could do worse. At least you won't be standing in a drive-through or manning a deep-fat fryer," Dad says, taking the opportunity to once again show off the silvery scar on the back of his hand that he got from his teenage tenure at Burger Barn. "I bet Del pays better than the Golden Arches, too."

"You don't have to, of course," Mom adds again. "You can apply for whatever you want. But this is a job with no application, no interview. And you get to wear jeans."

I glance around the restaurant, taking in the employees on shift tonight. I've never paid much attention to them, even though they show up all over my childhood photo albums. They're a mix of sullen high schoolers, some of whom I vaguely recognize from Brook Park High, and some older people who look like they're either about to quit or are resigned to staying here until they die. They *are* all wearing jeans, the only uniform being their ubiquitous red I'M HOT 'N CRUSTY T-shirts and a black ball cap with *HnC* stitched in red. As uniforms go, it could be much worse. And Mom and Dad are right. I *do* need a job. My parents give me a small allowance that has been fine for things like movie tickets or the random dinner out, maybe even the occasional new pair of jeans if I save up and scout the clearance racks.

But they don't bankroll me. They can't. My dad is a middle school social studies teacher who only recently finished paying off his student loans, and my mom has always stayed home. Before I was born, she was a teacher, too. She taught home ec, though I think they called it Family Life Sciences or some other nonsense. She taught cooking, sewing, personal finance, and a bunch of other subjects that are probably a hell of a lot more useful than algebra or trig. But after I was born, she quit. My mom loved teaching, but I'm pretty sure she was always waiting for the position of stay-at-home mom to open up. And when it did, she slid right on over and has been dominating the industry ever since. My mom was always the crafting, baking, story-reading, pretending-playing, home-cooked-meal kind of mom. When I started school, she was room mom and field trip chaperone, and she has done a couple of tours as PTA president.

But as I got older, she had a little less to do, and so instead of slipping into retirement, she started a side hustle as a baker and cake decorator. She's *really* good, but since she works out of our home kitchen, the extra cash it brings in isn't enough for me to keep up with Tamsin's weekend shopping trips. And definitely not enough to cover gas and insurance when I finally get my license.

I for sure need a job. I just didn't want it to be *this* job. I was hoping to get *away* from Hot 'N Crusty, not join its staff. As we shuffle out the door back to Mom's Subaru station wagon, I'm already formulating a plan to find another gig. And I'll have to do it fast, because something tells me my parents are fine with me working wherever, but they won't wait forever.

CHAPTER
TWO

My new driver's license is shiny, the edges sharp. I got it this morning (after which I spent way too much time gloating to Dad that I passed on the first try), so it's hardly spent any time in my wallet. I can't stop staring at it. It feels like a plane ticket to my future. I'm one step closer to being an adult. One step closer to leaving Brook Park. One step closer to never being the Hot 'N Crusty Bathroom Baby again.

"Lemme see that," Tamsin says, taking the white plastic card out of my hand. She peers down at the postage-stamp-sized photo that's obscured by holograms and watermarks and all manner of other anti-fake-ID technology, and wrinkles the milky white skin of her nose. "You should have let me do your makeup before you went to take the test."

"I didn't want to jinx it," I tell her. I take the license back and squint at the photo. I have a zit on my chin, and my hair—usually stick straight—is taking up more real estate in the photo than it probably should. But I kind of like it. You can't see my freckles, and my green eyes pop against the gray backdrop at the DMV.

"You're too superstitious," Tamsin replies, tossing her fiery red hair.

"I think I'm just 'stitious enough," I mumble.

"Can you blame her? We can't all fail as epically as you," Colin says.

"I maintain that *that* was bullshit," Tamsin replies, her voice rising in pitch and volume. Tamsin would sooner die than join the debate team, which is a shame, because I'm pretty sure her righteous indignation would be enough to thoroughly dominate the state tournament. "I had *plenty* of space to make that right on red. That car was nowhere *near* hitting me, and that woman was clearly hangry or undercaffeinated. Or maybe they shouldn't have hired such a nervous passenger to administer the test. It was like driving with my great-grandmother."

"If ever there was a time to drive like your great-grandmother was in the car, I'd think the driver's test would be it, Sis," Colin says with an eye roll. Not like he has room to talk. Sure, he passed his test on the first go, but two weeks later he wrapped his pickup truck around a telephone pole. He walked away with barely a scratch, but Mr. Roy confiscated his license for six months as punishment. He only just recently got it back, along with a brand-new truck he hopefully will not total this time.

Tamsin's "birthday extravaganza" plan turned out to involve an evening at Pearce Lake. It's been a pretty low-key affair for something she dubbed an "extravaganza," but this sort of thing is exactly my speed. Which is comforting, because it means that maybe Tamsin gets me after all. It's still warm for late September, so we ate burgers and dogs that Eli cooked on his dad's Smokey Joe, then waited for the sun to set so the boys could unleash an entire box of fireworks that lasted a good twenty minutes and only nearly burned Colin's eyebrows off twice.

Since then, we've mostly just been hanging out, the doors open on Tamsin's forest green Range Rover, a playlist coming from the speakers. The boys have been getting in a little batting practice with some sticks they found on the lakeshore, sending rocks splashing out into the water. Baseball season doesn't start until February, but they all play fall ball for a regional traveling team. Which means year-round they're perpetually batting with whatever found objects are lying around, like an athletic tic. If the boys are in the vicinity of something they can use as a bat, you've got to be prepared to duck or risk getting beaned in the forehead.

Mac drops his stick and ambles up the sand, shoes in hand. The moonlight casts a silver glow over him, as if the universe knows a guy like that deserves his own personal spotlight. I remember the first time I really noticed him. It was the first day of freshman year, and he'd come back from summer break a good five inches taller, his hair shaggy, his braces gone. He looked grown into his body, sauntering around with a rangy, relaxed gait that I now know so well I can recognize him just by the sound of his big feet hitting the ground behind me. I fell pretty hard right away, but I didn't actually get to *speak* to him until last year. Natalie's dance studio had just closed, so she switched over to the Madison School across town. She ended up in the same class as Tamsin and Cora. The four of us started hanging out soon after, and when Cora started dating Eli, suddenly our group expanded by three dudes, Colin and Mac coming along for the ride. Our first day back from winter break sophomore year, Mac slid into the chair next to mine at what would become *our* lunch table (a fact I still cannot get over), and I swear I nearly melted into a puddle of Beck right there on the speckled linoleum floor. He flashed that impossibly white, impossibly straight smile and introduced himself.

"I'm Mac," he said as he opened his milk carton, and in what has to be the single greatest conversational achievement of my entire life thus far, I managed not to reply with, "I *know*."

I've been a goner ever since.

He smiles that same smile at me now as he makes his way up the shore toward me. I smile back in what I hope is a totally cool, relaxed way and not in an "oh my god I want to tackle you straight into that water and make out like a demon" way. I suck in a breath, wondering if he's going to join me on the picnic blanket where I posted up, but then Tamsin lets out an epic squeal that gets everyone's attention.

"It's live!" she says, waving the glowing screen of her phone around. It's just after midnight on Saturday, which means the Sunday paper is now online. And because no one robbed the bank downtown or drove their car into the community pool, there's my birthday photo, front and center. My parents are grinning, Del looks like he just won the lottery, and my smile only barely makes it to my eyes. It's far from the worst photo of the lot (the sixth grade shot, where I'd attempted my own bang trim the previous evening, is particularly brutal).

The glow of the screen illuminates Tamsin's wide grin. "You look good, Beck. That purple tank is a good color for you."

"Thanks," I say, letting the compliment wash over me. The top was from Tamsin. She'd given it to me that morning at school, wrapped in matching purple tissue paper and an explosion of ribbons.

Mac leans over her shoulder to peer at the phone, and I try not to melt into the ground as he stares at the photo of me. Does he like the purple tank? Can he see the zit on my chin that was just erupting but I've successfully beaten back with the drying stick Cora gave me? Does he like the way I curled my hair so that it framed my face, something Natalie and I learned from watching a YouTube video?

"You're so lucky. Free pizza for life? That's, like, *goals*," he says.

I immediately deflate. Of course he's not actually looking at *me*. His eyes are on the extra large pepperoni pizza in front of me. Because pizza is irresistible. Whereas I'm just . . . me. Being overshadowed by pizza is basically the story of my life.

"I think I'd rather be born at Margaritas," Eli says. "A lifetime supply of tacos sounds amazing."

"If you were born at Margaritas, they'd be closed by

now. They couldn't afford to feed you, you human dumpster," Cora says.

I've heard about ten thousand variations on this conversation throughout my life, of course. Everyone has an idea of just what unlimited supply they'd like to have. Ice cream? Cheeseburgers? My uncle Nate often says he hopes his future wife has their baby at a bank, as if unlimited cash is on the table. Me? I wish I could have been born at MacArthur Toyota. Mac's dad is always giving away free cars for charity events and stuff, so had I made my messy debut in their glossy white auto showroom, maybe I'd be the Prius Princess instead of the Hot 'N Crusty Bathroom Baby. I could be driving a sweet new car to celebrate my birthday instead of getting ready to sling pizza for a couple of dollars over minimum wage. And I probably would have spent every birthday of my life with Mac. Why couldn't my mom have had a craving for a test drive instead of a slice?

A breeze blows past, and I shiver, pulling my hands into the sleeves of my Brook Park Trojans shirt. I'm glad we're not experiencing a second summer. If it were a little warmer, I have a feeling Tamsin would probably be encouraging everyone to skinny-dip. She's always pushing our group to be a little bit wild. And skinny-dipping is something I could happily go my whole life not doing.

While stripping down to my undies in front of Mac sounds all right in theory, I'm hoping to get a few more romantic milestones out of the way first. Maybe kiss him before he sees the pink cotton llama undies I'm sporting tonight.

The playlist blaring out of Tamsin's car shuffles, and an old boy-band song comes on. Tamsin and Cora immediately jump up from their blanket on the sand, falling effortlessly into the rhythm and choreography.

"C'mon, Natalie!" Cora cries, waving her up to join them on their makeshift stage at the lakeshore. "You know you know it!"

Natalie groans beside me, but after a beat of protest, she jumps up and falls into step beside them, shimmying and spinning and executing some pretty impressive arm movements. I wonder if it's a dance class combo, or if they made this up while hanging out when I wasn't around. I know it happens. Sometimes I have to help my mom with cake deliveries, or they're on trips for dance competitions. It's never on purpose, so it's fine. Really. I just try not to think about it.

As the girls drop to their knees in this coordinated slide-and-spin maneuver, the boys drop their rocks and sticks to watch the impromptu performance, their whoops and cheers bouncing around the still lake water like skipping stones.

"Beck, you should join dance with us!" Tamsin says, grinning down at me on the blanket. She's shimmying in little circles, but it's not a loose movement like Natalie's and Cora's. That's because Tamsin is practically a prima ballerina, tall and slender and stork-like. She can leap and pirouette, but when she does dance team moves, she always looks like a badly animated mannequin. It's only barely a flaw, because she somehow still manages to revel in her ballerina grace in a way that's magnetic. Everything about Tamsin is. Maybe it's her confidence. Even when she's twerking like someone's midwestern grandma, she still manages to look cool.

Tamsin's invite is nice, but it ignores the fact that I have the moves of a drunken flamingo. I inherited my dad's coordination, which is so lacking that even the hokey pokey eludes him. *You want me to put* which *foot* where *now?*

"Yeah," Cora says, still shaking her hips to the next song on the playlist. "Tuesday and Thursday. You can ride with us."

I gulp, because now I have an actual reason why I can't join dance. One that has nothing to do with my complete and total lack of rhythm or ability to move my feet and arms simultaneously.

"Love to, but can't. I have to work," I reply.

"Oooooh! Where?" Cora asks.

I spent all of Friday after school shuttling around with my mom in a last-ditch effort to find another job. I started at the cool boutiques downtown, and the bookstore off the square, but they seem to only hire adults and the stray college student with good availability. I can only work after school and on the weekends, which severely limits my employability anywhere that doesn't have a deep-fat fryer. So just as I suspected, my only options were of the fast-food variety. There was an opening for a bagger at ShopRite, but it only paid minimum wage, and I'd have to wear a red button that said, "Thank you, no tips please." Del offered to pay me three dollars more, plus tips. As much as I want to run screaming from Hot 'N Crusty, I need the money. And I need to not wear polyester while dunking frozen french fries in hot oil.

"Wait, are you . . ." Natalie trails off, knowing better than to bring it up directly.

"Oh my god, you're working at Hot 'N Crusty!" Tamsin squeals. "Are you going to have to wear that awful T-shirt?"

I sigh. Might as well lean into it now, I guess. I throw

up some halfhearted jazz hands, then think better of it and cross them over my chest, tucking my fingers into my armpits. "You're looking at the newest staffer at Hot 'N Crusty Pizza," I say, but any trace of enthusiasm gets trapped in my throat. I feel like I've just taken a giant step backward from my friends, and true to form, I've tripped over my own feet on the way.

"Please tell me you get to wear a crown instead of the baseball cap. They call you the Pizza Princess, right? You should totally demand a crown." Tamsin's giddy fascination with my employment is bordering on morbid, like I'll be slicing up bodies in the morgue, and she's hoping I'll let her come watch. Well, not so much bodies, more like my reputation. There will be no running from the whole bathroom baby thing come Tuesday, when I officially start. "Does anyone cool work there?"

I shrug, because I've never paid all that much attention to the staff at Hot 'N Crusty. It never occurred to me that one day they'd be my coworkers. Even though half the staff is around my age, I think I've been subconsciously thinking that if I didn't notice them, they wouldn't notice me, and any potential connection would be severed.

"I think that guy from calc works there. Fred or Ford? Or something?" Colin says. "You know, tall guy, super smart? Like, *major* nerd. He seems nice, though."

"Ugh, hopefully it's not just a bunch of antisocial trolls," Tamsin says, rolling her eyes like *she'll* be burdened by proxy working with Fred-or-Ford and his compatriots. Tamsin's not *really* a jerk, but she sure can play the part sometimes.

I'm saved from having to answer—or even consider the awful possibility that Del really will try to get me to wear a tiara—when Mac drops down onto the blanket next to me. He's so tall and broad that he barely fits. His feet hang off the fleece, his heels digging into the sand. He's got nice feet, for a dude, the nails trimmed and not at all like the gross talons my dad sports. He leans back on his hands, his wrist brushing mine. A gasp catches in my throat, though I try to let it out slowly, a sigh I hope no one can hear. Mac's all energy, heat radiating off him like a furnace. He glances up at the inky black sky, a scattering of stars shining through since we're a few miles outside of town. He lets out an enormous yawn.

"Tired?" I ask.

He nods. "Coach has gone on this big cardio kick and has us doing high intensity interval training and plyo. It's seriously kicking my ass."

I have no idea what he's talking about, as my sole source of exercise is taking Pup, our ancient basset hound, on a leisurely walk around the block. It also doesn't help

30

that I lose all ability to ask, because at that moment, Mac leans his head to rest on my shoulder. I freeze as if he's a hummingbird and the slightest movement will scare him off. I breathe in the smell of his shampoo—something in the Axe family that I'd normally roll my eyes at, but in this moment is irresistible. I will my body to be still, to enjoy the warmth of him and the way the blond curls that fluff out from beneath his ball cap tickle my cheek. He smells like fireworks—literally and metaphorically. I want to pour that smell into a candle that I can burn to visit again and again. This is the closest I've ever been to him, and it's thoroughly lighting me up. But I can't stop shivering with nerves and excitement.

And then just as soon as it began, it's over. Mac sits up and grins at me.

"You need a jacket," he says, reaching back for a Brook Park Baseball hoodie that Colin abandoned on a log earlier. Mac tosses it into my lap, enveloping me in the synthetic evergreen scent of whatever soap the Roy family housekeeper buys for Colin. I pull it over my head, because if I don't, Mac will wonder why I was shivering like I was sitting in the Arctic. And then maybe he'll figure out that it was because I'm completely and totally in love with him, which I don't want him to know even though I desperately want him to know. I'm not sure how I'm ever supposed to take this to the next level if I'm trying to hide something I very much need him to know (which is that we really should be more than friends). I'm terrified that he just thinks of me as a friend, that to him I'm no different from Eli or Colin. I'm terrified he'll say, "*Oh, that's sweet, Beck, but . . . no.*" And so instead I pine away silently because the knowledge that the door *could* be open is better than the potential of it slamming hard in my face. Schrödinger's Crush, if you will.

But Mac isn't paying attention to my shivering. He's not looking at me at all, because Natalie is approaching with a Tupperware box full of cupcakes. There are flickering pink candles stuck down in the white frosting.

Once again, I play second fiddle to snacks.

"Happy birthday to you," Natalie sings, her voice low and sort of husky, and then my other friends join in. They gather around me, their faces illuminated by the flickering candlelight. Eli has his arm around Cora. Tamsin bumps my hip with hers. I let myself look at Mac one time, my eyes sweeping lazily across his face like it's an accident. Just for a moment I let myself take in his warm, casual grin. Then I quickly avert my gaze to the cupcakes. And when the big moment comes, the song at its finale, I allow myself one last, tiny look at him before I suck in a breath and make a wish.

I wish Mac would kiss me.

And then the flame is out, and the boys are shoving their hands into the box. Natalie swats them away.

"The birthday girl goes first," she says, offering them to me. I pluck out the one from the middle of the box, licking stray frosting off my finger. "My mom made them, so they're carrot cake. And I can't promise there's not kale hidden in them."

Natalie's mom is a nutritionist who runs a modestly read food blog about convincing your kids to eat vegetables. Her food always *looks* amazing, but usually tastes sort of like someone shouted the name of something delicious from another room. These cupcakes, though, are moist and shockingly sweet.

"You can thank me for the frosting," Natalie says as she finally lets the boys attack the box. "I snuck in some honest-to-god white sugar while she was taking a call. Bless my mother, but she has truly convinced herself that applesauce is a legitimate sweetener. And she is very, *very* wrong."

"Tell her I said thanks," I say. "And thank *you* for bringing them."

"It's my best friend's birthday, of *course* I'm gonna bring cake!"

Colin reaches for seconds, having hoovered his first like someone was going to take it away from him.

"Yeah, thanks, Natalie. These cupcakes are the business," he says. Nat's cheeks redden, because even though she denies it, I'm pretty sure she has a five-alarm crush on Colin. She's been far too enthusiastic about going to watch the baseball team practice, and she turns that exact shade of red whenever Colin drops his tray onto our lunch table every day. Colin, being a dude, seems completely oblivious. But he also doesn't seem to have eyes for anyone else, so it could definitely happen. I make a mental note to ask her about it later.

We hang around for another half hour, until a police car comes by to scout for alcohol and tells us we should probably be getting home. Cora, Eli, and Mac pile into Tamsin's Range Rover with Colin, since they all live in the same neighborhood. Legacy Park is one of those new subdivisions that's built to look old, as if Brook Park was always a place with enormous stone mansions boasting saltwater pools in their backyards and a big tennis center in the middle. You know, like in the *olden* days or whatever. We wave goodbye from Natalie's car, where we blast disco, singing along at top volume to "Dancing Queen" as we drive back through the woods.

"Tonight was fun!" Natalie says, gripping the wheel of her mom's old Volvo. She glances over at me. "It was fun, right?"

"It was!" I say, and I'm not even lying. Natalie always seems worried that I'm miserable hanging out with Tamsin and Cora and the guys, which I'm definitely not. Tonight *was* fun, and *hello*, I'd go skydiving if it meant Mac would be there. I'd even wrestle greased pigs at the state fair and do it with a smile on my face if it meant hanging out with Mac. "I'm glad it wasn't quite as intense as Tamsin made it sound."

"Oh, believe me, I talked her down," Natalie replies. "She originally wanted to go to that karaoke bar in Singleton and make everyone dress up like it was prom. I caught her researching party buses."

Even the thought of that makes my stomach seize up. Karaoke in a prom dress? With Mac? No thanks. The only thing worse than my dancing is my singing. Don't get me wrong, I'd do it. But I'd be more comfortable jumping out of a plane. I'm much more a blend-into-the-crowd kind of person. The idea of a spotlight makes me break out in hives.

"You know me well," I tell her, the most comforting words that have come out of my mouth all night.

"Hell yeah, I do," she replies, and then she waggles her eyebrows, giving me a mischievous side eye. "Soooooo . . . you certainly looked cozy with Mac tonight."

My cheeks flush, and I light up with a grin to match.

Everything I was trying to contain back on the lakeshore suddenly comes pouring out of me like the Niagara Falls of squee. Because if you can't tell your best friend every single, solitary detail of your crush, who can you tell?

"*Right?*" My voice rises, like, six octaves, and I'm surprised the windshield doesn't shatter. "I nearly *died* when he put his head on my shoulder. Maybe I did die. Am I deceased? Is this what the afterlife is like? Driving around with my best friend listening to disco?"

"I think he's smitten," she says. My heart skips a full beat at the thought. "He just doesn't know how to deal with it yet. I think something could happen soon."

I twist around in my seat and get caught on the seat belt, nearly choking, trying my best not to reach over and shake her. She is driving, after all. "Okay, but do you, like, *know* something? Because if you know something, you have to spill. Did Colin say anything to Tamsin? Has Mac said anything about me?"

She grins, but shakes her head, and my hopes fall just a little bit. "I don't have an inside scoop, just a hunch."

I have to spend the next half a mile trying to slow my heart rate. My disappointment is actually doing a pretty good job of it. I remind myself, like Mom always says, *no news is good news*. He hasn't said he *doesn't* like me. He just hasn't said he does. Ugh, crush limbo is torture. I opt for a subject change.

"While we're on the subject, then, what's going on with you and Colin? You were making eyes at him all night!"

Now it's Natalie's turn to blush, something she's never able to hide with her Scandinavian milkmaid looks. "I have no idea what you're talking about."

"Are you kidding? You looked like a damn strawberry when he was complimenting your mom's cupcakes. *You* are a smitten kitten."

"Shut up!" she says, her grin a mile wide. "Yes, okay? I like Colin. But nothing is happening there. He's totally oblivious."

"I'm sure he won't stay that way for long," I tell her. "Especially not if Tamsin finds out."

"You *cannot* tell her," Natalie says forcefully, and I smile. Our friend group may have expanded, but Natalie and I are still a team. We keep each other's secrets. And thank god for that. She's never told anyone about the summer in fifth grade when I shaved my arms because I thought my arm hair was too dark, and I've never told about the time on the third grade field trip to the aquarium when she peed her pants a little. I just gave her my sweatshirt to tie around her waist, and I'll take that secret to the grave.

"I would never," I say. And then I reach out to turn up the volume just as the opening piano run of "I Will Survive" hits the speakers. We sing all the way home like our voices are fueling the car. We hold hands and raise them in the air and close our eyes and toast to our crushes and our secrets and our friendship.

And later that night, as I'm falling asleep in bed, I think that it was my favorite birthday ever.

CHAPTER
THREE

I grip the wheel on my dad's old Toyota, which he let me drive to my first day of work, since my shift starts after he gets home from school. It's my first time driving without one of my parents in the passenger seat. The first time without my dad cracking jokes next to me or my mom gripping the door handle and pressing an invisible brake. I pulled out of the driveway and traveled the first half a mile from my house terrified I'd go flying off the road at any second. I drove slow, my eyes wide and scanning the road for stray cats, small children, or potholes. But soon my nerves settled, and then all of a sudden I was just driving, like I'd been doing it my whole life. I listened to the *Cruisin'* playlist that Natalie and I made back when we were freshmen. It's full of songs about, well, driving and cars, with a few exceptions made for songs that just sound like freedom. And that's what I felt for most of the drive, like suddenly I was free to go and do and be. I could drive to Canada if I wanted to. Or Mexico. Or either of the oceans. You know, if I wanted to then be grounded for the rest of my natural life.

But sitting here in the parking lot of Hot 'N Crusty, watching the glowing green digital clock on the dashboard as the minutes tick close to 4 p.m., I don't feel free. I feel like I'm going to walk into that dark and sticky dining room and the door is going to slam shut behind me like a prison cell.

Needless to say, I'm not too jazzed about my first day of work.

At 3:55, I climb out of the car and lock it behind me. I take a deep breath, staring up at the red and white neon sign above the door.

And then I head inside.

The dining room is mostly empty, save for a few random customers. There's a mom in the corner eating a slice of pizza while nudging a stroller back and forth with her foot, a baby asleep inside. The music on the crackly sound system, a mix of eighties power ballads and nineties boy bands, is turned lower than usual, probably to accommodate.

"There she is!" Del calls from the kitchen, and the mom in the corner shoots him a dirty look. He gives her a face full of apology, mouthing *sorry*, and creeps over, dropping what he's doing in the kitchen to greet me at the door. "Hot 'N Crusty's newest employee. Welcome to the team, Beck! Everybody, come say hi to Beck!"

There's a pause. The rest of the employees are mostly back in the kitchen soaking up the predinner lull, and they don't seem sure if Del is serious. But when he waves them over again, so enthusiastically I'm worried his arm might detach from his shoulder, they start to shuffle out.

"Beck, meet the team," Del says as they line up haphazardly along the counter in front of the register. He points first to a guy who looks like he's several years out of college, but still somehow exudes an air of teenage insolence. He's tall and thin, but hides his height with an impressive stoop, his spine rolled and his shoulders hanging out around his ears. He leans against the counter like standing is just too much effort, and casually pulls his long, frizzy dark hair into a messy ponytail. "This is Joey Rizzo, our resident pizza chef. He's a full-timer, been here since he was in high school. He's our longest-running staffer—he was actually here when you were born!"

Okay, so he's definitely several years past college, then, if he's worked at HnC for sixteen years. And yet the more I study him, the more ageless he becomes.

"I stayed *very* far away from that mess," Joey mutters, glancing up from beneath hooded eyes. This is apparently the only greeting I'll be getting from him. He barely makes eye contact, like looking at me will bring back the more vivid memories of that night. Honestly? I don't blame him. The only good thing about my birth is that I don't remember it at all.

"Joey is not so good with blood. Luckily he's got no problem with marinara!" Del's laugh booms through the nearly empty restaurant, like this is the funniest joke he's ever told. The baby in the corner begins to cry. Oblivious, Del gestures to a trio of guys about my age. I recognize them from school. I think I had gym with the gangly white guy with the thick glasses. "These are our busers: Frank, Jason, and Greg. They run food and do dishes, and sometimes pitch in on the line when we're busy."

Del doesn't pause to specify which boy is which, and it almost doesn't seem necessary. The very tall, very skinny guy with the wide grin and thick glasses must be Frank, the super nice super nerd from Colin's calculus class. Next to him is a short, stocky boy with pale skin and messy brown hair. He looks like a coiled spring. And beside *him* is a black guy with black-rimmed glasses and a frown, his arms crossed over his chest. I have no idea which is Jason and which is Greg. I just know that neither seems to care for me much. They're eyeing me like I'm a toddler they've been forced to babysit. The one in the middle, who I think I've seen at a National Honor Society meeting freshman year, actually rolls his eyes.

"And this is Julianne," Del says, pointing to the lone girl of the bunch, standing at the end of the line. She opts to stare at her fingernails instead of looking at me. "Julianne runs our register and is our front line when it comes to customer service. She's the best. She's going to be doing your training for the next couple of weeks."

I know who Julianne Scarborough is. Everyone does. She was homecoming queen last year, but not like that. A bunch of assholes got together and nominated her as a joke, and then she actually won. I'm not sure if the win was an act of cruel bullying or if people were trying to be nice to make up for the initial nomination, but in the end does it really matter? Before the homecoming fiasco, I'd never even noticed her, which is I think how she must prefer it. She's got long dark hair that she lets just sort of exist, which means it usually falls over her pale face. She wears a lot of dark colors and sits alone in the cafeteria, always focused intently on some thick book that's not for school.

But I don't *actually* know her. I've only heard the stupid rumors: that she's a witch, or in a cult, that sort of nonsense. She's always seemed a little weird in a way that I couldn't put my finger on, but I could never tell if that was a symptom or the disease. If people were saying I was a witch, I might be sort of quiet and shifty, too. I heard she reads spell books at lunch, and that she has a cat that talks back to her. I also heard she sits in the front row of every class but never says a word. Which, when people are whispering about your magic cat, could you blame her?

"If you have any questions for me, just shoot me an email, as the kids say." And Del actually does finger guns. I hear someone from the buser crew choke back a laugh. "I'm not usually here on weeknights, but I wanted to come by to say welcome and introduce you to the staff. I hope Hot 'N Crusty feels like your second home, since it kind of was your first!"

I nearly groan at the joke, but manage to hold it in at the last minute, rearranging my face into an approximation of a smile.

"Where ya off to, Del?" The shorter one—who I think is Jason—asks, leaning back so his elbows rest on the counter behind him. He cocks an eyebrow, then glances over at Greg. There's something unsaid zipping between them, but Del seems oblivious.

"I've got a date, actually," Del says. "I tried that Tinder that you mentioned. Took a while, but tonight I'm meeting this woman, Sheryl. She's a teller over at PT&D Bank. She seems really nice. From her messages, anyway."

"Sounds promising," Greg replies with a wide smile, his voice full of amusement and something else, this time directed toward Frank.

"Hope springs eternal!" Del says, bouncing on the balls of his feet. "Okeydokey, I'll see you all tomorrow. Call me if you need anything. And, Beck, welcome to the team!"

As soon as the glass door swings shut behind him, Jason, Frank, and Greg burst out laughing.

"You owe me ten dollars, because I got him to actually use Tinder," Jason says to Frank, who rolls his eyes as he reaches into his pocket for his wallet.

"But you owe *me* that same ten dollars, because you didn't think he'd ever actually get a date out of it," Greg adds. He holds his palm out and wiggles his fingers.

"Five dollars says he keeps referring to it as 'That Tinder,'" Jason announces as he takes the ten-dollar bill from Frank and hands it immediately off to Greg.

"I'll take that bet," Frank replies. "I'm pretty sure next time we hear about Tinder, he'll be calling it Tingler or Tumbler."

"Can I get in on that action? Because twenty dollars says he never sees Sheryl again after tonight," Joey says, suddenly emerging from his stoner haze. "In fact, I'd put down a cool fifty dollars that she leaves before they've finished their meal."

"Too rich for my blood," Frank says.

"I'm not taking that bet, because there's no way in a frozen hell that Del gets a second date. I'd rather just light my money on fire," Jason says.

"Leave the poor man alone," Julianne snaps. It's the first time I've ever heard her voice. "He's going on dates, which is more than I can say for the three of you."

Jason opens his mouth to protest, but she cuts him off before a sound can escape. "Please don't with your crush from space camp," she says.

"It was *robotics* camp, and I dated him all summer," Jason says with a glare. "We just didn't want to do the long-distance thing."

Julianne rolls her eyes, then levels me with her gaze. "Come on," she says, and heads back through the swinging door to the kitchen. I follow her, because what other choice do I have?

At the back of the kitchen, there's a wooden door that sits half open. Julianne bumps it with her hip and gestures me in with a cock of her head. The room is the size of a broom closet—it may actually *be* a broom closet—but Del has turned it into his makeshift office. There's a small desk with a computer on it, a metal filing cabinet with labels written in faded script, and a time clock on the wall that appears to be the most modern piece of technology in the room. Julianne is bent over rifling through a cardboard box that's open beneath the desk. When she stands, she's holding a fistful of red fabric.

Oh god. My uniform.

"I'm guessing you're a small?" she asks, though it sounds more like an accusation. She holds out the shirt. "They're men's sizes, and the cloth is stiff as a board. If you wash it with a bunch of fabric softener, after about sixty or seventy washes it *kind* of stops feeling so much like sandpaper."

I grimace as I take the shirt in my hand. Her vivid description seems spot on.

"I keep begging Del to order something softer and with a more flattering cut, but he's too much of a cheapskate."

I take hold of the sleeves and hold the shirt up, though I already know what it says. I'M HOT 'N CRUSTY. In all caps. Heavy, black font. Unmistakable. Right across my nonexistent boobs.

"And here's a cap, one size fits no one," she says, offering me one of the black baseball hats. It's cheap, with the plastic adjuster in the back. Then she hands me a short black apron to tie around my waist.

"Thanks," I tell her, and she steps out, pulling the door shut behind her. I guess I'm just supposed to change here, next to the ancient computer. As I whip off my tank and pull on the T-shirt, I realize this is it. I'm really becoming one of them. I also realize that Julianne was right. This is the cheapest, itchiest, stiffest T-shirt I've ever worn. It also smells like the burnt bottom of a pizza. As if having this awful catchphrase emblazoned across my chest isn't awful enough. I feel pricks of sweat in my armpits almost immediately. Is this thing even cotton, or is it just made of industrial misery?

Just as I'm starting to feel like the walls of the office are closing in on me, Julianne knocks. I open the door, shoving my tank into the bottom of my purse. She steps back into the office as I adjust the ball cap, pulling my long, thick ponytail through the hole at the back.

"Okay, so here's the time clock. Punch in when you get here. Your number is the last four digits of your social. It's super easy, just pound, your number, then pound again," she says, her fingers waving over the hashtag sign. She steps aside so I can punch in, which I do, and the machine beeps back, my name appearing on the screen along with the time. "Congratulations. You're officially getting paid to be here."

Well, at least there's that. I've spent plenty of time at Hot 'N Crusty over the course of my life, but I've never actually made any money off it, unless you count the lifetime supply of pizza. Which my dad points out isn't taxable income, so it doesn't actually count. It's the tiniest sliver of a silver lining.

"So, I'll show you stuff until customers start coming around five. Then you'll just have to, like, watch and not get in the way."

"Sounds good," I say, as if there isn't a big boulder of dread sitting in the pit of my stomach.

Pizza Princess, reporting for duty.

By the time Julianne locks the door and flips off the neon open sign that hangs in the window, I'm completely gassed. I'm so tired I'm pretty sure I could lie down on the sticky tile floor behind the register and fall immediately into a deep sleep, only to dream about extra banana peppers and the guy who demanded a free pizza because he swore up and down that there was a stray olive on his cheese-only pie. I'm pretty sure it was just a large piece of basil, but I'm no expert.

It wasn't even that busy. Tuesdays usually aren't, according to Julianne. This is just one of a metric ton of tidbits she mumbled at me throughout the course of the night. I feel like a balloon she kept filling up with information until I was in danger of exploding and scaring all the small children who paraded through here tonight, leaving footprints of marinara on the tile floor. It was a constant, running commentary, either about how things are done ("If you make incorrect change, the *no sale* button will open the register."), or backstory on the people who work here ("Del is divorced and has two grown kids, and I think he's having a major midlife crisis. He's been dating like it's going out of style. Or trying to, anyway."). I know that the commercial ovens in the kitchen are heated to 800 degrees, even though I'll probably never be operating them. I know Jason is applying to every single Ivy League school, and Julianne is terrified of what will happen if he doesn't get into at least one of them. I know that the elderly couple who arrived at 5 p.m. on the dot and split one slice and a Caesar salad have repeated this ritual weekly for as long as Julianne has worked at Hot 'N Crusty, and I know that she started a year and a half ago on *her* sixteenth birthday.

She rattled all of this off without ever looking at me. She was always either wiping down menus, rolling silverware, or studying her nails, which are bitten down to nubs. Sometimes she resorted to just staring at her shoes. I don't know why she talked to me at all, since she seemed to have so little interest in me. But it all seemed to just pour out of her without even realizing she was doing it. It makes me wonder if, when I'm not there, she's still talking anyway. Maybe that's the origin of the talking-cat rumor.

But now it seems there's something I'm missing.

Because now that the restaurant is closed and all the patrons are gone, the staff is gathering at the counter. Jason looks oddly pleased with himself, while Frank looks sort of twitchy. Greg is just frowning, which I've already learned is his default position. About midway through the evening I had a flash of recognition and realized he's in my enormous bio class, which BPHS accidentally over-filled and had to haul in extra desks to accommodate. I missed him, because he's squeezed into the front right corner, while my desk is sardined into the back left.

"Mine is *really* good tonight, you guys," Frank says, bouncing on the balls of his feet. He grins, his teeth clenched and his lips wide so that it looks like his mouth is about to wrap around to his ears.

"The last time you said that, all you had was a dirty diaper," Jason replies. "Your barometer needs some serious adjustment."

"Less talk, more action, people," Greg says. He drums on the counter like a carnival barker. "Show us whatcha got."

I glance over at Julianne, waiting for some kind of explanation, but she's too busy grinning like she's holding a winning lottery ticket. And I'm struck by the fact that it's the first time I've ever seen Julianne Scarborough smile.

They're all just staring at each other, grinning and waggling their eyebrows. It looks like that scene in last year's *West Side Story* production when the Sharks and the Jets are about to rumble or whatever. I swear, if someone breaks into song, I'm walking out that door and never coming back.

"Will someone please tell me what's going on?" I say finally, because frankly, I'm tired, and I'm pretty sure there's marinara sauce in my left ear. I just want to go home.

"Every night we play a game where you bring the weirdest thing you found on a table," Julianne says.

"Photographic evidence will suffice if it's something

you actually have to dispose of in order to clean the table," Jason says, laying out the rules like he's in Mission Control.

"Like the time Frank had the photo of the table where the toddler threw up his pizza and also his mother's engagement ring, which he'd swallowed earlier that night," Julianne says.

"I still deeply regret looking at that photo," Greg says, turning slightly green.

"Everyone shows their hand, and then we vote on the winner. You can't vote for yourself, that's how we keep it fair," Julianne says.

"It's not fair when alliances are formed," Greg grumbles.

"Some of us grew up watching *Survivor* with our parents, and are therefore more ruthless than others," Frank says, blatantly pointing at Jason, who looks not at all cowed by the charge.

"And what does the winner get?" I ask.

"The winner gets to designate the closing duties. Which means the winner doesn't have to clean the bathrooms or take out the trash, because those are the suck jobs and no one in their right mind would ever choose them," Jason says, looking smug. Something tells me he doesn't end up cleaning the bathrooms very often.

"Seriously, less talk. Let's see 'em," Greg says.

Frank goes first, pulling out a white orthopedic sneaker that looks well worn, yet shockingly clean.

"Child's play. We find shoes all the time!" Jason says.

"Kids' shoes, sure. Kids are always leaving shoes behind. They don't care. But this is an *adult* shoe. A grown-up actually walked out of here sans shoe," Frank says.

Jason rolls his eyes, completely unconvinced. "That could have easily fallen out of a geezer's gym bag. Next?"

Greg reaches in his pocket and pulls out a small piece of paper. "I present to you an index card," he says, clearing his throat as if he's about to read some Thoreau. "Written at the top—in shockingly terrible penmanship, I might add—is 'Reasons I'm Dumping You,' and below that is a numbered list. Number two reads, 'because you insist on using a soft *g* to pronounce *gif*,' and three says, 'because you peed your pants on the Fourth of July.'" Greg drops the index card on the counter. It's crumpled, the edges soft like whoever wrote it spent a lot of time worrying it in their hands. Good lord, who brings notes to their breakup?

"To be fair, the soft *g* is correct," Jason says.

"It just sounds wrong, though," Frank replies.

"Okay, okay, not bad," Jason says, reading over the

list. Then he pulls out his contribution. At first I recoil at the bundle of fur he's holding, thinking it's a dead guinea pig or something, but as he drops it on the counter, I realize it's a toupee. A golden blond rug of hair that only barely looks human. If I had to guess, I'd say it's 100 percent synthetic. Put that thing in the pizza oven, and it'll melt into a puddle of plastic.

"How do you *always* find hair?" Frank whines. "I swear, it's like you're bringing them in with you. Do we need to start checking your pockets at the start of your shift?"

"This is his *third* toupee," Greg tells me with a scowl. "And I've lost track of the hair extensions."

"Are we ready to vote?" Jason asks.

"Excuse me, boys, but I haven't presented mine yet," Julianne says. Gone is the glowering, grumbling girl hiding behind her hair. Julianne has come alive.

"Oh, *you're* playing tonight?" Jason says.

"Yes. Despite my serious handicap, being relegated to the register for most of the night—"

"Which is why we rarely give you the suck jobs, Julianne. It's only fair," Frank says.

"Thank you, Frank. I appreciate it." Frank blushes a little under Julianne's gratefulness. "But I don't need your charity tonight. Because despite only busing three tables,

I managed to score a real winner." She reaches under the counter and drops a paper plate soaked through with grease, upon which rests a cold, congealing slice of pizza. It lands on the counter with a soggy thud.

Jason scoffs. "I'm sorry, you're bringing *pizza* to this game? Seriously? I know you're not at the tables often, but you do realize we *sell* this, right?"

"Gentlemen, I present to you my selection from table eight," she says, ignoring him. Thanks to my training, I know table eight is the round banquette in the back corner. It's usually favored by families or rowdy groups of unchaperoned tweens. "On this plate is a piece of pizza, yes. But not just *any* pizza. This is pizza that came from *somewhere else.*"

There's a beat of silence while everyone looks at the slice.

"No fucking way," Jason whispers.

"Way," Julianne replies. She leans back against the counter, crossing her arms over her chest with a satisfied smile. "We do not sell stuffed crust pizza here at Ye Olde Hot 'N Crusty. Someone brought this in from *outside.*"

Even I can barely suppress a gasp.

"What kind of asshole goes to a pizza place and brings pizza from *another* pizza place?" Greg says, bending down to observe it like a NASA scientist.

"I wish I knew, friends, but I didn't see who left it. Now should we vote?"

"Why bother? Julianne clearly wins," Greg says with a shrug. He reaches for his note card and shoves it back in his pocket.

"She's got my vote," Frank says, taking the shoe and tossing it into the cardboard box behind the counter that's used as a lost and found.

"That's two!" Julianne says. She flashes me a big, open-mouthed smile, like *can you believe it?* But then she remembers who I am and the smile drops before she turns to Jason. "You're welcome to vote, but either way, I believe you have lost. And so I'd like to direct you to the cleaning supplies. Those bathrooms need some attention."

Jason groans, but does as he's told. Apparently the rules of the table game are sacrosanct. Greg gets trash duty, and Frank is in charge of mopping floors. Joey apparently always does the kitchen close. He asks for help if he needs it, but tonight he's good. Julianne sticks to counting out the drawer, carefully detailing every moment of the experience for my personal Hot 'N Crusty handbook. I'm surprised she didn't send me off to do trash, but maybe after her big victory, she was feeling charitable. But she actually doesn't assign me *any* jobs, so I'm left standing there awkwardly as she starts wiping down the plastic-covered menus.

"You can leave if you want," Julianne says as she dunks a washcloth into a tub of soapy water.

"You sure? I can help with the menus or something." I really *do* want to leave, but I also feel bad that everyone's doing jobs while I just stand here like a decorative fern. I don't want special treatment or anything. I don't want them to hate me.

"It's fine. There's nothing else to do anyway."

"Okay. Thanks," I say. "And for all the training. I hope I can remember it all."

"It's not the jet propulsion lab. Unless you're a total idiot, you'll be fine." It almost sounds like a compliment.

"Sure. Great," I say. I'm already picturing myself sinking to the bottom of a deep pool of marinara and diet soda, while everyone stands around going *jeez, couldn't you figure it out?* I didn't realize I needed to work on my fitness to be a Hot 'N Crusty employee, but I am full out exhausted.

I make my way back through the kitchen, where Joey is washing a stack of metal trays from the pizza ovens in the industrial sink. The floor is covered in soapy water, like he just dumped a bucket down and hoped for the best. As I pass by the stainless-steel ovens, I catch my reflections in their doors. My ponytail has quadrupled in size from the heat and humidity of the kitchen, and several long bits of frizz have made their escape from beneath my hat and are plastered to my forehead and neck with sweat. My jeans are covered in splatters of marinara dipping sauce from when I dropped an entire bowl of it while delivering breadsticks to a table. There's a white film of grated Parmesan cheese on my nose from who knows when, and there are dark sweat stains in the armpits of my shirt. I sort of look like I was thrown from a moving car into an Italian swamp. I am—*literally*—Hot 'N Crusty.

"Hey, hot stuff," I mutter to my reflection before I hurry away to the office to clock out. But as soon as I step in, I suddenly forget how the damn thing works. It's the last four of my social, that part I know, but do I hit the star button? Pound? Do I do it before, or after? Or before *and* after? I make a few attempts, but the thing just beeps angrily at me. My brain feels full of garlic and a night's worth of pizza orders, numbers swirling with pepperoni and mushrooms and red onions. There's no room for how to punch out. I think the last extra large, extra garlic, extra onions (zero make out, apparently) shoved it out.

"Are you lost?" A deep voice jolts me out of my fog of exhaustion. I look up from the time clock to see a tallish guy standing in the doorway. He's wearing the Hot 'N Crusty T-shirt, but it's mostly hiding beneath a faded denim jacket that looks so worn in, it has to be velvety soft to the touch. His ball cap is nowhere to be found, leaving his mop of dark wavy hair free to flop over his dark eyes. He shoves his hair back with one hand, revealing deeply tanned skin and freckles.

"I just, um, I was, uh," I stammer, trying to figure out how to get out of this situation without looking like a complete idiot.

"Who are you?" he asks, although it comes out as more of an accusation.

"I'm Beck," I say, and then after a pause, I hold out my hand like I'm in a job interview. Oh my god, I'm such an effing loser.

He grunts again, this time with a little bit of a laugh, one that's definitely directed *at* me and not *with* me. "Right," he says with a knowing nod. My hand hangs there between us until I finally let it drop, my palm sweaty. "The pizza princess."

I bristle at the mention, whatever nerves I was feeling at first catching a glimpse of him now fading away. "It's just Beck, actually."

"That short for something?"

"Rebecca," I say. I'm named after my grandmother,

though he looks like he couldn't possibly care less. "I just go by Beck."

"Whatever." He shrugs, then nods at the keypad on the wall. "You gonna punch out, or are you trying to commune with the time clock?"

"Uh," I say, and I feel my cheeks turning red. Why is this guy being a dick, and why am I all flustered? I shake my head, trying to steady my brain, and end up just stepping aside. "Go right ahead."

He looks at me like I'm the two-headed cow at the state fair, then leans in close to the keypad. I feel his presence near me like an alarm. He smells like pizza and gasoline and something else that I can't quite name. I feel warm standing this close to him, and I'm not sure if it's the close quarters and the cooling-down ovens outside, or if it's something else.

He punches four numbers, the thing beeps, and then he leaves without a word or a second look. I lean in to look at the screen before the text disappears. TRISTAN PORTER, it reads, then the time. The name sounds sort of familiar. I think he goes to Brook Park, but isn't in my grade. He must be a senior. I don't think I've ever seen him before, though. I mean, I think I would have noticed him. He's a dick, but he's sort of cute. Although I didn't notice him at all tonight, and he apparently works here.

"Did you forget how it works?" Julianne asks, appearing in the open door, her hat in her hands.

"Oh, uh, no. Just waiting my turn," I say, suddenly worried I'm disappointing her by forgetting my training. "Tristan was just here."

"He actually showed his face?" She leans past me and punches the clock like a reflex. "Dude's like Loch Ness. Every night he slips in and out the back door. I think it's his mission to complete an entire shift without ever speaking to anyone. He may not even talk to the people he delivers to."

Ah, so he's the pizza delivery guy. "Does he go to Brook Park?"

"Yeah. He's a senior. Though I think he might do co-op or something? I never see him."

"Seems like a theme."

"Yeah, he's not much of a joiner," Julianne says, then she fixes me with a glare. "Not that I blame him."

There's no mistaking the implication. I'm to blame for what happened to her. Or at least I represent the problem. I've seen her sitting alone in the cafeteria or drifting silently through the halls, hiding behind a curtain of hair, and I've never reached out, never done anything about it. I don't know what to say. I've never been mean to her. Not on purpose. But I've also never gone out of my way to be nice to her. I've certainly never defended her. And I've probably laughed at a joke Colin or Tamsin made about her.

But none of that would matter if I said it out loud. I'd still be me with my lunch table, and Julianne would still be at hers.

"Yeah" is all I can think to say, and she huffs out this breath that sounds like rolled eyes look. Just total disgust. But she doesn't say anything else, either.

Suddenly my exhaustion drapes over me like a flannel blanket. I want to go *home*.

"See you Friday," I say, because my feet won't let me move without saying something.

"Sure," she replies.

It's not until I'm halfway home that I realize I forgot to actually clock out.

CHAPTER
FOUR

I spend the rest of the week at school thinking that I smell garlic—and that it's coming from me. I can't tell if it's in my hair or if I'm having a stroke, and I can't tell which option is preferable. When I get to the cafeteria on Friday and see pizza sitting on the hot lunch line, my stomach turns. Sure, Brook Park High's pizza is rectangular and the pepperoni looks like little rabbit pellets that are more like jerky than actual pepperoni, so the whole thing bears almost no resemblance to the food I sling at Hot 'N Crusty. But still. At this point, pizza is pizza, and I don't want anything else to do with pizza unless there's a paycheck involved.

Unfortunately, I was so exhausted from my shift last night that I opted for the extra three slaps on the snooze button and didn't get the chance to pack my lunch. With no other option, I quickly head to the salad bar, where I hide a sad pile of iceberg lettuce beneath a mountain of croutons and shredded cheese, then smother the whole monstrosity in honey mustard dressing.

As I make my way through the crowd with my tray, I spot Julianne sitting at a round table in the far corner of the cafeteria. I can barely see her face, since she's staring down at an enormous hardcover book on the table in front of her, her thick, dark hair cascading down around her shoulders and hiding her face like a frizzy curtain. There's only one other person at her table, a guy wearing an *Apex Galaxy* T-shirt who's passed out on an open binder, the notebook paper speckled with drool. I quickly look away before Julianne can look up and notice me. I don't know why, and I feel sort of gross about it.

When I get to my usual table, Natalie is the only one there, so I take the seat right next to her.

"What's that?" Natalie asks, eyeing my plate.

"Salad." I poke at it with my fork.

"Only if we're drastically expanding *that* definition," she replies.

"Which do you think your mom would say has more

nutritional value, my plate of croutons and dressing, or the cafeteria pizza?"

"I think the mere prospect of choosing between those two would cause her brain to short-circuit. She'd need to consume, like, three green juices and some cauliflower rice just to get it working again."

And then Eli and Colin show up, both with plates stacked high with rectangles of pizza slathered in ranch dressing. When Eli drops his plate onto the table, a glob of ranch plops down onto the faux-wood linoleum top. He reaches down with his finger, swipes it up, and sends that finger directly to his mouth. I grimace.

"I take it back," Natalie says as she wrinkles her nose in their direction. She gestures to their plates with her fork. "That right there would cause her to keel over dead on the spot. Frankly, looking at it is enough to clog *my* arteries."

"Don't knock it till you try it," Colin says, lifting a dripping piece of pizza to his mouth and taking an enormous bite.

"Hard pass," Natalie replies, her mouth turning down into a frown, one I'm pretty sure I mirror.

I'm watching in horror as Eli folds a piece of pizza in half so that it acts as a trough for the river of ranch dressing when a familiar figure catches my eye over his shoulder. It's Tristan. He's wearing the same denim jacket, his hair full of flyaways from what looks like a very recent nap. He's holding a carton of milk and a bag of chips. As if he can feel my gaze, he glances up in my direction. Caught staring, I raise my hand in a little half wave, but he either doesn't see me or he doesn't want to, because he turns away and heads straight for the back door of the cafeteria. It'll take him into the back corridor by the auxiliary gym, and eventually dump him out by the band room and the football field. We're not supposed to leave campus for lunch (or anytime during school hours without a pass), but it looks like he either doesn't know that rule or, more likely, doesn't care about it. I watch him disappear through the door, wondering where he could be going. And wondering if he's going alone. And feeling weird that I'm wondering about him at all.

"Who were you waving at?" Tamsin asks as she drops her lunch bag on the table on the other side of Natalie. Because of course Tamsin saw.

"No one," I reply. I reach up above my head and rotate my arm for show. "I slept funny last night. Just stretching."

Her eyebrows shoot up into her hairline, but she lets it fly. She's got more pressing gossip.

"Did you hear about Mackenzie Morales's car?" she asks no one in particular.

Colin clutches his chest, a comically stricken look on his face. "Oh no. Not the Audi!"

Tamsin nods deliciously. "Yup. She was apparently trying to film Carpool Karaoke when she rear-ended a UPS truck. They had to call a tow truck to yank it out from under the bumper!"

"Is she okay?" Cora asks.

"Oh, she's fine," Tamsin says, waving away the worry. "She's milking a bruise on her cheek from the airbags, but I think she's just glad it distracts from the epic hickey Miles Jensen gave her."

"Rest in peace, you sexy little sports car," Colin mutters, wiping away imaginary tears.

Tamsin tosses a piece of her ciabatta at him, where it bounces off his forehead and into a puddle of ranch dressing. "You know her dad will have her in a fresh new ride by tomorrow."

"A ride which you can observe from afar, because you ain't *never* getting in the passenger seat of Mackenzie Morales's car," Eli says.

"Speaking of rides, who am I picking up tonight?" Tamsin asks the table.

"Me," Cora says, and Natalie adds, "Me too." It's when Mac raises his hand for a ride that my heart plummets into my faux Frye boots. Because you know who *doesn't* need a ride, smashed into the back seat of Tamsin's Range Rover with Mac?

"Beck?" Tamsin asks.

I shake my head. "I have to work."

"What? No!" Natalie cries, like I'm shipping off to war. Fridays are usually our main hang. During the fall, we go to the game, then out for dinner, then usually off to the Dairy Barn for dessert until it gets too cold to tolerate standing in a parking lot eating ice cream. Then we all crash at Tamsin's for a slumber party, which my mom approves of because it hasn't yet occurred to her that Colin being Tamsin's twin brother means that the guys are also having a slumber party, and we all just generally end up crashed out on whatever leather couch or easy chair we land in when the DVD starts. And I'd be lying if I said I wasn't planning for the night when I wind up spontaneously sprawled out on a couch with Mac. Maybe I'd be the little spoon. Maybe he'd kiss the back of my neck, his arms wrapping around me to pull me in close. Maybe I'd turn my head . . . You know, if I ever manage to work up the kind of courage it would require to implement a plan like that.

"Sorry, guys, I'm on the schedule for every Friday and every other Saturday from now . . . well, until kingdom come, I guess."

"Are you serious? That sucks," Cora says.

I shrug, because the truth is, I'm not totally heart-broken. I mean, yeah, I'd much rather hang out with my friends than work at HnC, but football is really not my favorite thing. The game is interminable, and now that the fall weather is starting to settle in, it'll be freezing cold up in the stands once the sun goes down. Sitting on frozen concrete for three hours listening to the pep band play the *Star Wars* "Imperial March" every time there's a first down (which is the only way I know there *is* a first down, because I'm still unclear on what a first down even is) is not my idea of a fun Friday evening. Even with Mac there.

Besides, I can still meet up with everyone for the fun stuff after my shift is over. My dream of falling asleep on the expansive leather sectional in Tamsin and Colin's basement, my head on Mac's shoulder, is still within reach. My body lights up like a pinball machine at the thought of his warm, heavy body pressed against mine.

"So what's it like there, anyway?" Tamsin asks, leaning forward on her elbows. "Is it terrible?"

"It's, you know, work. It smells like pizza, and I have to talk to a lot of strangers, but it's really nothing special."

"Is everyone nice?" Natalie asks.

"Yeah. That kid you guys were talking about, Frank,

works there. He's nice," I say to Colin and Eli. "And these two other guys, Jason and Greg, bus tables. I think Greg is in our grade?"

"Oh yeah, Greg, uh—" Mac snaps his fingers, trying to pull the last name from the recesses of his memory. "Wooten? Greg Wooten? That sounds right. He's in my AP US class. He seems cool. Sort of mumbly and sarcastic, but cool."

Yeah, that sounds like Greg.

"Please tell me you're not the only girl," Tamsin says, and I gulp, because I was kind of hoping not to mention it. But why not? Hiding Julianne's existence would probably make me as bad as the people who make fun of her, like I'm admitting she's someone I'm ashamed to be around. Maybe this could be some kind of atonement. Maybe it'll make her not hate me.

"Julianne Scarborough works there, too."

"*No*," Tamsin says, gasping all dramatic-like. "She's so weird! I remember in seventh grade she was, like, obsessed with our social studies unit on the Salem witch trials. Seriously, *obsessed*." She doesn't even bother to keep her voice down. Julianne is clear across the cafeteria, so there's no danger that she'd overhear, but other people could. It could get back to her. If anyone talked to her.

"She's actually nice," I say, but even I can hear my

voice coming out at only half strength. *Nice backbone, Beck.* And okay, she wasn't exactly nice to *me*, but she was nice to all the customers. And to the guys.

"I didn't say she was mean. Just that she was weird," Tamsin says with a shrug, like that makes it better. Like *weird* doesn't come with its own mountain of baggage. I don't even know what to say to that, so instead I stab at my honey mustard croutons and hope this conversation ends as quickly as it started.

The rest of the lunch period passes with way too much talk about baseball from the guys and some in-depth discussions about exfoliation (namely, chemical versus physical, or, Cora's treatise on why the St. Ives Apricot Scrub is murder for your skin). I may not be very into makeup, but skin care is my jam. It's the one time I feel like I can full-on girl-out with Tamsin and Cora and Natalie, who— bless them—spend a lot of time talking about primping, and even more time doing it.

The thing is, my friends are really pretty. All of them, even the boys. They could easily be TV teenagers, played by twenty-somethings, only they're not movie-magicked into perfect skin and shiny hair. They've just got it. It's like they took the express train to Puberty Town, skipping all the stops at Awkward Alley and Acne Valley along the way. The boys all have a relaxed, bordering on lazy, loose-yet-muscled look of high school athletes, and with the attitude to match. I suspect it's because baseball involves an awful lot of standing around (though I would never say that to their faces, because they are *very* defensive about the slowness of their chosen sport). My friends are all absolutely gorgeous, and I can never tell if their good looks have rubbed off on me or if I just look majorly out of place.

Because my parents started me in school right at the birthday cutoff, I'm almost a year younger than everyone else in my grade. I feel flat-chested and knobby-kneed and *very* Ramona Quimby around them. But hope springs eternal, as my mom always says, so I choose to believe that I can be pretty by association. Or at least not an awkward baby, which is how I feel 99 percent of the time and is 100 percent why I keep my crush on Mac a government-clearance-level secret. I'm terrified he thinks of me as someone's little sister, because that's what I know I look like.

Lunch ends, and on the way out of the cafeteria, we drop our trash and separate back to our respective classes. Natalie and I have English together, but everyone else is headed to the science wing in the opposite direction.

I'm halfway out the door when an arm reaches over my shoulder, holding it open for me. I glance up over my shoulder and see Mac smiling down at me, his bicep flexing right in my eye line. I feel like someone lit a sparkler where my heart should be.

"We'll miss you at the game tonight," he says with that smile that causes my insides to liquefy.

"Yeah, um, it's a, uh, real bummer," I sputter. God, it's like I'm grabbing words blind out of a paper bag. My heart is pounding somewhere around my throat, like the sound is trying to escape out of my mouth. I'm three seconds from completely short-circuiting. *Get ahold of yourself!* "I'll try to meet up with you guys after my shift."

"Cool! Glad to hear it," he says, and then he's off, headed toward Ms. Worthington's bio class, not that I know his schedule by heart (except that I totally do).

I have *got* to learn to be a normal human girl sometime between now and tonight.

Unfortunately, Ms. Williams has plans for the rest of the period that don't involve me strategizing how to avoid acting like a total dork in front of Mac MacArthur.

"As you know, junior year is all about the college search, so that when you get to senior year, you'll be all ready to apply," Ms. Williams begins. She's perched on the edge of her desk, leaning back on her hands with her ankles crossed out in front of her in that "I'm not a regular teacher, I'm a *cool* teacher" pose she does. And to be fair, Ms. Williams *is* a pretty cool teacher, it's just that sometimes her attempts to convince us of that are laughably transparent. But we let it slide, because she let us read *The Disreputable History of Frankie Landau-Banks* instead of *The Scarlet Letter*. "To that end, we'll be spending the fall semester working on exercises to help you write your admissions essay as well as how to narrow down your choices and formulate your plan when it comes to potential colleges and universities."

Brook Park High is obsessed with college. As a typical upper-middle-class suburban school, we start talking about college choices in freshman year. Everything is about preparation, first for the PSATs, then the SATs (which some ultradedicated people take as sophomores, which my dad thinks is not only insane but a waste of money). By senior year, everyone is submitting applications and chewing their fingernails off waiting to hear back. The end of senior year is a parade of precollege celebration, from printing all our scholarship offers and college choices in the local paper to announcing our college plans as we cross the stage at graduation. The term *gap year* is not something that has ever crossed the lips of a student here. Sure, there are people in every class who don't go to college, but unless they've enlisted in the military, everyone sort of acts like they don't exist.

"I want to start today with some small group dialogues to help you begin talking about your college plans," Ms. Williams says, and then she counts us off into small groups. The next minute or so is spent scraping desks across the linoleum floor as we all get into little pods, prepared to discuss the questions Ms. Williams is currently passing out to the class.

I find myself in a pod with Lucy Hernandez, Byron Frankel, and hulking Wyatt Hawkins, who's in line to be the first string quarterback for the BPHS Trojans should Jackson Lewis break his arm or fail a class. Sitting next to him makes me feel like Polly Pocket.

Lucy immediately launches into her plan, supported by notes she refers to from her phone. Lucy is for sure going to be our valedictorian. She wants to go to Stanford and become a billionaire tech genius. She made this app for when you're at the movies that uses your location and scrapes data from movie websites to show you what movie starts immediately after yours ends, so that you can figure out what movie to sneak in to next. If you start early enough, the app can create a mini film festival for you that takes you from matinee to midnight on only one ticket. Probably not something you can put on your college applications, since it basically encourages stealing, but definitely evidence that someday Lucy will be able to buy and sell us all.

Next up is Byron, with his perfectly straight teeth, moisturized skin, and ballet dancer posture. He's going to audition for every major musical theater program in the country (one of which is apparently in Oklahoma. Who knew?). He's busy laying the groundwork with dance classes, a vocal coach, and a third summer at Backstage, a camp in upstate New York that boasts more than a dozen alumni who've won a Tony. Also, Lin-Manuel Miranda follows him on Twitter.

And rounding out our little posse is Wyatt, who, based on his sort of Neanderthal persona and the fact that his chief interest is football, I figured would at least fall on my side. You know, Team Not a Clue. But nope, even Wyatt's got his future planned out. He's going to the U, where he'll get a degree in secondary education so that he can be a high school football coach. The only sign that he was wavering at all was when he couldn't decide between social studies or physical education as a concentration. Not super flashy, but at least he's got a plan.

Because when it's my turn to share, I find myself stumbling and stuttering. I have *no* plan beyond "college: I want to go there." Obviously I'll apply to the U, because hello, in-state tuition. But any sense of a college plan starts and ends there. I have no idea what I want to do when I get there. But I can't *wait* to go to college, which until now has seemed like enough. To no longer be saddled with all the shit that comes from growing up and going to school with the same people for thirteen years. It seems like the place where I can finally figure everything out. So my plan has always been:

Step 1: Go to college

Step 2: Figure it out

Because the one thing I know for sure is that when I get to college, I can stop being the Hot 'N Crusty Bathroom Baby. *That's* what I want to major in.

But that doesn't fly, at least not with Lucy and Byron, two of the most driven human beings on the planet. They immediately launch into counselor mode.

"How about starting with what you're *not* interested in doing?" Lucy suggests, tapping away at her phone. I bet she's looking for an app that will help me plan my future. Or hell, she's probably *making* one.

"Um, probably nothing with science. It's not really my jam," I say. Which is true. I barely scraped by in biology, and chemistry has been an utter disaster for me. The only reason I'm toughing it out is because it'll mean my required credits will be done and I can spend my senior year science-free.

"What do you like to do with your free time?" Byron asks.

Watch a twenty-year-old space soap opera with my dad and pretend to care about my friends' intricate choreography, which is set to pop music that I don't particularly like.

"You could open a pizza place," Wyatt says, nodding his head on his beefy neck. "Call it Pizza Baby."

Ugh. I'd rather spend the rest of my life performing chemistry experiments.

I'm saved from my career planning team when the bell drones its electronic tone and everyone starts rearranging their desks back into rows.

"On Monday we'll be talking about Shirley Jackson's short story in your text, so make sure you've read and are ready to discuss!" Ms. Williams calls over the sounds of feet stampeding for the door.

Ah, a short story of dystopian murder. At least I'll have something to say for Monday's class. Anything's better than another college inquisition.

CHAPTER
FIVE

My first Friday shift should be filling me with dread, but I can't stop thinking about the way Mac's arm hovered over my shoulder as he held the door open for me today at lunch. I can't stop hearing his voice telling me he'd *miss me*. Okay, he said "*we'll* miss you," but he included himself in that. And his smile. And his breath, which somehow wasn't terrible after all the pizza and ranch dressing he'd scarfed down. And yeah, I'm bummed to be walking into the greasy cocoon of Hot 'N Crusty instead of scooting up close to Mac on the bleachers, but even that isn't dulling my shine.

That is, until I see the SUV with the WCVB logo

wrapped around it in very shouty colors parked right next to the front door.

I notice her immediately. She's so polished that she practically glows in an impeccably tailored Barney-purple suit and a blond bob sprayed with enough product to withstand a Category 4 hurricane.

"Rebecca!" She smiles, and a line of perfectly white teeth—which only the best dental work in four counties can buy—nearly blinds me. She's standing near the counter, but very intentionally not touching it—or anything else, I notice. I have a feeling that if she could avoid letting her designer heels touch the sticky floor, she would, but hovering over the floor is not one of her skills.

"Molly," I say. I swallow hard, trying not to let what I'm really thinking read all over my face. Because *what in the blooming hell are you doing here* is not polite. And even though Molly Landau is the absolute last person I want to see in Hot 'N Crusty, my mother instilled in me the importance of always being polite.

"I called and called and called, but could never manage to track you down," she says, enunciating words like she's tasting every syllable. She's got an accent that's somehow Midwest meets mid-Atlantic by way of mid nowhere. "You're a very busy bee!"

"Well, school, work," I say, keeping it purposefully vague. My mom told me she called. Gave me every last message. Mom would never pressure me to do any press I don't want to do, but she did tell me I should give Molly the courtesy of actually declining. I should have listened, because this would have been *so* much easier over the phone.

"Well, it was no problem to pop down here and find you," she says, and her tone gets extra saccharine, which I think means it definitely *was* a problem. "Anyway, I'm just here to talk to you about doing an interview. Something to commemorate your sweet sixteen and the fulfillment of Del's promise of a job. I think it'll be a fantastic package, a *where are they now* with a lovely little twist."

"What's the twist?" Julianne asks from behind the register. Her sardonic tone slices through the air.

Molly smiles, and it looks like she's been cued. "That she's right back where she started, of course!"

Tell me about it.

I take a deep breath and steel myself, because I really hate confrontation, something I sense Molly was counting on with her surprise appearance. "I'm really sorry you had to come all the way down here, but I'm not really interested in doing an interview," I tell her.

Molly presses her red lips together in a thin smile, her

perfectly waxed eyebrows narrowing *just* slightly. "Do you mind if I ask why not?"

Because I'd sooner climb into one of the pizza ovens than talk into a camera? Because the potential of another viral clip of me—in the era of YouTube and Twitter—makes me want to start walking down Highway 41 and not stop until I hit the ocean? Because no person should ever have to spend this much time thinking about the moment that they exited their mother, much less talk about it on television?

The only thing about my birth that I'm grateful for is the fact that social media wasn't yet a *thing* when it all went down. The internet was still in its tween years, making a lot of noise and trying to figure out who it was going to be. There was no meme-ified version of my arrival into the world. The story was olden times viral, meaning it was on TV and in magazines and on a few websites, but there were no retweets or reblogs or reshares of me.

Still, if you search my name, the first few results are all spots from Molly Landau that went on to live forever on YouTube. She did a package on my first birthday. And then she showed up again for my fifth, getting some B-roll of me blowing out my candles while Del and my parents looked on. But even at five, I'd refused to have a microphone clipped to the collar of my pink dress so that I could answer questions in front of a camera. And my parents never pushed me. When Molly asked again for my tenth birthday, I flatly refused, telling my parents they could go ahead and put me down as a *no* for all future television requests. The newspaper photos were one thing, but talking in front of a camera? No thank you please.

I didn't want to do it then, and I certainly am not going to do it now, when I'm wearing an I'M HOT 'N CRUSTY T-shirt and a matching baseball cap (not to mention the blooming whitehead right in the middle of my chin).

"It's just not for me," I tell her, trying to match that mysterious accent she's got going on. But instead I think I wind up sounding a little stoned. I remember my mom's instructions: *Be polite, but remember that "no" is a complete sentence.* So I smile as warmly as I can. "But I appreciate your interest."

From the way her jaw is twitching, it looks like it's taking a Herculean effort for Molly Landau to keep that local Emmy-winning smile plastered on her oddly ageless face. But she's a professional, so of course she doesn't crack.

"Well, that's unfortunate," she says, and I don't know if it's the Botox or just good training, but her face manages to remain placid. "I really think a story like that could bring a lot of joy to people. The news is so negative these days, and I know folks would love to see an update from a bright young woman like yourself. It would be a great opportunity for you to talk about things that matter to you, maybe give a platform to a pet cause. And of course, it would make a wonderful addition to a college application."

She cocks an eyebrow at me, and I can tell she's really giving it the business. But as my mom likes to say, "no" is the end of a conversation, not the start of negotiations. (See? My mom really is great at pep talks.)

"Again, I appreciate that, but it just isn't something I'm interested in," I say. "Thank you for stopping by."

She nods, and I can practically hear her teeth grinding from over here.

"Can I get you something to eat?" Julianne asks, leaning over the counter with a snide smile. I like this feisty, screwing-with-a-local-celebrity Julianne. "We could box it up to go."

Now Molly's professional mask slips, her lip curling slightly. I wonder when Molly Landau last ate pizza. Or any complex carbohydrate.

"No, thank you," she says. She hoists her leather tote bag higher onto her shoulder and pivots on her impossibly high heel. "I need to get back to the station."

As she passes me, she reaches out for a handshake, but of course there's something extra, too. Because when I grasp her hand, I feel her press a crisp card into my palm.

"Do call me if you change your mind," she says, her beauty queen smile back with a vengeance.

"Thank you," I say. I take the card and slide it into my pocket. "Again, I'm sorry you had to come all the way here for nothing."

With one last smile and a quick glance around the dining room, she's gone.

"Damn. You like, leaned *in*," Julianne says when the door shuts behind Molly's purple pencil skirt. I can't believe it. I think Julianne just paid me a compliment.

I blow out an enormous breath, my shoulders sagging, and it's at that moment that I realize my hands are shaking. My shift hasn't even started yet and I'm already sweating. I feel like I just walked out of the ring with a prizefighter and didn't get knocked out. I don't know how I managed to do that, except that the only thing worse would have been agreeing to do her ridiculous "package."

"Thanks," I say to Julianne with a smile.

I may have played at being confident and strong, but I don't come by it naturally. I hope Molly doesn't come back. I don't know if I have it in me to say no again. I might just have to quit and convince my parents to move to another town.

"I hate confrontation," I tell Julianne, "but I hate being on TV even more."

"Do we embarrass you, Pizza Princess?"

I look up from the counter and see Tristan hanging out in the doorway that leads into the kitchen. He's smirking, because of course he is. And for maximum annoyance, he skulks back out through the kitchen before I can even try to say something back.

And my shift hasn't even started yet.

"Yo, Del, how was your date?" Jason asks as Del emerges from the kitchen. I didn't realize he was here, and thank god he didn't come out while Molly was here. The two of them tag teaming would have been much harder to say no to.

Del wipes his hands on his jeans, leaving a streak of flour. He must be helping Joey prep dough for the weekend, since dough is best after it's been hanging around in the walk-in fridge for a few days. These are the facts that fill my head now.

"Her cat was sick, so she had to leave early to take him to the vet. But I sent her a text message about seeing a movie this weekend, so hopefully we'll get another try," Del says, holding up both hands to show his fingers crossed. My heart breaks for the man. I mean, sure, he's a bit of a goofball, but seeing him fail to recognize the "my cat is sick" date ditch tactic is like watching a puppy try to talk through a glass door.

And then I watch Del turn and try to walk through the swinging door to the kitchen, only to miss and half crash into the doorframe. The poor man is *so* tragic.

I follow him back to the office and clock in, securing my ball cap over my hair and dropping my purse in the corner. Then I return to the front where Julianne is carefully turning all the cash in the same direction in the register drawer while Lena, a day waitress who sometimes takes an extra evening shift on busy nights, is wiping down trays. I grab a rag and help her.

"What do you think Del is doing wrong on his dates?" I ask, still feeling a truckload of sympathy for him and wanting to forget my local news showdown.

"I think the date format does him no favors," Lena says, dropping her rag as she secures her long braids in a tight bun on top of her head. "Del is . . . a lot, and when you trap all that energy and rampant positivity in a chair and aim it at another person sitting across the table, I'm guessing it can get a little relentless."

"That's super insightful," Julianne says, and I'm surprised that there's no sneer, no gazing at her shoes.

Talking to Lena, Julianne seems like a different person. Hell, with anyone in Hot 'N Crusty but me, she's a downright social butterfly.

"Also, that mustache is just tragic," Lena adds, and we all nod.

"You should be a life coach," Julianne says, bumping the cash drawer closed with her hip. It gives back a little ding of protest. "You should be *Del*'s life coach."

"That is a made-up white people job," Lena says. "I'm in school to be a family therapist. And Del cosigned my student loans, so no, I will *not* tell my boss he's a bad date. Now excuse me, I need to deliver some breadsticks." She turns and takes a basket from the pass-through and drops it on a freshly wiped tray. As soon as she's gone, Julianne reverts back to her default setting with me: sullen with a side of withdrawn. But I can't shake the look on her face while talking to Lena. And I start to wonder if maybe Julianne might warm up to me, too. I pin the notion to my mental corkboard. It would be an ongoing project, that's for sure.

The night is a total blur of activity. I remember Del telling me Friday nights are always nuts, and it doesn't take me long before all the training that was stuffed into my brain just sort of clicks. I stop worrying about messing things up because I'm too busy *doing* things. I take orders. I bus tables. I scoop what feels like eleven tons of ice into a billion red plastic cups, filling them at the soda fountain behind the register. I swipe debit cards and learn to studiously avoid eye contact as the person fills out the tip line, or busy myself as they reach for the tip jar positioned next to the register.

I had a few stumbles, of course. There was the great vegan standoff with a dreadlocked white girl who clearly wandered into the wrong restaurant.

"I'd like a large pizza with nut cheese," she said.

"With what?" I didn't know what nut cheese is, but it sounded like an affliction for which you seek urgent medical care.

"Nut cheese," she said again, slowly like maybe I didn't speak English. "It's vegan cheese."

Vegan cheese? What's the point? "Um, I don't think we have that." I glanced over my shoulder to check the board over my head, but I knew the answer. Hot 'N Crusty doesn't even have gluten-free crust. I wouldn't put hard money on Del stocking any kind of cheese-substitute. "I guess we could go no cheese if you want to make it vegan."

"You really should have a dairy-free option," she replied.

"Well, um, we don't."

"You *should*." She crossed her arms over her flannel shirt and cocked an eyebrow at me.

We stared at each other for a few brutal seconds, enough time for me to contemplate how much it must have hurt when she had that ring shoved through her septum. Did she think I was lying about the nut cheese? Or maybe that some would magically appear if she scolded me long enough? Or maybe she wanted me to get in my car and drive over to the ShopRite and pick up a bag of it. Whatever it was, she wasn't budging, so finally I just told her I'd find Del. He offered her a cheese-less pizza and a discount, which she took, grumbling about nut cheese the whole time.

There was also the moment when a tray of eight sodas needed to be delivered to a table. The busers were busy, so I took a step toward it, even putting my hands on the edge of the tray with the kind of blind confidence of a person going ice-skating for the first time. Luckily, Julianne stepped in before I could wind up covered in about a hundred ounces of sticky liquid. Which I filed away as a sign that Julianne didn't totally hate me. I mean, if I were her enemy, she probably would have sat back and enjoyed watching me take an impromptu soda bath. Julianne herself only made it out from behind the counter before Frank practically sprinted across the restaurant to pull the tray from her shoulder. Though I don't think that one was about avoiding a disaster so much as a very enthusiastic act of chivalry. It hasn't escaped my notice the way Frank tends to blush when he's around Julianne.

By the end of my shift, I'm practically dead on my feet. I shoot Natalie a text to see where everyone is, then shove my phone back into my pocket. I wander outside with my keys in my hand only to realize my mistake. Because when I press the unlock button, there's no beep. And there's no beep because there's no car. I didn't drive myself to work tonight. Dad needed the car for some Quiz Bowl thing he had at school, so Mom dropped me off. I was supposed to text her just before my shift ended so she could be waiting to pick me up, but I forgot. Now I'm going to have to sit on this stupid curb and wait for her.

I drop down onto the concrete and fish out my phone again, typing an SOS to Mom, when the door opens and Julianne comes outside, locking the door behind her. She catches sight of me on the curb and stares at me for longer than is comfortable.

"Do you have a ride?" she finally asks. It's the definition of *begrudging*.

"I just have to text my mom. She'll be here soon. We only live, like, five minutes away."

"Okay," she says.

The boys tumble out of the restaurant, laughing about the box of industrial-sized condoms and a stapled printout of how to use them that Greg found on a table (for which he won the right to assign Jason to haul out the mountain of Friday night trash).

"Hey, Beck, you coming out with us?" Frank asks when he spots me.

"Uh, I—"

"Her mom is coming to get her," Julianne says, too quickly. But for once, Frank isn't tuned in to Julianne's frequency.

"You should come. We're gonna get some food," he says. "We can give you a ride there and then home."

At that moment, my phone lights up with a text message from my mom. Apparently she, too, forgot that she'd be my ride and just put something in the oven. She'll be here in twenty.

So my options are to sit in the empty Hot 'N Crusty parking lot for twenty minutes waiting for Mom, or hitch a ride. For food. And as my stomach lets out a prehistoric growl, I realize that I'm starving.

"Yeah, okay, food sounds good," I say as everyone starts piling into cars.

"My car's full, so you're with Julianne," Jason says as he twirls his keys on his key chain and moseys across the parking lot to a newish Honda. "There's a giant box of robotics supplies riding shotgun until I drop them off with Mr. Grant."

I glance at Julianne. I'm tempted to let her off the hook, tell her I'll ride shotgun with the box, or maybe even just skip altogether. But then I realize this is a prime opportunity to get her to warm up to me. And so I just wait. And finally she shrugs.

"Yeah, fine, you can come with me," she says.

So instead of telling my mom I'll wait for her pound cake to finish, I ask if it's cool if I go out with some work friends. And instead of an actual reply, I get a string of emojis that includes two thumbs-up, a party hat, and three smiley faces with heart eyes (when it comes to emojis, Mom's take is that more is always better).

I climb into Julianne's car, something old and gold and designed for old ladies to drive to church. The bumper is hanging off slightly in the front.

"Accident?" I ask.

"Cart corral" is all she says, and I'm left to fill in the gaps.

Then she studiously adjusts her mirror and clicks her seat belt before her keys even approach the ignition, like it's Coach Quarles in the passenger seat with his driver's ed clipboard. And when they do finally make contact, the public radio station my dad listens to comes through the speakers at a pleasant volume. I recognize the bluegrass show from plenty of rides in the passenger seat of Dad's Corolla.

It's about a twenty-minute drive to Madisonville, and I feel every minute of it. Julianne tells me (in as few words as possible) that we're headed to Stefano's. Beyond that, it's just silence and banjos on the radio.

Madisonville is home to Warren West College, a small, competitive liberal arts school. It looks like a movie set for college, all stone and brick pathways and honest-to-god ivy. My parents want me to apply. I tell them I see myself at someplace bigger. But what I really mean is farther away. I open my mouth to ask Julianne where she plans to go to college—a reflex—before I remember that she doesn't want to talk to me. At this point, I think riding quietly might be the quickest way to her heart.

Stefano's is a long, one-story building with ivy growing over it, the Stefano's sign glowing in red neon on the stone exterior. It's a building of indeterminate age, but it's definitely seen some things. Inside, rows of wooden booths with super high backs give everyone their own little cubby in the restaurant. I follow Julianne to the table in the back, a square booth with bench seats on three sides, the high, dark wood making it feel like its own little cubby. The way she strides back there with confidence tells me this is "their" table, in the same way the round table two from the center of the cafeteria is "ours" at school. The boys are already sipping on red plastic cups the size of their heads, the menus still in a pile in the center of the table. It occurs to me that while I've spent Friday nights at football games and hanging at Tamsin and Colin's house, they've been spending their Friday nights here. This is *their* ritual. And now I'm a part of it. Or crashing it—I can't tell quite yet.

"I got you a Coke," Frank says, gesturing to the cup next to his. Julianne slides in with a smile and a thank-you that seems to light Frank up from the inside. He tears his gaze away as I slide in next to Julianne. "Didn't know your drink. Sorry, Beck."

"It's okay," I reply, and when the waitress arrives, I order a water with lemon. It's become a habit, since Tamsin is always dragging us to pricey cafés where a Coke comes in a glass bottle and costs like three dollars. But water is always free.

The boys are chattering on about something, leaning in and intense, and I prepare myself to relax and tune them out (like I do when Mac, Colin, and Eli get deep into fantasy baseball conversations), when I hear the mention of Spacefarers and an upcoming galaxy war. They're talking

about an episode of *Apex Galaxy* that Dad and I just finished, one where the Navstar Force pulls a classic Trojan
horse operation on the Exos.

"Did you know that was Blake Garcia playing the Exo
guard in the cold open?" I say, and I swear there is an
actual record scratch as the boys halt their conversation
and swivel their heads in unison to stare at me. Jason's
mouth is literally hanging agape.

"You watch *AxGx*?" Greg asks. I recognize the abbre-
viation from the message boards I've read late at night
when I can't sleep, though I never realized it was pro-
nounced *AxGax*.

"Yeah. With my dad," I say. "He was into the '88
series back in the day. We finished that one over the summer and just started the reboot."

"It's not a reboot, it's a companion," Jason says. I can
tell he's trying to regain some high ground, but he's still
too stunned to find out we share a fandom to actually put
the requisite sneer in it. I bet he's on the message boards,
one of the screen names who posts a lot of corrections
and *actually*s. I bet he's even a mod. But I don't ask,
because I've never told a single soul that I visit the *Apex
Galaxy* message boards—not even my dad.

The waitress brings my drink and takes our order—
two extra larges, one cheese, one half pepperoni,

half mushrooms and onions—and then the table goes silent. It's like suddenly the boys are too nervous to nerd out in front of me, even though just moments ago they were seconds from achieving peak dork. It makes me feel like a total interloper. I'm throwing off their rhythm. So I try to fix it by talking.

"So you guys seriously finish working five hours at a pizza place, and then you go out . . . to another pizza place?" I ask.

"Okay, we love HnC—" Julianne says. I'm shocked to hear her speak, but I can't dwell on it, because Jason cuts her off.

"Speak for yourself."

Julianne rolls her eyes. "But we all freely admit that it's not exactly the *best* pizza." She drops her voice a little as she says it, like someone might be recording her. It's like she's committing some kind of act of pizza treason and doesn't want to be caught.

"It's fine. Serviceable," Frank says with a shrug.

"It's the perfect pizza to eat with your soccer team when you've won the fourth grade championship," Greg says.

"When did you ever play soccer?" Jason snipes.

"It's a metaphor," Greg shoots back.

"It's the kind of pizza you have at your birthday party in middle school," Frank clarifies.

"It's cafeterialicious," Jason says.

"Anyway," Julianne says with an eye roll, "to try and compare Stefano's to HnC is like comparing a Ferrari to a Dodge Dart."

"Okay, but you're seriously not tired of pizza?"

"Beck, you've clearly never been to Stefano's," Frank says.

And I haven't. I know what it is, of course. I've driven past it when I've been to plays at the college with my parents, but it always seemed like a place that wasn't for me. It's for students at the college, for people infinitely cooler than me. People who know something I don't. It never occurred to me that I could just *go* there. Like I would belong.

The pizza arrives. Two huge pies, and right away I see what they mean about Stefano's being different. This pizza has a thick, doughy crust, and the edges are crispy with cheese overflow.

"They use cast-iron pans, like for deep-dish pizza, only it's not deep-dish," Frank explains as I pull a slice of pepperoni onto my plate. The cheese is hot and gooey, and I have to break the strings with my fork to detach it from the rest of the slices. Before I take a bite, though, I reach into my purse and pull out a Lactaid.

Jason gasps. "I'm sorry, are you telling me that the Pizza Princess is . . . *lactose intolerant*?"

"I prefer Bathroom Baby," I say back, shocked that I reached for the joke. Shocked that the entire table laughs *with* me. "I usually just avoid cheese, but this looks good, so I'll make an exception."

"So *that's* why you only ate the crusts on your birthday," Julianne says.

I hadn't even noticed her there on my birthday. But she noticed me. She noticed my aversion to cheese. And she's not making fun of me.

The pizza tastes as good as it looks: salty and cheesy and yeasty, with a nice acidic bite from the tomato sauce. I'm embarrassed to hear my own moan escape as I chew.

"She gets it now," Julianne says as she attacks a slice of mushroom and onion.

"I do," I reply. And conversation slows as we all tuck into our slices while they're still steaming, riding that fine line between delicious and painfully hot mouth burns. We're quiet again, but this time it's silence with a purpose. I don't feel like an intruder. I feel like we're all quietly sharing this delicious moment. It feels oddly familiar, like slipping on your favorite sneakers.

And then the quiet chewing gives way to conversation, and I find myself happily tossing out *Apex Galaxy* fan theories between bites. Jason is over his shock now and is happy to loudly debate me over whether Captain Evangelion is a turncoat (I say no, he says I'm blinded by his blue eyes and washboard abs . . . He may be right).

I'm actually having fun when Tristan shows up. I suppress a scowl, but he doesn't. His just shines right on through as he slides into the opposite side of the booth next to Greg. He'd be facing me, if he actually acknowledged my presence. As much as I hate that he has any kind of influence over me, I suddenly feel very sour. And I'm reminded once again that I don't belong.

The conversation carries on around him, but he doesn't say anything. He just silently starts in on a slice of mushroom and onion. He's yet to say a word to anyone, just a few nods of greeting to the guys when they said hey. Is he nice to *anyone*?

And then he reaches into his messenger bag and produces a small wooden box, just a little bit bigger than a cigar box. The wood is unpainted, but it looks polished such that if I touched it, it would have a velvety smooth finish. There's a pair of brass hinges on one side, and an intricate gold latch on the other. He passes it across the table to Julianne without saying a word.

She takes it in her hands and gasps. She lifts the lid, and inside I see that it's divided into compartments with narrow pieces of wood cut and interlocked together. There's a small piece of mirror set into the lid, and a delicious woody smell wafts from the box.

"Tristan, it's beautiful! Thank you! My mom is going to absolutely love it," she says, running her hands over the delicate woodwork inside.

"You made that?" I say, but he just shrugs in response.

"Tristan is super talented," Julianne says, like I've accused him of stealing it. "I'm going to give this to my mom for her birthday." She carefully closes the lid and cradles it gently in her lap. "How much do I owe you?"

Tristan shakes his head, waving her off.

"No, seriously, let me pay you. This is gorgeous!"

"It's on the house," he says, staring down at his plate as he rubs the back of his neck. It's hard to tell on his tan skin, but I can see a hint of blush creeping into his cheeks, which surprises me. "It was good practice. That's the first jewelry box I've ever made. Really, you were helping me."

Julianne sighs, running her hand across the box's lid. She smiles. "Thanks, Tristan," she says, her voice soft.

"It's fine," he mutters, before returning to his pizza crust.

"Hey, Beck, have you gotten to the episodes with

Ataria yet?" Frank asks, pulling my attention from Tristan and his act of surprising kindness.

"I actually just saw her first episode the other day," I tell him. Ataria is an alien who has magical powers that she can't seem to control. Her first episode was treated as comic relief, but there was a hint at something darker. "She comes back?"

"Don't spoil her!" Greg yelps, punching Frank in the arm.

"You can't spoil a twenty-year-old show, dude," Frank shoots back as he rubs the spot on his arm and groans.

"It's okay, I don't mind spoilers," I say, channeling the debate I've been having with Dad for the last year. He'd seen all the episodes in the original four seasons, but he never watched the reboot (or, *companion*). He's relentless about not being spoiled, but I love perusing the online forums and reading fan theories. Spoilers are inevitable. "Any show that depends solely on audience surprise isn't very good to begin with."

"That's what I'm saying." Jason slaps the table with his palm like we're debating in the United Nations. Getting agreement from Jason feels like a hard-won victory. I have to stop myself from fist pumping. "Don't worry, you're close. Ataria comes back in, like, three or four episodes? As soon as the producers saw her on film, they knew they had to have her back. She's magnetic. Her arc with First Lieutenant Ringold is classic."

"Beware. You've just climbed aboard Jason's ship," Greg says.

"Then we're about to fight, because First Lieutenant Ringold belongs with Ensign Oriana forever and ever the end," I reply. I know I'm quickly severing whatever connection Jason and I forged in that moment of spoiler debate, and I can't help grinning. I never get to talk about *Apex Galaxy* in real life. I once tried to bring it up at lunch, thinking at least I could get the guys to bite, but Tamsin just wrinkled her nose in disgust while Eli called me a Trekkie. I couldn't even manage to tell him *that's an entirely different show, you dipstick.*

Only instead of pushback over my preferred ship, I get silence, as all three boys' eyes go wide, Jason looking *way* too satisfied. I'm guessing I've stumbled on a *major* spoiler.

"Don't tell me," I say, plugging my ears. Apparently my spoiler stance is flexible, because if I'm about to find out that Ensign Oriana dies I will thoroughly lose my shit. "I will go down with this ship!"

Everyone at the table laughs, including Tristan, who is straight-up cackling.

"What?" I ask, leveling him with what Natalie calls *the eye*.

"I just didn't realize you were such a nerd," he says with a shrug.

"Hey!"

"It's a compliment," he says, and as I look around the table, where Julianne is leaning toward Frank talking about some books where fairies astride dragons wage war with humans while Jason and Greg start in on the origin of the Exos and their relation to the Synchros, I realize that he's right. At this table, being a nerd means being part of the squad. And I'm surprised at how good that feels.

The waitress returns to clear away empty plates and drop the check, a subtle hint to GTFO. I pull out my phone to check the time and see a text from Natalie from nearly an hour ago.

> We'll be at Cora's till midnight. Boys have early practice. Come when you can!

But it's already 11:30. By the time I get back to Brook Park, I will have missed them completely.

"There's no *way* Rigel gets commander. He lacks

Academy training," Jason says, thoroughly leaving any trace of inside voice behind.

I glance back down at my phone, then back at the table. Then I fire off a reply to Natalie.

Sorry I missed you guys! Work went late.

And then I school Jason on why Rigel is *absolutely* qualified to command the Navstar Force thanks to his apprenticeship with Admiral Fox.

CHAPTER
SIX

I hate Friday shifts. And I have to work every single one.

I didn't think missing football games would be all that bad when I started at Hot 'N Crusty, but I've yet to make a postwork hang happen. And this week is Bearden Week, when we play our big rivals from the next town over at Bearden Falls High School. I say "we" like I'm going to suit up and kick a field goal, like I've ever given half a crap about football. But that's what Bearden Week and all its spirit days and pep rallies and sign painting will do to you. Suddenly you're bleeding school colors while chanting the fight song like you're about to follow Braveheart into battle.

Only, Hot 'N Crusty has taken both my life and my freedom. Because all my friends are at the game. And I'm not. Which means I'm not taking the next steps with Mac, whatever those are. Natalie swears they're coming, but I'm starting to think the thing holding us back now is this stupid job. I mean, the only time I get to see him anymore is at lunch, and the Brook Park cafeteria, with its sticky linoleum floors and the smell of gravy in the air at all times, is not exactly the stuff of romantic dreams.

Nope, once again I'm at the counter beside Julianne taking orders from the steady stream of customers that are parading through Hot 'N Crusty. First it's the families trying for early dinner before the kids melt down for the night (only about half of them make the deadline, as evidenced by the sheer volume of pizza crusts and spilled soda beneath the booths). Then we get everyone who skipped the game, plus some stray college kids on a date night. And I can tell when the game is nearly over because people in blue and white, temporary tattoos on their cheeks and pom-poms stuffed in their back pockets, start streaming in.

All evening I've been getting updates from Natalie about the game. It was close, and everyone was jacked up to eleven. By the fourth quarter, my phone was pinging with random strings of emojis and increasingly insane selfies. Natalie and Cora faux biting their nails. Tamsin with her mouth so wide I can count her fillings. Colin and Eli and Mac cheering at the field, their arms overhead, a sliver of tan skin peeking out above the waistband of Mac's jeans that yes, I stare at for *way* too long. For the first time in my life I was sad to be missing an actual football game. And then we won. Natalie sent a selfie of the whole gang crammed together in the frame, cheek to cheek, taken with the aid of Mac's long arm held high overhead. Everyone was grinning.

Everyone except me.

I text Natalie and ask her what everyone's doing now. I still have another hour until close, and then at least another half hour after that to do closing duties. And then I click back to the photo of Mac and take another quick peek at his abs.

"Excuse me, can I order, please?" The annoyed tone of voice comes from a girl I recognize from ecology class freshman year. She spelled *fir tree* with a *u*. She's wearing someone's letterman jacket and practically swimming in it, her black hair pulled up in a high ponytail and secured with an explosion of blue and white ribbons.

"Yeah, go ahead," I say, and punch her order in on the touch screen, scanning her card and flipping the screen around for her to sign. My phone feels like a brick in my pocket. I'm dying for Natalie to text back, to figure out how I can meet up with Mac and his abs. But when I finish with ecology girl, I check my phone. No text.

I don't get a text back for nearly an hour, and by then my shift is almost over. My nerves are tied up in knots as I gradually try to psych myself up for seeing him. Maybe this is the night. Maybe tonight I can make a move. Tonight. Tonight. Tonight.

When my phone finally buzzes in my pocket, I leap like it's an electric shock. I pull it out of my back pocket with such gusto that it goes shooting out of my hands and skitters across the floor, coming to a stop under a booth where Fur Tree and her boyfriend (the hulking owner of the letterman jacket) are parked on the same side of the table, attached at the tongue, making out like it's their last night on earth. I creep up and drop to my hands and knees, reaching for the phone, and end up accidentally brushing the exposed ankle of the girl, who yelps. I dive backward onto my butt, my phone thankfully still in my hand.

"What the hell, creeper?" she cries, staring down at me.

"Sorry," I say, holding up my phone. "Just dropped this."

And then I scramble to my feet, ignoring the damp

spot blooming on my butt from lord knows what was in a puddle on the floor. I'm too busy tapping and swiping until I can see my text message.

> Night ended early. Have to help with mom's gluten-free piecrusts at the ass crack, and Colin failed a calc test so he's grounded. Eli and Core left for a late movie. See you tomorrow? After I get released from pie jail?

I notice she doesn't mention what Mac's doing, but without everyone else, there's no good, organic reason for us to hang out. Not unless I *really* want to put myself out there. So I guess tonight is just another bust.

You win again, Hot 'N Crusty.

In my text message haze, I managed to forget to bring anything to the table game. Jason wins with a retainer in a cup of soda and sticks me with trash duty. I think the only reason I don't wind up on bathrooms is because Jason seems to be feuding with Frank over something *Apex Galaxy* related. I escape the suckiest of suck jobs, and instead wind up with the suck-lite job.

I'm muscling the last bag of trash out the back door to the dumpster. It's weirdly heavy and unwieldy, but I try to ignore it. I don't need my brain trying to figure out what's in there that's causing it to sway like a steamship.

Some things are better left a mystery. I just need to heave it into the dumpster. No thinking, just swing. Only when I swing, something in the bag gives way, and I feel my shirt get wet before I even realize what's happening. Within seconds, I'm coated in garbage juice—what smells like a noxious mix of soda and marinara.

"*Ugh!* Gross!" I drop the remains of the bag, and all the wet napkins and other detritus that were once inside it topple out onto the pavement. I'm going to have to clean all that up eventually, but now I can only focus on trying to get as much of the garbage juice off me as possible. I grab my shirt and pull it away from my body, wondering if I can whip it off without getting the grossness in my hair. Or if anyone will be around to see me standing by the Hot 'N Crusty dumpster wearing just my bra.

I glance around the parking lot, which is thankfully empty, and then across the street to the Margaritas parking lot. They stay open later than we do, so they're still fairly bustling, though the action seems to be mostly inside. Except for the couple coming out and heading to their car. I squint, wondering if I know them. If they're strangers I'll never see again, then maybe it doesn't matter if they see my heather gray cotton laundry-day bra. They look like they might be older, but when they walk to a familiar hunter-green Range Rover, I realize they're not strangers. Not at all.

They're decked out in blue and white from the game. I can see Tamsin's sparkly makeup from here, a temporary BPHS tattoo on her cheek that, on her, somehow manages to look chic. Mac walks Tamsin to the driver's side door of her car. But before she can get in, he puts his hands on her hips and spins her around, leaning her against the door. He takes a step closer, right into her personal space, his hands still resting on her hips. Tamsin is slight, but tall, so Mac only has to duck his head a little bit to kiss her—which he does, quickly at first. But then she snakes her hand up around his neck and pulls him down, so that soon they're engaging in a full-on make out. For just a quick moment I sigh at the sight, like I'm watching a movie and imagining myself up there making out with the leading man. Only it's not a movie, and it's definitely not me.

It's Mac and Tamsin.

Tamsin and Mac.

Making out.

Everything suddenly clicks into place, my focus becoming razor sharp. Because of course they are. Of course Mac likes Tamsin, with her skinny jeans and her lithe dancer body. Of course he wants her, with her Range

Rover and her giant house and her red hair and her big personality. I was such an idiot for even thinking there was a universe in which he had a crush on me.

But it really seemed like he did.

Apparently I was wrong.

I drop down onto the curb, forgetting that my shirt is soaked with garbage juice that's now adhering to my torso. Soon it'll be soaking into my bra. There are wet napkins and soggy pizza crusts all around me, and if a breeze comes by, the torn trash bag is going to blow across the parking lot like a tumbleweed. But I don't notice any of that, because I'm too busy feeling sorry for myself. When I feel the first tear wind down my cheek and drop from my jaw, I realize that I'm crying. I'm hurt. And the more I think about it, the angrier I am. At myself, and maybe at Mac, because he totally made me think he had a crush on me. I know I didn't imagine that. Natalie saw it, too. And for a moment— just a really short, brutal moment—I wonder if Natalie knew. If that's why she didn't mention Mac and Tamsin in her text. But it's a dark thought, and I shove it out of my mind as fast as it arrives. Natalie would never do that to me. *Right?*

The slam of the metal door jerks me out of my misery spiral. I swipe at the tears on my cheeks and glance up to see Tristan, the black straps of the red delivery bag in his hand. Great. Because *this* is what I need right now.

"What's wrong with you?" he asks.

"Nothing." I glance up at him and try to arrange my face into something that resembles casual, but I'm pretty sure I fail. He studies me for a moment before following my gaze, turning over his shoulder until he's got them in his sights, too.

"What, is he your boyfriend or something?" He tosses it off like a joke, but too soon, dude. Too soon. I hiccup back a sob.

"Clearly not," I finally manage to sputter.

He turns and gives me an up and down, taking in my tear-streaked face, my wet, stinky shirt, and the literal pile of trash I'm sitting in.

"But you like him?" he asks.

I don't say anything. I feel like the scene pretty much speaks for itself. And having to share this moment with Tristan feels like the universe really giving me the middle finger.

There's a long beat of silence, then he says, his voice dripping with condescension, "You shouldn't waste your time or your tears on Mac MacArthur."

Am I seriously getting crush advice from Tristan Porter? Tristan, who can barely spare a kind word—hell, *any* word—for me? *He's* going to advise me on my love life? What in this lifetime or the next possibly qualifies him to comment on my friends or my crush? No way. Eff that.

"Why the hell not?" I shoot back, feeling my anger and misery finally point in a productive direction—at his smug, stupid face. It feels good to let it fester in his general direction, because at least it can distract me just a little bit from what's still going on across the street.

"Well, to start with, his name is *Mac MacArthur.* Nobody with two first names is worth whatever this is," he says, waving at me and then at the mess around my feet. What a fucking metaphor.

"Shut up" is my biting retort. I sniffle, willing the tears to stop, but of course the more I try to tell myself to stop, the more they come. The more I feel embarrassed by them, the harder they fall. I guess the seal is broken now, and all I can do is stare at my shoes and cry. I am completely defeated. "You have no idea what you're talking about, so just leave it, okay?"

Tristan sighs. He shifts back and forth on his feet, shaking his hair out of his eyes. Then he shifts the pizza bag to his left hand and takes a deep breath. "The *Golden Girls* theme song makes him cry. In third grade, he peed in his sleeping bag at camp to avoid walking to the bathhouse, which, by the way, was right next door. And he once referred to the Beatles as 'whatever.'" He makes the requisite air quotes, adopting the laid-back, faux-surfer tone that's Mac's specialty. I never realized quite how stupid it sounded until I hear Tristan mocking it.

A smile starts to tug at my lips. It makes me feel better, but just a little. Because, dammit, I still like him. If he walked over here right now and told me that kissing Tamsin was just performance art or rehearsal for a play or, hell, even practice for kissing *me*, I'd wipe the crusted marinara off my T-shirt and pucker up.

I swipe at the tears on my cheeks, which thankfully have slowed to a halt.

"How do you know all that? About Mac?"

"We used to hang out." His voice is flat. I couldn't be more surprised if he told me they were long-lost brothers. I can't reconcile a friendship between the two of them. Mac, who is basically a human golden retriever, and Tristan, who seems like a more-pissy-than-usual stray cat.

Across the street, I hear the slam of car doors as Tamsin and Mac get into the Range Rover. The engine roars, and then they're pulling out of the parking lot. Probably off to suck face in front of her house until curfew.

Ugh.

"Are you okay?" Tristan asks.

I sniffle again, then take a deep breath, nearly gagging

on the smell of the open bag of trash next to me—and all over me.

"I'm fine," I say. I rise from the curb and dust myself off, then start trying to shove the detritus back into what's left of the torn bag. Tristan puts the delivery bag down on the curb and comes over, wordlessly taking the trash bag from my hands and holding it open so I can scoop up the garbage.

"If you really want to make me feel better, you'd let me hold the bag," I say.

"I'm not that nice, Pizza Princess," he says.

Pretty soon, I've gotten most of it off the ground, and Tristan gives it the final heave into the dumpster.

"Thanks," I say.

"No problem," he replies, which is literally the nicest thing he's ever said to me. "Listen, I gotta go deliver this pizza before it gets cold. But forget that guy, okay? You don't need him."

I nod, unable to work up any kind of smile. I want to believe him.

But I really, really don't.

I turn to head back into the kitchen when I hear a strange *chugga-chugga* sound, and then an old van comes careening around the corner of the restaurant. It's one of those hippie vans from the sixties that make you think of Woodstock and Haight-Ashbury and free love.

It's Tristan. The windows are down, and some wild electric guitar is blaring from the tinny speakers, making the song practically unrecognizable. And even if I knew it, it's gone before I can identify it, because the tires go squealing out of the parking lot, taking the turn so fast I'm surprised the van doesn't tip over. Before it disappears down the road, I see the back window is decorated with a collection of brightly colored decals and bumper stickers, none of which I can read or recognize. He's gone too fast, leaving me alone again in the back parking lot.

CHAPTER
SEVEN

Natalie's been texting me all morning, and I haven't responded once.

They started out normal, then got sort of pathologically perky. Lots of exclamation points. She even deployed the unicorn emoji. Three times. That's when I knew she knew. And that's when I knew I didn't want to talk about it.

Because, honestly, I have no idea what to say. Natalie and I have spent hours breaking down Mac's flirting. She knows how deeply I want him and all my crazy fantasies, which now seem next-level pathetic. Like how I wanted to go to prom with him and get him to wear a bow tie and white dinner jacket like James Bond. Or how I cropped a group picture so it looked like we went to see *Spider-Man* by ourselves. See? Pathetic. And now she knows it was all for nothing, that I was completely imagining it all.

And so I tuck my phone under my pillow and sprawl out on the floor of my bedroom with my laptop, notebook, and US history textbook. I have an essay on manifest destiny due on Monday, and I'm going to make sure it's the best damn essay I've ever written. Because the only thing that could possibly crowd out all the dark thoughts about Mac and the images of him kissing Tamsin is some mind-numbingly boring colonial history.

When Mom stops in to ask if I want to go with her to the grocery store, I point at my textbook. When Dad pops his head in to ask if I want to "binge some *AxGx*" (I deeply regret telling him about that nickname), I shake my head. By two o'clock, I've ignored roughly eleven billion text messages and managed to avoid saying any words out loud. Except for the random swears I mutter every time the image of Mac and Tamsin slices its way into my brain—which is often.

But when I hear the doorbell ring once, then twice, without hearing Dad answer, I know I'm about to break my streak. Especially when I pull the door open and see

Natalie standing there with a foil-covered dish in her hand and the hardest-working smile in the history of friendship on her face.

"You weren't answering my texts, so I had to go old school and just show up," she says.

"Please tell me you don't think a casserole is going to make this better," I say. I nod to the dish as I step aside and let her in. I'm suddenly aware that I'm wearing a ratty old pair of flannel boxer shorts and one of my dad's T-shirts from the U. My hair is still hanging on to the messy bun I threw it into last night, but at this point I'm pretty sure it's mostly supported by tangles. And my breath is, I'm guessing, eau de sewer system.

"Natalie! Good to see you," Dad says as he strolls into the foyer. I shoot him a glare for not answering the door, and he winks at me. Because he's a crafty bastard, my dad, and something tells me this was his plan all along. My parents like to pretend they're not meddlers, but they definitely are.

"My mom sent this over," she says, passing the dish to Dad. "She was working on her vegan potpie recipe, so she made four, and they don't freeze well, so here you go!"

Dad lifts the foil and gives it a tentative sniff. "Vegan potpie? Dare I ask?"

"The sauce is made from almond milk and pureed

cauliflower. It's also low-sodium and keto, whatever that is. And the good news, the crust is gluten-free!" Natalie just barely sells that last point, her smile morphing into a pained grimace. "It's, um, not bad?"

"Natalie, be straight with me. How starving do I need to be to eat this?" Dad asks.

"Forty-eight hours trapped in your car at the bottom of a ravine, at least," Natalie replies.

Dad nods, his suspicions confirmed before turning to me. "Then this can go to book club with your mother," he says. "I'm going to put it in the fridge and throw some bagel bites in the microwave. Beck, now that you've rejoined the land of the living, my *AxGx* offer still stands!"

"What's *AxGx*?" Natalie asks.

I shake my head. "Just this show he's into," I say. I start padding toward the stairs in my sock feet, Natalie following close behind. As soon as we're in my room, I flop down on my bed. Natalie, standing on my rug, reaches into her purse and pulls out a cellophane bag.

"I brought provisions," she says, and holds up the clear cellophane bag filled with my very favorite candy. Which means she *definitely* knows, and is here for a very specific reason. Because we each have our pick-me-up junk food, something we'd never eat in front of anyone else. It's something we deploy when we're in desperate need of cheering up. Like when Natalie's mom decided to try Whole30 and made the whole family play along. Or when they killed off Rivers on *Golden Hours* (RIP, you golden vampire god). It's a never-fail, please-send-help, pull-in-case-of-emergency option when things are looking really low.

And as I stick my finger through a hole in the flannel boxers I usually sleep in, I know things are *really* low.

She tosses me the bag of circus peanuts. They bounce next to me on the bed, and I snatch them up and tear the paper top off the bag, pull one out, and take a sugary bite.

"Delicious," I say as the sugar melts over my tongue. Because as low as I feel, I can already tell my pick-me-up is working. Just a little.

Natalie shakes her head, walking over to the bed and nudging my hip with her knee. I scooch my butt over, and she flops down next to me. I offer her the bag, and she plucks one out, but clearly only for observational purposes. She holds it up and closes one eye to stare at it closely with the other. "A neon orange marshmallow that's shaped like a peanut but tastes like bananas. It makes no culinary sense."

"A chicken potpie made with neither meat, dairy, nor wheat. Now *that* makes no culinary sense."

She drops the circus peanut back into my bag. "You'll get no argument from me there."

"And you have no room to talk, Ms. Sixlets. Who eats bootleg M&M's?"

I munch in silence for a few minutes, squishing the peanuts between my thumb and forefinger before taking a bite. Somehow they just taste better when they're this dense little sugar bomb. It's weird, I know, but it's a technique I've honed over several years of bad days and road trips (the only other acceptable time to eat circus peanuts).

"Sooooooooo," Natalie says after my fifth circus peanut. And I'm almost a little glad she's talking, because I know from experience that after the sixth, my stomach starts to get very angry at me. Not that it deters me from eating the whole bag and ending up filled with sugar and deep regret. But I guess that's just part of the fun. At least "filled with deep regret" matches my current mood. "I'm guessing you heard?"

"Heard? Oh no," I say, swallowing both the bite of circus peanut and the cosmic bitterness that's lodged in my throat. "I *saw*."

"Wait, what?"

"Yeah. Tamsin and Mac. Sucking face in the parking lot of Margaritas last night. It was hard to miss."

She groans. "Oh god."

"How did you find out?" All manner of dark thoughts flash through my head. Like how long has this been going on, and how long has Natalie known, and was everyone just keeping it from me? God, fit me for my tinfoil hat.

"I started to suspect when they kept touching each other during the game last night. Nobody needs to hug like that after every single touchdown. Then Tamsin called me this morning to spill the details." Of course Tamsin didn't tell me. I'm Natalie's friend, and Natalie is Tamsin's friend. Is it the transitive property that says I'm only Tamsin's friend by default? I don't know, I'm not particularly good at math. But it sounds right.

"So last night was a first?" I ask, testing the waters of how much I actually want to know.

"Yup."

Well, at least that's good news. My friends haven't been carrying on or concealing a torrid love affair behind my back while I was stuck in pizza hell. But it's cold comfort. I still ended up in a wet pile of trash watching my crush make out with someone else. "But not a last?"

"Nope."

I sigh. "Well. There that is."

"I'm sorry, Beck. I really didn't see this coming."

I bark out a bitter laugh. "Yeah, me neither."

I pop another circus peanut in my mouth, letting the sugar melt on my tongue and blinking back tears. I manage to win the battle, but only just.

"Are you going to be okay?" Natalie asks. "I mean, is it too early to say that you can do way better than Mac?"

I take a deep breath, ignoring the protestations of my stomach (which are due to equal parts artificially banana-flavored sugar and the rotating image of Mac and Tamsin in full-on make-out mode). I blow it out and nod my head, flopping onto my stomach and looking over at my best friend, who showed up as soon as she heard and brought me my emergency parachute junk food.

"He thinks the Beatles are just 'whatever,'" I say, channeling my best Tristan channeling Mac. I try the sneering tone on for size, try to settle down into it like a comfy chair. I don't need Mac. I can do better than him.

Except I do.

And I'm afraid I can't.

"Yeah, who needs that?" Natalie says, burrowing into my shoulder. And at least, for now, I have this. I have my best friend. So I'll let her think this is fine. Just fine.

CHAPTER
EIGHT

By Monday, I manage to part myself from my pajamas and clean myself up. My hair no longer looks like a family of field mice are hosting a family reunion there. I walk into school not looking like I spent the weekend in a self-loathing sugar coma, trying to mask my pain with colonial history and what ended up being an epic *Apex Galaxy* binge with Dad (I finally got to Ataria's return, and the buser boys were right—she's epic). I pop my locker open to retrieve my chemistry book and feel like maybe I'll be able to get through the day without replaying the image of Mac licking the inside of Tamsin's mouth.

But when I slam my locker and pivot on my heel

to head to first period, I realize that wiping away that one image isn't good enough, because I'm staring at the Groundhog Day of make outs at the end of the hall.

Tamsin is pressed up against her locker, Mac leaning in and ducking his chin so he can kiss her, one hand bracing himself over a shoulder against her locker, the other resting on her hip. They look like a movie poster for a teen romance, one I'd definitely watch if it came on at 3 p.m. on a Sunday and I'd already seen that episode of *House Hunters International*. And in that moment I know that I have to get far, far away, because there's no way I can control my face. I can feel my lips pursing, the corners turning down like I've just stepped in dog crap. Before I can bolt, I see Ms. Stone come rushing across the hall to break them apart. PDA is strictly against Brook Park High rules, and I never thought I'd be so grateful for that. She waves the manila folder in her hand between them, and Mac leans back with a grin. Tamsin ducks her head, her cheeks turning red.

Well, isn't that just a sight.

For the next week, I have to watch them hold hands in the halls, whispering and giggling like they're in their own private romantic comedy. And as soon as the last bell rings at the end of the day, they're sucking face like he's about to ship off to war. It's deeply disgusting.

And, curiously, all the attention he paid to me is gone, too. All the flirting, the quiet little jokes, the accidental and not-so-accidental contact. All of it disappeared into the ether, replaced by constant attachment to his new girlfriend. Which makes me wonder what all that was for, anyway. Because he definitely *was* being flirty. I don't *think* I was being crazy to think he might like me, too. But the more I flip back through the mental slideshow of my interactions with Mac, the more I realize that there's one constant to all of them: Tamsin was always there. Which makes me wonder if it was all just show. Was he trying to get her attention? Because that's a really shitty thing to do.

I can't believe I ever liked him.

I can't believe I still do.

Friday rolls around, and the football team has a bye week. Everyone seems antsy, trying to come up with replacement plans. Parties, movies, date nights. By last period, the whole school is basically a walking social calendar.

I, of course, don't have that problem, because I have a date with Hot 'N Crusty.

"Do you want to try and meet up with us?" Natalie asks. "You can text me. I can let you know where we are. I'm sure we'll still be hanging out."

Awesome, so I can see my friends, but only if I'm

cool with watching the new royal couple suck face all night.

But I don't want to explain all that to Natalie. First of all, it sounds pathetic. And my rational mind tells me that the first step to getting over this is to pretend it doesn't bother me. Fake it till you make it (out of this black hole of suck). I assured her I was over Mac, that my attraction to him was temporary and circumstantial. That I'm happy for Tamsin. That they really do make a cute couple. It's obvious they belong together.

Well, I've certainly got the faking-it part down.

I shrug. "We'll see. If I don't get out too late, I'll text you," I say, but I already know I won't. There's no way in a frozen hell that I can act normal around Tamsin and Mac, especially not if we're all hanging out on the couches in the basement. I can't imagine having to watch whatever action movie Colin throws on just to avoid having to see the pair of them spoon.

No thank you please.

The night passes in a tomato-scented, sticky-floored haze. I mostly spend it in a deep funk, taking orders with the fakest of smiles and sleepwalking through all my work. I don't even realize it's time for my fifteen-minute break until Julianne taps me on the shoulder and I jump a good ten feet in the air.

"It's just your break, jeez," she says. The sound of her disdain sends tears pricking at my eyes, which is embarrassing, a fact that only makes me want to cry more. And then something amazing happens. Julianne seems to unwind. Her brows, usually knit together in a permanent display of frustration, and the corners of her mouth, which seem to fall naturally into a grimace, all seem to release at the exact same moment. "Hey, are you okay?"

It's just enough to bring me back to myself, to swallow the tears and square my shoulders, letting out a long, low breath.

"Yeah, I'm fine," I say. I offer her a smile, and to my total shock, she returns it. I grab one of the red plastic cups from the stack next to the soda machine and fill it with water, then shuffle through the kitchen and to the back door. When I get to the parking lot, I drop down on the curb next to the dumpster and take a deep breath of garbage stank and think *yup, this tracks.*

But of course I can't just sit out here and enjoy some lukewarm water that vaguely tastes like Sprite while sucking in the scent of hot dumpster. Of course, it would have to be interrupted by the sound of a glorified tin can on wheels, chugging along with Tristan behind the wheel. He throws the van in park next to the dumpster and mercifully shuts off the roar of the engine.

Excellent.

He gets out with only a grunt by way of greeting. But tonight I'm fine with it, because all I feel like doing is grunting, too. Whatever moment of bonding we had the other night is long gone. That was clearly a one-time show. So when he goes inside to retrieve the next delivery, I go back to my water and my sulking.

But then the hairs on the back of my neck stand up when I see a familiar forest-green Range Rover glide through my peripheral vision. Tamsin's car stops at the front door, and she hops out. She appears to be on a mission, and my heart leaps into my throat wondering if she's coming to see me. She never bothered to confide in me the details of her hookup with Mac. I think their walking love story through the halls of Brook Park High did that enough. And besides, as we've plainly established, Tamsin is not my friend. She's just a friend by proxy. So I never got the details, even if I wanted them. I just absorbed the news like every other rando at school.

And then I see that her passenger seat is occupied.

Mac, of course, because heaven forbid they spend a moment apart. The engine is idling, and I can hear the thudding beat of whatever dance track she's got playing in there. Mac's gaze travels the parking lot, and before I can leap up and hide behind the dumpster, he spots me. A look crosses his face that I can't name, and then he's getting out. And then he's walking toward me. Oh god, he's coming to talk to me. And when Tamsin comes out, she's going to talk to me, too. And then I'm going to have to talk to them *together*, and seriously, what god have I angered? There's approximately zero chance I'd get through the encounter without saying something embarrassing . . . or worse, crying.

I know he's seen me and I know he's already on his way over here, but I can't help it. My fight-or-flight response kicks in, and I jump up from the curb and spin on my heel, ready to bolt back into the restaurant. He won't come in the back door to the kitchen to follow me, surely. And even though it's, like, six levels of awkward to run away, that's a problem for later. My problem for *now* is figuring out how to avoid talking to Mac, which is a problem I can solve. By running away like an absolute chicken.

Only just as I reach for the door, it flies open, Tristan

pushing it with his back, the giant delivery bag that keeps the pizzas warm held out in front of him. When the door is open wide, he spins, ready to let it fall shut behind him—except I'm in his way. The corner of the pizza box catches me right in the chest, and I groan. I'm not sure if it's because it hurt (it did) or if it's because I know I'm caught (which also hurts, but more metaphorically).

I thought I managed to contain the sound, but I guess I don't because Tristan's eyes go straight to mine. I wonder if he can see the terror on my face. I'm sure it's all there. My dad has always said that my greatest weakness is that everything I'm thinking and feeling is displayed on my face like a ballpark scoreboard. And when Tristan looks over my shoulder to see Mac coming toward me, his eyes flip back to mine. I know for sure that I look like I'm being chased by a serial killer in the climax of a horror movie. Attack of the Shameless Flirt.

And I'm about to become a victim.

I brace myself for the awkward conversation I'm going to have, but then Tristan shifts the warming bag onto his shoulder like a tray. He steps forward, the metal door clanging shut behind him, his free hand reaching for my hip. It rests there with a warm pressure that I can feel through the scratchy cotton of my I'M HOT 'N CRUSTY

T-shirt. The chill of it races through my veins like the time I had to get a saline IV before getting my wisdom teeth out. He leans in close, but stops just short of his lips brushing mine. I can feel his hot breath, which smells like spearmint, as he whispers, "Is this okay?"

I feel like I'm standing on the edge of a cliff being asked if it's okay to be pushed off. And you know what? I think it is. I give a little nod, because if what I think is about to happen is going to happen, all of a sudden I *really* want it to happen.

I suck in a breath as his lips press to mine. My very first thought is *I hope my mouth doesn't taste like flat Sprite*, and it turns out to be my very last thought as my mind clears like the surface of Pearce Lake. I shiver, which sends my body closer to him, my hands pressed to the center of his chest. His I'M HOT 'N CRUSTY T-shirt is still scratchy, but more worn in than mine. He tastes like spearmint and smells like matches and auto grease and pepperoni. My hands, operating completely on their own, go to his face, resting at his jaw, which is slightly stubbly.

The kiss isn't particularly long or deep. I doubt an observer would call it passionate. But it knocks the breath out of me all the same. And when he pulls back, I feel the absence almost as much as I felt the kiss itself.

He's just inches from my face now, then he rests his forehead to mine, his eyes locking in on me. "I hope that was okay," he says. Then his eyes flick over my shoulder to where Mac was just standing.

Mac. I completely forgot about Mac. I forgot everything. I forgot my *name*.

"Yeah," I whisper, because it's the only word that I can extract from the mush of my brain.

He steps back, the sudden space between us feeling like a giant canyon. He gives me a final up and down. "You sure you're cool?"

I nod, and then ever so slowly turn to look over my shoulder.

Where I'm met with the back of Mac's head as he walks away.

He's walking away.

He saw Tristan kiss me and peaced out completely.

If my head wasn't swimming, my heart pounding, I'd be wondering what the hell that means. But instead, I'm too busy wondering what the hell *this* means. Because Tristan Porter just kissed me, and holy *wow* was it good.

"I've gotta go," Tristan says. I whip around and see him nodding to the delivery bag still held aloft on his shoulder. "Before this gets cold."

"What the hell just happened?" I ask. The words fly out of my mouth before I can run them through any kind of mental filter.

He shrugs. "I dunno, you looked like you needed saving." He nods toward Tamsin's car, where Mac is now parked in the passenger seat. The front door to the restaurant flies open and Tamsin bounds out, a pizza box in her arms. She climbs into the driver's seat and passes the box to Mac, and Mac must not say anything about me, because she drives away without ever once looking over.

I turn back to Tristan.

"So you *kissed me*?"

"Look, it's not a big deal."

I've only kissed two other people. There was Drew Cassidy in a movie theater in seventh grade. We were watching some heist movie that I didn't care about at all, and missed the last half of it thanks to a very sloppy make out that tasted like fake butter and required several napkins while the credits rolled. Drew and I "went out" for exactly three weeks, but we never actually kissed again or saw each other outside of school. And then there was Jabari Reed at camp the summer before freshman year. He kissed me during a hike when we were supposed to be identifying trees. It was actually a good kiss, but camp only lasted a week, and he lived two hours away. So that was the end of that.

Tristan makes number three, and that kiss was . . . well, I wasn't thinking about oak trees, that was for sure.

"It *is* a big deal," I tell him.

"It's really not. Don't freak out, okay?"

And suddenly the reality of the situation comes crashing down. Tristan kissed me, and Mac saw him do it. Which means if Tamsin doesn't already know, she will soon. At which point I will never *ever* hear the end of it. So maybe the kiss wasn't a big deal to him, but it was a big deal to me, and that's separate from the way it made me feel.

"So, what, I'm supposed to tell my friends that you randomly kissed me in a parking lot, but don't worry, everyone, it didn't mean anything. Tristan said so."

He sighs, and I can't believe he has the gall to be frustrated when he created this situation. "Why do you need to tell your friends anything?"

"Because they're my friends! Do you not have any?"

Tristan glares at me. Fully glares, but as soon as he realizes he's doing it, he stops. Back comes the carefully disinterested face. He holds up his free hand in surrender, backing away slowly toward his van with his delivery. "Look, it was just one kiss."

"What were you *thinking*?"

"That watching Mac kiss that redheaded girl made you cry, so maybe this would be good revenge? Turnabout's fair play, or whatever. My toolbox was sort of limited. I'm holding an extra large Hawaiian." He nods toward the pizza box. "You really need to relax."

"*Relax*?" I don't do well with people giving me one-word orders about how to be. Relax, smile, chill, those kinds of things. It's like waving a red flag at a bull. I'm surprised there's not smoke coming out of my nose right now.

"What do you want me to say? This isn't the part where we hatch a plot for me to pretend to be your fake boyfriend. It was just, I don't know, you looked like you didn't want him to come over here. I kissed you, and he didn't. So it worked, right?"

"That was *really* short-sighted." Suddenly any trace of appreciation for the kiss is disappearing in a sea of Tristan being so . . . *Tristan*. The boy is a walking sneer. Sure, he saved me for the moment, but he just made things exponentially harder. Because I'm definitely going to have to explain that kiss. Hell, I'm surprised Tamsin isn't already texting me wanting to know what the hell is going on.

"Don't make me regret it," he says.

Okay, now I'm *pissed*. "You don't get to kiss me and then tell me how I'm supposed to feel about it! What about if *I* regret it?"

He holds up his one free hand in surrender again. "Sorry, okay? It won't happen again. I can promise you that." And then he opens the door to the van, deposits the warming bag on the passenger seat, and heads around to the front to the driver's side. Whatever conversation was to be had about our kiss, it's over now, apparently. I have a feeling that when he returns, he'll be back to his chilly, monosyllabic self.

And the kiss will be forgotten. At least by him.

But I won't forget it.

Because even though Tristan royally pisses me off, my lips are still tingling and my heart is still pounding from it. That kiss was definitely *something*.

I don't see Tristan for the rest of the night. I don't know if it's because he's avoiding me, or because it's just a busy Friday night. When my shift is over, I read Natalie's text about coming over to Tamsin's and then close it. There's no trace of anything that would tell me she knows about what happened with Tristan. Which means Tamsin doesn't know, because Mac hasn't told her. Yet. But I still don't want to risk it. Instead, I text my mom and ask for a ride home. After the kiss, I don't even want to go to Stefano's. Julianne actually looks bummed when I decline, but I can't imagine sitting in a booth across from Tristan after that. If he's serious that the kiss was nothing, then I need to start working on my poker face, which I definitely don't have down tonight. Already I can feel my cheeks flush every time I think about it.

It's best if I'm just alone with my wild thoughts.

CHAPTER
NINE

I spend another weekend in social hibernation, this time working on an essay about *Inherit the Wind* for my English class. Sure, I could crank this thing out in an hour the night before it's due (which is what I'd normally do), but I decide to toil away at it for two full days like it's the manifesto that could free me from prison. Anything to avoid picturing the kiss with Tristan.

No, not picturing. *Reliving.*

Because anytime I let my mind wander too far from that literary criticism, I'm right back there, feeling his lips pressed against mine. They were a little rough, coupled with the scruff on his chin and cheeks, but they were warm. Just thinking about it for even half a second has me feeling all fluttery and sighing and *ugh*.

It doesn't help that I'm also panicking that at any moment my phone will burst with a torrent of text messages asking who my make-out buddy is and *oh my god are you going* out *now???*

There's a question I absolutely do not want to answer. What would even happen then? What if we actually became a *thing*? Would Tristan join my friend group? I'm trying to picture it. I know he used to be friendly with Mac, but something happened there. Something that may mean a big group friendship ain't happening. So then what? Would there be a wall between my friends and my boyfriend? And why am I calling him my boyfriend when we kissed once and he promptly told me it didn't mean anything and to calm down?

So . . . *Inherit the Wind* it is!

By Sunday afternoon, my mom creeps into my room with a slice of banana bread on a paper towel. So *that's* what I've been smelling coming from the kitchen for the last hour.

"Knock knock," she says, after she's already taken a full three steps into my room without ever actually knocking. "I brought you a study snack."

She lays it on the bed next to my laptop, and I bend down to inhale the warm banana smell. "Thanks, Mom,"

I say. Then I return to my laptop, the universal sign for *I'm busy, thanks, bye.*

But Mom doesn't take the hint. Or deliberately ignores it. She sits down on the bed next to me, careful not to jostle the banana bread or my laptop. "So where's Natalie this weekend?"

"Dance team competition with Cora and Tamsin," I say, although they're probably back by now. Pre-TM (Tamsin and Mac), we would normally be bingeing something on Netflix or lying out by Tamsin's pool flipping through SocialSquare together on our phones. Post-TM, I'm an academic hermit. At least my heartbreak will improve my GPA.

"And how's work? Going okay?"

Okay, so this is definitely mercenary banana bread, because here comes the interrogation.

"It's fine," I reply. Which is true. It turns out that working at Hot 'N Crusty is the least of my worries. Talking freely about *Apex Galaxy* has been a perk, and there seems to be an Arctic thaw occurring where Julianne is concerned. I wouldn't say we're friends, but she doesn't seem to hate my breathing guts anymore. Plus sometimes my coworkers kiss me.

"I ask because this is the second weekend in a row that you've hidden in your room like a fugitive. Did something happen?"

Hoo boy, what a question. My mom knows how to cut right to the heart of it. But instead of sitting up and tucking my knees under my chin and outing with my boy troubles like I *know* she wants, I simply sigh. "Just school. They keep telling us how important junior year is, so I'm giving it the ole college try." *Wow. I'll take clichés for five hundred, Alex.* It almost sounds true, too. I might just be the only girl on the planet whose boy troubles send her running into the arms of a 4.0 GPA.

I sell it hard enough that I think even Mom is buying it, despite the fact that her bullshit detector is usually pretty finely tuned.

"Well, I don't want to see you stress yourself out so much that you forget to actually enjoy life. Are you *sure* there's nothing else? Things with your friends are okay?"

"It's fine, Mom." And to try and distract her from her concern, I break off a hunk of banana bread, the dark, caramel-y crust part, and pop it into my mouth. It's still warm from the oven, and dense and moist. I let out an involuntary groan.

Mom's eyes light up. "Good?" she asks.

"The best," I tell her, reaching for another bite. "Is that coconut?"

"Yes! I toasted coconut flakes and mixed them into the batter. I'm working on perfecting a few recipes so I can expand my catering options. You know, for meetings or baby showers. That sort of thing."

"This is truly epic, Mom," I tell her, and I mean it. This isn't even a mode of distraction. This is bar none the best banana bread I've ever eaten. "You should open a bakery. Seriously."

She *hmmmmm*s with a little smile, like she's trying to brush off the compliment while still seriously thinking about it. Which would be crazy, to imagine my mom opening her own place. Having her not just be *here* all the time. Although that would mean fewer mom's intuition interrogations. So maybe it wouldn't be the worst thing in the world.

She drifts out of the room while I finish off the banana bread, happy that for a full five minutes, I didn't imagine Tristan's lips once.

Until now.

Dammit.

I arrive at school on Monday with the best damn essay I've ever written and a pit in my stomach the size of a Honeycrisp apple. But my secret appears to be safe, because at the lunch table, there's no fanfare or waggled eyebrows or even knowing looks. And no looks at all from Mac, who seems intensely focused on his corn dog nuggets.

Still, I spend the whole lunch period—and the whole rest of the day—nervous that the dam is going to burst and the news will explode out of somewhere. Hell, maybe there was someone else in the parking lot. Maybe Tristan told someone. Although that would require him to actually talk to another person, and thus far I've seen no evidence of that. Still, the news could come from anywhere, and I walk around expecting it to leap out at me from behind a locker.

But it doesn't. Not on Monday, or Tuesday. And then a whole week has gone by, a week in which I sit mostly quietly at our lunch table and watch Mac and Tamsin flirt and the boys eat copious amounts of disgusting fried food, and nod and smile while the girls scroll SocialSquare and point out makeup looks they want to try.

As for Tristan, he's definitely not talking. Not about the kiss or anything else. Like I suspected, he immediately returned to using only nods and grunts, with the occasional prickly, one-word answer whenever he needed to communicate with me, which didn't turn out to be very often. He was back to slipping in and out of the kitchen door mostly undetected.

I say mostly, because I managed to detect him quite a lot. Over the last week, I've practically become a human Tristan detector. And I'm not happy about it. But every time I see the back of his denim jacket disappear around a corner, or that floppy, wild hair falling over his eyes, my stomach leaps into my throat like when I ride the Death Drop at Six Flags. And then suddenly I'm time traveling back to the parking lot, next to the dumpster, feeling Tristan's lips on mine so vividly that I actually have to reach up and brush my own with my fingertips to make sure I'm not hallucinating.

It's been a real treat, I tell you.

I'm so mad at him for doing this to me. Working at Hot 'N Crusty was annoying, sure, but until the kiss, there was something to be said for it being a fairly drama-free environment. But now I feel like I'm constantly flashing back to Tristan's lips on mine, the smell of sawdust and gasoline mingling with the hot, sour smell of the dumpsters. It's a weird cocktail, that's for sure, and I'm embarrassed to say that if I could bottle it, I'd consider spritzing it on my pillow at night when I lie there trying to fall asleep, but only succeeding in replaying the kiss.

It's almost enough to make me forget about Mac and Tamsin, which is a small blessing. But then the next thing I know they're nuzzling noses or clasping hands and leaning into each other like they're surgically attached. It's beyond gross. Or maybe I'm just jealous.

Emotions are weird.

These are the things I think about all day, every day, while watching my friends suck face and Tristan skulk in and out of the Hot 'N Crusty kitchen with deliveries.

And then it's fall break.

Natalie's family always goes to Fort Lauderdale to visit her grandparents, while Tamsin and Colin head off to Grand Cayman with their parents. Cora is seeing Broadway shows with her mom and grandmother and also doing a massive amount of damage to her father's credit card, and Mac is in Colorado with his parents and younger brothers skiing and missing Tamsin. I'm guessing, judging from the fact that they haven't been apart for, like, five minutes since they got together. They've been leaving heart emojis on each other's SocialSquare posts like it's going out of style.

We never travel for fall break, which I used to hate, but, honestly, now I'm glad to have nothing to do but binge *Apex Galaxy* with Dad and eat Mom's kitchen experiments, which have been growing in frequency since the banana bread. She's been working on her croissant recipe, and I'm not mad about it. But after three solid days of *AxGx* and baked goods, I'm ready to get out of the house. When Julianne texts to tell me everyone's getting together to watch movies at Frank's house and I'm invited "or whatever," I'm typing yes faster than First Lieutenant Ringold can order, "Engines at flash jump."

Frank's house is a seventies basement ranch not far from my neighborhood. There's an old, deflated tire swing hanging from an enormous tree in the front yard and a mailbox painted like a ladybug at the curb. A woman who must be Frank's mom answers the door, though it takes me a few moments to place her because she looks *nothing* like Frank. She can't be five feet tall, for starters, with curly blond hair and heavy—yet perfectly applied—makeup. She's dressed in black jeans and a tight black tank top, and it's not until I see her name tag that I realize she works at one of the makeup counters at Dillard's down at the mall. Which explains why her makeup looks so flawless. Her cheeks are so luminous it looks like she's traveling in her own beam of light. But when she smiles,

I can see that she has Frank's wide, oversized mouth, even if he seems to have inherited nothing else.

"You must be Becca!" she exclaims, her arms wide like she's resisting a bodily urge to hug me. And that's when I realize what Frank *did* get from his mother: the joy and enthusiasm of a room full of golden retriever puppies. The thread of recognition makes me smile.

"It's just Beck, actually," I say. "It's nice to meet you."

"Everyone's downstairs," she says, nodding to the open door that leads to the basement. "Tell Frank I put the pizza bagels in the oven, so he should listen for the timer."

The basement turns out to be Frank's room, though it's divided in half between his living space and what looks like an epic entertainment center. There are two full-sized arcade games against one wall, and a giant flat-screen TV at one end with all manner of controllers and consoles coming out of it. There's a floor-to-ceiling bookshelf that's stuffed with completed Lego sets and Funko Pops. I spy a completed *Apex* ship roughly the size of my head and am impressed. There are leather couches and armchairs, just like at Tamsin's house, only these look like they've been through a war and have been patched up with varying ages and colors of duct tape. Jason, Frank, and Greg are parked on the couch, each with a controller in their hand, playing some kind of space game that I can't look at for too long or the graphics will start to make me motion sick. Julianne is in an armchair scrolling through her phone. She looks up when I enter, and she actually smiles.

"Thank god. There's so much testosterone down here I was worried the television was about to grow testicles."

"That's an image that will live in my brain for a while," I say, laughing for the first time in days.

"You're welcome," she replies.

I didn't realize how much I needed human contact—how much I needed *this* human contact—until I walked in the door.

"Frank, your mom says the pizza bagels are in the oven."

"Thanks," Frank says, never taking his eyes off the screen but steering hard with his shoulders, like it'll control the game. And then the screen lights up and Jason throws his controller at the floor while Frank waves his in the air. "Five bucks, dude! Your five bucks is *mine*!"

"Whatever," Jason mutters, but he digs into his pocket until he produces a crumpled pile of receipts and a very abused-looking five-dollar bill. "But I want a rematch."

"After the movie, dude," Greg says. "I'm ready to watch a possessed tree attack a white girl."

"Despite my *intense* protestations, we're watching *Evil Dead*. Again," Julianne says. "I hope that's okay."

"It's fine," I say, having never been particularly affected by horror movies.

"You can throw your stuff on my bed," Frank says, pointing over his shoulder while he juggles like four different remotes to bring up the movie. I've got my purse slung over my shoulder and my jacket over my arm, so I turn around to dump it and come face-to-face with rows and columns of the same photo of a smiling, gray-haired white man with cosmetically enhanced teeth and gold-rimmed glasses surrounded by a 1-800 number and CALL NOW in bright yellow letters. The images cover the entire wall behind Frank's bed, floor to ceiling.

"What in god's name is that?" I ask, unable to tear my eyes away. The repeating images are almost mesmerizing. The man's beady eyes, even behind his glasses, seem to follow me.

"It's the Wall of Justice," Greg says.

"It's Ken Lunn," Frank says.

"It's the back cover of about a hundred phone books," Julianne says.

"Two hundred and thirty-three phone books, Julianne," Jason says. "Have some respect."

And then the niggling feeling of recognition takes hold. Because, yup, that's definitely the full-page, full-color ad on the back of every phone book distributed in town, most of which go straight to the recycle bin. Ken Lunn's face also graces a handful of billboards around town, the side of a few buses, and a banner ad on the fence in one of the end zones at the Brook Park High football stadium. Ken Lunn is an aging personal injury lawyer who drives around town in a red convertible sports car whose license plate says JUSTCE and whose hair is for *sure* surgically attached to his head.

And I swear, right now, Ken Lunn is staring deep into my soul, possibly trying to claim it as his own.

"But . . . *why*?" is all I can say, unable to tear my eyes away from the tableau.

"Frank lost a bet," Greg says.

"We found a shrink-wrapped pallet of phone books by the dumpsters behind the Shop 'n Save last summer, and Frank bet there were two thousand, and I said there were only eight hundred, and it turns out I was right, so I skinned enough of them to wallpaper his bedroom and thus the Wall of Justice was born," Jason says.

"I like to think he watches over me," Frank says.

Oh, he's watching, all right.

"Okay, horror movies don't scare me, but *this* does," I say, pointing at the Wall of Justice.

"I'd worry if you *weren't* scared of the Wall of Justice." The gruff, gravelly voice has me spinning around, out of the tractor beam of Ken Lunn's evil gaze. Tristan is just emerging down the basement steps, clad in his uniform of ratty denim jacket, holey jeans, and a T-shirt. This one is yellow and worn and reads DOGWOOD ARTS CHILDREN'S CHOIR 1994. My heart comes skidding to a stop. It's officially the most he's said to me since his tongue was in my mouth, and *that* thought kicks my heart back into gear, thudding away at triple time.

Frank fires up the movie, but it doesn't take long to realize that, just like at Tamsin and Colin's house, the movie isn't the main event. It starts out with some gentle yelling at the characters on-screen, who are making absolutely abominable decisions (as horror film characters usually do). But soon the discussion moves to other Bruce Campbell movies, then other Sam Raimi movies and their intersections (*Spider-Man* and the ever expanding Spiderverse). Then we take a sharp left turn into *Apex Galaxy* nerdery, which I am more than happy to join in on. The boys tread lightly to avoid spoilers, even though I assure them I don't care, and we dissect ships (of both the relation and space variety), notable character deaths, and Easter eggs, which creator Ben Derreygronde loved to plant seven ways from Sunday. We're halfway through dissecting the meaning of ACR-1559, a call sign that reappears throughout the series, when the infamous tree scene finally hits the screen.

The whole time, Tristan lies on the carpet, a pillow tucked under his head, while he silently stares at the screen. But even though his eyes stay on the movie and he never chimes in, he somehow still feels very much a part of the action. I can't *not* notice him. And I can tell that he's listening. He always seems to stretch and angle his ear toward the person doing the talking. At least, he always does it when I'm talking. It's the laziest active listening I've ever seen.

"Oh hey, I forgot to tell you guys," Jason says, reaching for a cold and drying pizza bagel from a plate on the coffee table. "I worked lunch on Tuesday, and Del brought a *date* in. Like, he actually brought a woman for a date in his own freaking restaurant!"

"How'd it go?" Julianne asks. She's on the couch next to Frank, who I notice keeps leaning toward her, then jerking himself back on his side of the couch like there's an electric fence between them.

"Well, he pulled her chair out for her and then sneezed in her hair, and I'd say that was the high point," Jason says.

"Poor Del. He's so nice!" Julianne laments.

"And completely hapless," Greg adds.

"We should help him," I find myself saying before I can think through it. Because surely I don't want to help Del date successfully. *Do I?*

"What, you want to *Parent Trap* Del?" Greg asks.

"After what I witnessed yesterday, I'm not confident he can be movie montaged into a good date," Jason says. "I heard him tell an honest-to-god knock-knock joke. And then he laughed at it. *Hard.* Like, my god, man. Have some dignity."

"He just needs to meet the right person. Someone who gets him. She'll put him at ease, and then it'll be cake," I say, wondering who that person might be. Not that I want to set Del up. But I mean, if the opportunity presented itself . . .

"No, what he needs is someone to tell him to take it down a notch or five. Del needs a strong woman," Frank says.

"The problem is a strong woman doesn't need Del," Greg replies.

The movie ends, and the boys resume their video game. Greg offers the fourth controller to Tristan, who shakes his head, and I wave it off, too. I pull my phone out of my pocket and check my texts. There aren't any, which oddly doesn't bother me like it once would. Then I start to mindlessly scroll SocialSquare. I haven't pulled my phone out once since arriving at Frank's. The conversation was just too good (plus Jason demands that we not scour IMDb for trivia, because he claims it's cheating the spirit of film criticism).

Tristan grabs a nearby trash can and starts sweeping crumpled paper towels and soda cans into it. Then he gets to the empty pizza bagel plate, now topped with only dried grease and a few stray crumbs. He picks it up, then nods down at my phone.

"Are your real friends back from vacation yet?"

The words feel like a slap.

"Excuse me?"

"I'm just surprised to see you hanging here for geek night. I figure the only reason you're not splitting avocado toast at the coffee shop right now is because the Brook Park royalty is out of town?" He arches an eyebrow at me, so smug it makes me want to slap his stupid face.

I can feel my blood boiling, pulsing hot beneath my skin. I clench my teeth, angry because he's partly right, and also angry that he's dissing my friends. No, not Tamsin and Natalie and everyone else. I'm pissed that he's dissing Julianne and Frank and Jason and Greg. He's acting like I wouldn't want to be hanging out with them if I had other options. Like I didn't have an awesome time nerding out with them. Like I didn't feel so *myself* tonight. *These* are my friends, too, and they're not runners-up. And how dare he imply that, even if I'm only just right this moment figuring it out?

"You're an asshole," I finally snap, then snatch the empty plate from his hand and stomp up the stairs to the kitchen. When I get there, I find Julianne pulling some sodas out of the fridge.

"You want anything?" she asks. "Frank's mom buys Fresca, which I thought would be disgusting, because grapefruit soda? Ick. But it's honestly pretty good."

"No, I'm fine," I say, but I sound like I'm spitting nails.

"What's wrong with you?"

"Someone should ask *Tristan* that question," I say.

"Okay, then what's going on with you two?"

"What do you mean?"

"Did you get in a fight or something? You're always glaring at each other or acting like one another is radio-active."

"No. I just think we don't mesh well together."

"Or maybe you mesh *too* well together?" She nudges my shoulder with hers. I temporarily forget my anger at Tristan, because it's a move Natalie has done to me a million times. It feels like friendship. I think Julianne might finally be my friend. Or on her way to it. But I'm too scared to ask her, or acknowledge it in any way, like when you catch a hummingbird in your yard and you go stock-still, afraid the slightest movement will scare it away. I don't want Julianne to revert to her scowly self with me.

"Ew. No," I reply. Because I don't want to date Tristan. I just want him to go back to how it was before. Which, okay, involved him being an enormous grouch, but at least I knew where I stood then.

"Look, Tristan's always been sort of . . . aloof. Distant, you know? He acts like he doesn't need or even *like* anyone, but clearly that's just some try-hard James Dean act. You seem to get him, and maybe that's not a bad thing."

"You mean like he's pulling my pigtails, recess-style?"

She wrinkles her nose and shudders. "No, because that's some bullshit patriarchy nonsense. I'm just saying he . . . *notices* you. And I don't think it would be the worst thing to lean into it a little bit."

Lean in? I think about it as I take a couple of sodas from Julianne and follow her back down the basement steps. What does that even mean? And why do I suddenly feel like I swallowed bees when I look at Tristan, who is tossing popcorn into the air and catching it in his mouth effortlessly (while next to him, Frank keeps pelting himself in the eye)?

Do I . . . *like* Tristan?

No.

No.

. . . Maybe?

Natalie: Back from Florida and only managed to burn
my shoulders a little bit!

Julianne: Drive-in tonight with everybody?

Tristan's attitude notwithstanding, last night was the most
fun I've had since I started at Hot 'N Crusty. And if I'm
honest with myself, maybe even longer. So as I flip back
and forth between the dueling text messages, it's Julianne's
I decide to reply to.

Beck: Sounds good. Can I get a ride?

It's ten minutes past five when, while waiting by the front window, I hear the familiar *chugga chugga*. I look outside to see the van shudder to a stop at the curb.

"What the . . . ," I mutter.

"Who's that?" Dad asks, peering over my shoulder from where he was sitting reading some book about war. "And what the hell is he driving?"

And then Tristan honks. Because of course he can't even drag his stubborn ass out of the car and knock on the front door.

"A van?" I reply.

"How old is that thing?"

"You're one to talk, Mr. Ancient Corolla."

"Hey, at least the Toyota was manufactured in your lifetime. I don't think that thing was even made in *my* lifetime."

I sigh. I'm already on edge thinking about making the long trek out to the drive-in with Tristan, who I called an asshole the last time I spoke to him (which he definitely *was*). The last thing I need is the Dadish Inquisition on the front step. So I grab my purse and reply as I'm headed to the door. "I don't know anything about cars, Dad. I've only known how to drive them for, like, five minutes, and I promise you I have no idea how to drive that one."

"Okay, but is it safe?"

"As you pointed out, it's survived several decades on the road, so I'm guessing it's okay." And before he can pester me anymore or poke enormous holes in my logic, I fling open the front door and step outside, practically bolting across the lawn to the van. I heave the door open and climb in, glancing back to see my dad's face practically pressed to the window. I give a little wave of assurance, and then the van pulls away, thankfully not backfiring or bursting into flames on the way.

"Sorry I'm late," Tristan says, his eyes focused on the road. *Well, hello to you, too.*

"I didn't know you were my ride," I reply.

"Julianne called. Something about chicken and you needing a lift," he says. I have no idea what he's talking about, but I'm definitely going to have some questions for Julianne later. I can't tell if this little setup is her warming up to me, or her punishing me. Or maybe a little of both. I'll know more when *I* know how to feel about it.

"I'm surprised you actually picked me up. I thought you'd just as soon run me over."

"Seriously?" He cocks an eyebrow at me, or more

accurately, at the road, since he still hasn't made eye contact with me.

"You seem to have an awfully low opinion of me, per our last conversation."

"*Per our last . . .*" He trails off, huffing out a sigh. "Listen, I'm sorry. I shouldn't have said that. I'm sort of . . ."

"An asshole?"

"Protective of my friends," he says, gripping the steering wheel hard as he turns onto Old Covington Highway.

"And I'm not?"

"I don't know." He shrugs, finally glancing over to catch sight of my glare. "I'm not good with new people."

"Will wonders never cease," I tell him, but I get what he's saying. And I decide to forgive him, because frankly, being mad at Tristan is exhausting. "Speaking of new people, just be glad I saved you from my dad interrogating you over this trash heap."

"Hey, watch your mouth in front of Cecilia."

I turn around, looking for this Cecilia, wondering how I could have missed a grandmother or an elderly neighbor hiding in the back of the van.

"Who's Cecilia?" I ask.

He reaches forward and pats the dashboard affectionately.

"You named your car? And you chose *Cecilia*?"

"First of all, Cecilia isn't a *car*. Cecilia is a 1978 Volkswagen Westfalia, but if you must refer to her casually, she's a bus."

Ah, so my dad *does* predate the van. I'll have to let him know *he's* the ancient one.

"And why Cecilia? Because she's old?"

"Show some respect," Tristan says. "She's named after the Simon and Garfunkel song, 'cause she's always breaking my heart."

I have no idea what he's talking about, but it feels like I should, so I just keep my mouth shut and my eyes on the road in front of me. There's a beat of silence, and I can feel a prickle from his glance.

"Come on, you know the song."

I'm sitting there trying to decide if I should just lie so I don't look like an idiot or risk looking like an idiot if he calls me on it, when he starts tapping out a rhythm on the steering wheel, his head bouncing a counterrhythm.

"*Cecilia, you're breakin' my heart,*" he sings—actually *sings*, which I did not expect. His voice is good, too, carrying the tune well while still sounding soulfully ragged. "*You're shakin' my confidence daily.*"

He sings a few more lines, drumming on the steering wheel, and I realize I do vaguely recognize the song. My dad is a major oldies fan, so his car is permanently tuned to Star 102.1.

"I love her, but she's always, *always* breaking down," Tristan says, giving the car—sorry, *bus*—another affectionate pat. "She was my dad's in college. He taught me how to keep her running before I even got my permit, and now she's mine."

Tristan pulls away from the last stoplight at the edge of town, and soon we're cruising down 411, the two-lane highway leading to the outer edges of the county. The windows are down, since the last gasp of warm fall is still hanging on, and the roar of the wind combined with the rumble of Cecilia's ancient engine ends our conversation, though I replay it several times over in my head on the drive. It's the first time Tristan and I have had a normal interaction that didn't include glowering or outright hostility, and I don't know quite what to make of it. It was almost like we were friends.

Friends who kissed that one time.

And then I'm spending the rest of the drive trying *not* to replay the kiss over and over in my head. But it's a losing battle. Instead I focus my attention on trying not to blush like a cherry tomato at the memory of being pressed up against Tristan behind the dumpster. Every once in a while I feel that familiar prickle that comes with Tristan glancing over at me, but he never says anything.

The Mendon Drive-In is about twenty minutes outside of town. You take the Old Covington Highway out past strip malls and gas stations until you hit the woods, and then you drive until you're sure you're in "I'm going to be murdered" territory. Just before you start to hear the twang of banjos, there's an old, wooden, hand-painted sign announcing you're just a quarter of a mile from the entrance. And then it appears out of the trees, as if conjured by magic.

You bounce down a little gravel road to the ticket booth, and there's almost always a line. You have to get there early if you don't want to miss the animated previews advertising the snack bar, and even earlier if you want a halfway decent parking spot. It's twenty dollars per car for a double feature, which, if you have a full load, is a pretty good deal. But tonight it's only Tristan and me in the bus, so I pull a ten-dollar bill from my wallet and hold it out to him to cover my share.

"You don't have to," he says, trying to wave the cash away.

"Don't be stupid," I say, placing the tenner on the dash. "It's not like this is a date."

The word hangs there in the expanse of the van, and I

feel like a giant idiot for bringing it up. Of course it's not a date, but as soon as you drop the word *date* with a guy, things immediately start to feel loaded. Suddenly you're both wondering if you should reaffirm it's not a date, or if maybe you should be reconsidering the whole not-a-date thing altogether. It's like the final *Jeopardy!* music is playing in my head, and I'm panicking, caught without the answer.

The car ahead of us pulls away, and it's our turn at the ticket booth. Tristan hands over his twenty to the woman in the booth, then takes the ten off the dash and shoves it into his jacket pocket.

Okay, not a date.

Tristan pulls through the entrance and winds down the snaking path toward the screen. He seems to have a spot in mind, eking past the cars that are turning down the first available row.

"I got a text from Frank," he says by way of explanation. "They saved us a spot."

Sure enough, right in the center of the middle row, Frank stands there in the grass with his hands on his hips, as tall and skinny as a road sign. At the sight of us (or, more accurately, the sight of Cecilia), he steps aside and begins waving us in with both hands like we're approaching our gate at the airport. Tristan pulls in at a diagonal, which is a technique I've never seen at the drive-in before, but when he shuts off the engine and hops out to throw open the sliding door to the back, I see that he's parked in the perfect viewing angle.

"Thank god you're here," Frank says, his forehead pricked with sweat even though it's not *that* hot out. "This lady in a minivan looked super bloodthirsty. She had a bunch of screaming kids in the back, and it seemed like she was looking for an excuse to commit a murder. Like maybe running me over would earn her a break in the state pen or something."

"Cecilia only goes as fast as she goes," Tristan replies.

"You made it!" Julianne leaps out of the bed of the pickup truck parked next to us. Jason and Greg are sitting in the back passing a bucket of fried chicken back and forth.

"Thanks for the invite," I say. "And for the ride?"

She shrugs, but there's a little tug of a smile on her face. "Sorry to pawn you off on Tristan, but Jason refused to go back for you." She says the last part loudly and pointedly over her shoulder.

"You were in the opposite direction! If we went back, the chicken would have been soggy by the time we got here," Jason says, waving a leg around in the air as a visual aid.

"No pizza tonight?"

"Stefano's is not a carry-out item," Greg says from the pickup truck, reaching in a box of potato wedges. "It's really best straight out of the oven."

"It does not box cure well," Tristan says.

"Box cure?"

"Yeah, you know how delivery pizza sort of marinates in the cardboard? It gets this almost smoky flavor, and the cheese gets delightfully rubbery."

"And also sucks up a lot of the grease," Frank adds.

"That's gross," I reply.

"It's true," Tristan says. I guess he'd know, as the delivery guy among us. He turns to me. "Hey, I didn't bring any food. Do you wanna hit up the snack bar?"

"Sure," I say, and wave to Julianne as we stomp through the gravel and grass toward the squat, cinderblock building that smells of grills and popcorn and sugar. Tristan gets in line and just sort of stares off into the distance. It's pretty crowded for a Thursday night, what with it being fall break, and the line moves slowly. Most everyone else who's not chatting with a friend is staring down at their phones. But not Tristan. He rocks a little on his heels, but otherwise he seems perfectly content to be waiting in a long line.

"How do you do that?" I ask him.

"Do what?"

"Just *wait*. Patiently, like it's the nineties or something." I gesture around to everyone else flicking their thumbs over screens.

He shrugs. "I don't really do social media, so there's nothing calling to me," he says. And I know that already, because I definitely attempted some light stalking and came up crickets.

"Still. I mean, there's email or the news or Candy Crush. Or you could read a book." Just the thought of being trapped in a line without my phone makes my fingers itch. Is he some kind of monster?

"Or I could just stand here and think my thoughts until it's my turn to order popcorn. And of course, there's always *this* scintillating conversation, which we wouldn't be having if we were looking at our phones."

Thinking his thoughts? Okay, he's definitely a monster. I want to ask him what he thinks about when he's standing there being quiet, but that feels too intimate, a word that makes the tops of my ears turn red. So instead I ask him if he wants to split a popcorn.

"Sure," he says, and when he steps up to the front of the line, he pulls my crumpled ten-dollar bill out of his pocket and orders two sodas, a large popcorn, and a bag of circus peanuts.

"You *don't*," I gasp.

"Hey, I don't want to hear it," he says. He takes the bag of candy from the cashier, rolls it up, and shoves it in his back pocket. "I take enough shit from my dad over these things, but they're delicious."

I hold my hands up. "Hey, I'm not judging. I love those things! I'm only judging if you're not sharing."

"Sure. I mean, if I don't share I'll just eat the whole bag myself and regret it."

"They must put something in them that makes you unable to stop until you're ready to barf."

"Just as long as you don't barf in Cecilia."

"Well, if it's only half a bag of circus peanuts, that won't be a problem."

"Hey, Pizza Princess!" A voice cuts through the cinder-block depths of the snack bar. I look up to see Carina, Del's sister. She's tall and broad like her big brother, like she could lift the snack bar and move it a few feet to the left if the need arose. I love her and her booming accent, but I don't love the public callout. "How's things? Del treatin' ya like the royalty you are?"

"It's work," I say, shrugging and feeling the blush creep into my cheeks.

"If he gives you any lip, you come find me," she says. She gets the attention of the bored teenager working the register. "Popcorn's on the house for that one." Then she winks and disappears back into the depths of the snack bar.

We carry our bucket of popcorn and sodas back to the van, and Tristan sets about getting his space ready. He's got a bunch of pillows and an old plaid comforter laid out in a nest in the back of the van. He climbs in and practically burrows into the setup, leaning back against the built-in kitchen counter in the back of the van.

The sun has just dipped behind the trees when the screen flickers to life, and suddenly there are dancing hot dogs and fountain sodas hopping across the screen. Julianne leaps into the bed of the pickup truck and takes her place leaning against the back of the cab. Frank is on one side of her, Greg on the other, with Jason splayed out near the open tailgate.

"We can make room," she says, scooting closer to Frank. And even in the dim light beaming off the screen I can see his cheeks start to turn red. She pats a sliver of space next to her.

I glance back at the open bus, where Tristan is pulling out an old radio and extending the antenna. He doesn't look like he's waiting for company, or like he even wants any, but for some reason I find myself wanting to join him in his little cave. And I don't think it's just the half bag of circus peanuts he promised me.

"It's okay, I'm gonna stay down here. More room," I add quickly, feeling the need to explain myself, but Julianne is already readjusting away from a slightly dejected-looking Frank. Like she knew what I'd say and was ready for it. She's a crafty one, I think.

I shuffle back over to Cecilia and stop at the open door. "Do you mind having company? It looked a little cramped in the truck."

"Sure," Tristan says, not looking up from the radio, where he's fiddling with the dial. The tape deck appears to be held closed with duct tape, and the antenna is slightly bent in the middle.

"What are you doing with that thing?" I ask.

"Drive-in plays the sound through a local radio station, but Cecilia's battery won't survive staying on that long. I have to bring backup."

"Good lord, where did you get that thing? 1984?"

"Probably," he says with a shrug. "It came with the bus."

He fiddles with the little dial, trying to get the station just right, but he's only able to achieve varying levels of fuzzy. He finally settles on the spot with the least amount of static, kind of a low, persistent buzz. It's the kind of sound that would normally drive me bats, but I'm surprised by how quickly it fades from my consciousness. I don't know if it's the cooling breeze now drifting through the bus or the musty smell of the upholstery or the glow of the screen in front of us as the previews begin, but just like the endless drone of the cicadas in the summer, the static is soon gone and only the thundering sound effects of some heist movie trailer fill the space between us.

"Thanks for the free popcorn," Tristan says as the screen lights up with the first movie.

"I didn't do anything," I reply.

"You're not the Pizza Princess?"

My cheeks flare, and I bury my face in my hands, groaning. "Ugh, don't remind me."

"I don't know what your problem is. Seems like a pretty good gig to me," he says, tossing a piece of popcorn in the air and catching it on his tongue.

The first movie of the night is one of the *Mission: Impossible*s. The newest one, not that I have any idea which one that is. I think they've made something like forty-three of them, and I've seen exactly none of them. All I know is that in this one Tom Cruise runs really fast and dangles from an airplane (or is that in all of them?).

We settle in to watch the movie, although I'm not actually watching the movie. Mostly I'm watching Tristan without watching him, which takes a lot of effort and concentration. It's an art form, really, and I might have finally found where my true artistic skills lie. There's no room in that equation for Tom Cruise. Tristan is watching the movie, in that his eyes are pointed at it, but I don't think he's really watching it, either. His mind must be somewhere else, or maybe he's asleep with his eyes open. He's staring at the screen, unmoving and intent, which is a whole lot more attention than a *Mission: Impossible* movie requires.

Thinking his thoughts. And what are those, exactly? He guards them like they're state secrets. It's amazing how little I know about him. Our school isn't small, but it's small enough that it's easy to absorb information about just about anyone. But I barely even knew Tristan was a student. How he's managed to float through four years at Brook Park High without being someone to be talked about is an achievement on par with summiting Everest. I try stealing another glance at him. Up close I can see that he's a little scruffy along his jawline, though the hair looks soft. I quickly look away before he can catch me, my eyes dropping down to his hands, which are clutched around a large soda cup. His fingernails are short, but there's still dirt or grease beneath them, and there's a small cut on his knuckle. Was that a pizza delivery accident? Or something else? What does he *do* when he's not delivering pizzas? And where does he go at lunch every day? Who *is* he?

That line of wondering occupies me for the next hour or so, until the vat of root beer I drank finally catches up with me.

I shift a little, but I'm worried I'm going to start annoying him, so I finally begin to unfold myself from the floor of the bus.

"I have to go pee," I say.

"I'll go with you," he replies, which I was not expecting, though it does confirm that his interest in the movie is probably hovering right around zero. When I glance at the screen, things seem pretty tense . . . not a time you'd really wander away if you were particularly invested in Tom Cruise (I *know* he's playing a character, but, honestly, unless his name *is* Mission Impossible, I have no idea what it is).

We walk slowly through the lot, weaving between cars and lawn chairs and picnic blankets as we make our way back to the concession stand. It's glowing in the back of the lot, but mostly empty, everyone else being focused on the movie—or the person they're making out with, which is definitely what was happening in the Jeep we just passed. That, or we need an ambulance because that was some unsuccessful CPR. But when we walk around the side where the bathrooms are, there's a strip of yellow caution tape looping around the door handle of the men's room and sweeping across to loop around the handle to the women's. OUT OF ORDER reads a crumpled sign printed on neon yellow paper.

"Crap," I mutter, because now that I'm faced with the possibility of holding it, I'm realizing that I really don't think I can.

"It's fine, there are porta potties," Tristan says, pointing to a row of them, forest green with white roofs a few paces behind the concession stand.

"No," I say, shaking my head. "No way."

"What?"

"I'm not using a porta potty. I'd sooner pee my pants."

"Are you serious? Why not?"

"Because they smell like a hell mouth. Because I've seen those viral stories about snakes in there. Because it's dark and tiny. Because *no.*"

"So what are you going to do? Because if you pee your pants, you're not allowed back in Cecilia. Not even to drive home."

"I'll just hold it," I say.

He lets out an exasperated sigh. He looks at me, his

eyes drifting down to my feet, where I'm sort of bouncing back and forth.

"I don't think that's going to work," he says.

"Why not?"

"Because there's a tub of soda inside you and you're already over there doing the cha-cha."

He's not wrong. I literally feel like there's a water balloon sloshing around where my bladder should be, but that doesn't change my stance on porta potties. I hold firm on my anti–porta potty policy (say *that* five times fast).

"I don't know what to tell you," I say, knowing I sound a little bit breathless. I close my eyes tight, like I'll be able to marshal some power over my bladder if I just concentrate really hard. Then I cross my arms over my chest for some good old-fashioned defiance. "I'm not going in there."

When I open my eyes, I see him scanning the lot. "You don't have to. Follow me."

I pray he's spotted a backup restroom somewhere as I follow him across the lot, toward the porta potties. Then he walks right past them, heading for the line of trees at the back of the lot. He disappears between the trunks of two enormous pines, his sneakers crunching over a bed of pine needles.

"You want me to pee in the woods?"

He stops and turns, giving me a pointed look. "You have a better idea?"

The thing is, I don't. My bladder feels like an overfull balloon, and with each step, it bounces with the threat of popping. I've got to *go*. And it *is* really dark out here. I glance back over my shoulder, and I can barely even see any of the cars. I don't hear any people. The sounds of the movie are muffled, and even the screen is just a ghostly glow between the thick branches of the trees.

Tristan pulls out his keys and clicks on a tiny flashlight connected to the ring. It's shockingly powerful, and he uses it to illuminate the path as we walk another ten paces or so into the trees.

"Were you a Boy Scout?" I ask at his gadgety key ring.

"No," he replies. Then he stops and points the tiny beam of light toward a small clearing. He doesn't say anything, but it's clear that that's my bathroom.

"Turn around," I tell him as I step gingerly over pine needles.

"I wasn't going to watch," he says as he dutifully spins on his heel. He takes a few steps away, but I stop in my tracks.

"But also, don't leave me," I say, the words coming out

quick and forceful, my voice climbing higher with each word. He's behind me, and I don't dare turn around.

There's a pause, and then I hear him say, "Fine."

I make it to the clearing and step behind a tall tree that seems wider than me. I slowly unzip my jeans and start to ease them down my hips, my eyes scanning the area like a SWAT team captain. I'm on high alert for anyone who might come stumbling through the woods to see me squat in the dirt. And as I'm thinking that, I can hardly believe I'm about to do it. Could I get arrested for this? Yeah, it's the woods, but it's the woods at the drive-in. That's for sure public urination. I'm starting to spiral, nearly ready to talk myself out of this. But then I start to go, and as soon as I do, *oh my god* I know it was the right decision.

That is, until I find myself standing in a puddle of my own pee.

"Oh, gross!" I say, jumping up and trying to leap away, which doesn't exactly work with my skinny jeans around my ankles. I pitch forward, arms outstretched, and wind up doing a very undignified tuck-and-roll, landing with my bare butt in a pile of leaves that are—thank god—dry.

"Are you okay?" Tristan calls.

"DON'T TURN AROUND!" I shriek. I glance over my shoulder. As promised, he's facing the other way. I rise gingerly to my feet, dust off my butt, and quickly pull my pants up. Then I walk over to Tristan, careful to avoid the puddle of pee on my way. I tap him on the shoulder.

"All done," I say.

He takes one look at me and instantly bursts out laughing.

"What?" I look down, hoping there's not pee soaking into my shirt or something, but I don't see anything. "What are you laughing at?"

"What the hell happened to you out there, Brix?" He reaches out and pulls two large leaves out of my hair. "Did you have an accident?"

"*No,*" I say, brushing at my hair and straightening my sweatshirt. "I'm fine. Everything is fine."

"Okay, well, it's my turn. And I don't need a chaperone, so feel free to head on back," he says, walking past me to find his own tree. "I'll see you at the bus."

I wend my way back to the bus (yup, that couple is still making out like he's her oxygen source). I climb in and take my spot on the shag-carpeted floor. Tristan returns just a few minutes later, and we settle in. The mission became possible sometime during our pee-in-the-woods adventure, and the second show in the double feature is just starting. This one is some terrible horror movie that seems like it's going to be low on actual scares and high on gore, as if the two are the same thing. I hate those kinds of horror movies, so I prepare myself to mostly stare off into the middle distance instead of watching. The temperature has started to drop, and Tristan pulls out a blanket and drapes it over me. I burrow beneath it and offer him the other end, and before I know it we wind up closer. Our knees are touching. He's warm, and my instinct is to lean into him like I would a space heater on a cold night. There's a mysterious electricity zipping between us, and I sit stock-still, trying not to disrupt the current. Or maybe get zapped. I'm not sure which. He shifts, and I swear he pulls his arm back to give me more space next to him. And without thinking, I take it. I tuck my shoulder up under his arm and lean back. But I don't lay my head on his shoulder. That's not what this is. That's not what we're doing.

There's a scream, and someone on the screen gets their head removed with a machete. I yawn, realizing that it's late, and there's a lot more of this terrible movie left.

Only there's not. Because the next thing I know, I wake up to the sounds of tires crunching along the gravel in front of the bus. Tristan is gone. I sit up in a panic, because my last image was of someone getting brutally murdered in the woods, and I'm having a hard time separating fiction from reality at the moment. Like, did I really curl up and sleep with Tristan? Did that actually happen, or was it all a dream?

Then I see him ambling across the gravel and I know it for sure. I *did* curl up into him like he was a recliner. Or a boyfriend.

Oh god. Should I be embarrassed? *How* embarrassed should I be?

He doesn't say anything as he comes around to the driver's side door. Finally I just ask.

"Where did you go?"

"Just tossing out some trash," he says, firing up the engine on the old bus. "You ready?"

"Where's everyone else?" The space next to the bus where Jason's truck had been parked is vacant. In fact, we're one of the last cars to leave the field.

"They already left," he says.

He doesn't mention that I've been asleep for probably an hour. He doesn't tease me about snoring or drooling. Which is weird, because that seems like something Tristan would do.

I climb into the passenger seat, and he cranks the radio. Since the windows are rolled up on the way home because of the chill, I can actually hear it. He's got his phone connected to the tape deck with this weird cord-and-tape thing. I think it's the Beatles, but I don't recognize the song, just the voices. He doesn't say a word for most of the drive.

Did something happen? Did I talk in my sleep? I'm used to Tristan being rude. I'm used to him being downright mean. I'm used to him being silent. But I'm not used to him being so distant.

"Remind me where the turns are, 'kay?" he says as he pulls out of the drive-in. Instead of the usual slow parade of cars, we're able to drive right out, since everyone else has left.

"Yeah."

And I do, but he only nods in reply.

When I climb out of the bus, I pause to thank him for the ride. I want to thank him for something else, but I'm not sure how to say it. I had a good time tonight, pantsless tuck-and-roll aside, but again, putting words to it would just make things weird. Or weirder.

And as soon as I slam the door shut, I mean the *instant* the metal clangs, he's putting the bus in gear and chugging away from the curb, not even a glance back, no waiting until I'm safely inside.

Maybe it's not weirdness. Maybe it's indifference.

I can't decide which would be worse.

Maybe after Mac I'm just desperate to feel close to someone. Maybe I had a little leftover crush, and like a poorly directed love potion, it landed on whoever happened to be the closest. I tell myself to shake it off. He's not the one. He's not even *a* one. Tristan is a jerk who has moments of greatness, but those aren't enough to make him someone I'd actually want to spend time with on the regular.

Inside the house, my parents are watching a movie, something slow and dramatic that's probably in contention for a bunch of awards. It seems like one of those movies that's three hours long but the script was only six pages because most of the screen time is devoted to characters staring at each other meaningfully. It's well after midnight, but they're still going strong. That's the thing about having young parents. They refuse to act old.

"How was the drive-in?" Dad asks.

"It was good."

"What was showing?"

"A *Mission: Impossible* and a slasher flick that I slept through."

"Who else was there?" Mom asks, her standard questions.

"People I work with," I reply.

"Oh, that's nice," she says. "Was Natalie there?"

"Nope," I say, putting an end to her fishing expedition. "I'm going upstairs to wash my face." Which is usually code for *I'm done now, good night.*

There's a brief pause, where I can tell my mom wants to ask me more, but instead she smiles. "Okay, see you in the morning."

But I don't wash my face. Instead I climb into my bed, still in my clothes, which smell like gasoline and popcorn. I pull out my phone and open SocialSquare. I don't follow that many people, just my friends, a few celebrities with truly delightful feeds, and some beauty influencers. I suck at makeup, but I do try to wash my face with decent drugstore potions. But not tonight, because tonight I head straight for Natalie's feed. She's the most avid social networker of all of us. As much as she denies her mother's influence, some of that blogging has definitely rubbed off on her. Her feed is always up-to-date, and usually really pretty, too. She knows how to artfully edit a shot and add the perfect caption to make her life (and by extension, ours) appear as if it were designed by J. Crew or profiled by *Vanity Fair*. It looks like they were all at Tamsin and Colin's house tonight. There's a snap of Tamsin holding up a gooey s'more, her face framed by the stone firepit her parents have in their backyard. I swipe, and there's Cora sprawled out on Eli's lap, the two of them spilling over the arms of a white Adirondack chair. Next is a picture of Colin and Mac fake sword fighting with a pair of metal skewers, each with a flaming marshmallow on the end of their fork. And last but not least is a little animated photo of Natalie, Tamsin, and Cora jumping jubilantly in front of the fire, their hair flying overhead as the fire flickers behind them.

Another perfect night.

I can't help but notice that no one bothered to invite me.

Over the break I worked two more shifts at Hot 'N Crusty: Friday and a Saturday double. Twelve hours, and I only saw Tristan twice. Neither time did he do more than give me a brief nod of greeting. Man, between Mac and this, my romance radar is seriously misfiring.

I guess I really was imagining it all.

Back at school on Monday, it's like nothing has changed. Tristan disappears out the back door of the cafeteria, chips and milk in hand. Julianne is reading in the corner. And I'm back at our round table, two from the middle, sitting next to Natalie while Colin regales us with his wakeboarding adventures and Tamsin flips through pictures of the hot lifeguard she's stalking.

"Did you do anything fun over the break, Beck?" Cora asks when it's clear we're all tapped out on ski stories.

"I just worked. Binged stuff with my parents," I say with a shrug. "Nothing special." And for the first time I'm keeping Hot 'N Crusty to myself not because I'm embarrassed, but because I just don't want to share it. I don't want to see Tamsin wrinkle her nose at the mention of Julianne or hear the boys say something rude about Frank, Jason, or Greg. And I don't want to avoid Mac's gaze when I bring up Tristan or worry that he's going to bring up the kiss he saw. I'd rather geek out on *Apex Galaxy* spoilers at our lunch table, and that's saying something.

The conversation continues around the table, but I'm not listening. Instead I stare down at my lunch, a fluffernutter sandwich my mom made, along with some pretzels and an apple. Yes, my mom still makes my lunch sometimes. And yes, I love it. Even the note she always writes me on my napkin. Today it's a Dr. Seuss quote: *Be who you are and say what you feel because those who mind don't matter and those who matter don't mind!* Oof, easier said than done, Mom.

"I missed you over break," Natalie says, leaning in so the conversation is just between the two of us.

"I could tell," I reply. I must still be lost in my own thoughts, because the response flies out before I can stop it. At the last minute I try to mask the tone with a mischievous smirk, but it doesn't fly with Natalie. She knows me too well.

"What does that mean?" she asks.

I shrug. "I didn't know you guys were doing a s'mores night over at Tamsin's." And as I say it, I realize how hurt I am. Even though I had a moment with Tristan and I *definitely* became friends with everyone else. Even though I actually don't wish I'd missed the drive-in or geek night to make s'mores and pose for filtered pictures. Even then, it still hurts to know that my friends had no problem ignoring me, or worse, simply forgetting me.

"I texted you," Natalie says.

"No, you didn't."

"I did!" Natalie reaches in her bag and pulls out her phone, glancing around the cafeteria to make sure Mr. Messer, the asshole football coach who also serves as cafeteria monitor, isn't looking. His favorite pastime is confiscating student phones during the school day, and I swear he spends his free time in his office, scrolling through your photos. When she sees him across the cafeteria busy harassing a girl over the dress code, she taps at the screen and navigates to her texts. And then she gasps. "Shit. Oh shit, I'm so sorry, Beck. I thought I sent it, but it never went through."

She flips her phone toward me under the table where I see a text typed out inviting me to Tamsin's on Thursday night. But there's the little red exclamation point in a circle next to it, indicating an error. It never actually left her phone. It should comfort me. And it does, a little. But not enough. She still never looked back at her phone after the initial text. She never wondered why I didn't show up. And she never sent another text to me the entire weekend. I slipped her mind like an errant calculus assignment.

"It goes both ways, you know," Natalie says.

"What does *that* mean?"

She stares at me. Hard. "You didn't text me, either," she says.

I don't know what to say to that. Because I didn't. Mostly because she's usually the social director of our friendship, and Tamsin is the social director of our friend group, so I'm always the one being invited along. That was just how it worked.

I don't realize I'm just sitting there silently, staring at my lap, until the electronic tone buzzes to let us know lunch is over. Natalie doesn't look mad. She seems to have sort of moved past it and is laughing a little too hard at a dumb joke Colin just made. Are we fighting? It seemed like maybe it was just a warning, but what if it's not? What does it mean if we're fighting? It would be so easy for us to drift apart. Natalie already has Tamsin and Cora. I could drift away from the lunch table easily. Would I end up with Julianne? Or would I follow Tristan out the back door to wherever he goes? Or would I have to find myself a solo seat and my own big book?

Things were weird with Natalie for the rest of the day. For the rest of the week, honestly. We didn't talk about the s'mores night again, or our notable lack of texting. To anyone else, it would look like everything remained the same. We still sat next to each other at the same table every day at lunch, but I'd stopped thinking of it as "our" table. I still got a ride home with her every day after school, but we mostly just talked about school, like the metric ton of college mail that had started arriving in our mailboxes. No crushes, no shared secrets. We didn't talk about Mac, and it seemed like all things Tamsin had also become off-limits. And I stopped asking her about her crush on Colin. The longer it went on, the higher the wall became. I checked for the three little dots that would tell me she was at least composing a text. I checked a *lot*. But it was always blank. The further I got from telling her about my night at the drive-in with Tristan, the harder it became to bring it up. The more time that passed, I became less consumed with the kiss and more consumed with what it meant that I hadn't told her yet. And that conversation scared me more than whatever was going on between Tristan and me.

Which, still, seemed to be nothing.

Tristan wasn't at work on Tuesday. Instead, Hunter, a stoner kid getting a business degree at the college, took his shift. I wasn't sure if Tristan was actually sick, or just avoiding me, and I didn't ask. It wouldn't have mattered if I did anyway. Tristan isn't the kind of guy to tell anyone. I was starting to know him enough to be sure of that.

By Thursday, I'm feeling fully adrift. My connection to Natalie feels like it's fraying by the day, and Tristan seems to want nothing to do with me, despite what happened last week. I have no idea who I am or where I belong. Even Hot 'N Crusty feels a little strange.

"Oh my god, you're the bathroom baby!"

The screechy voice yanks me out of my fog, where

I've been taking orders behind the register on autopilot. There's a woman standing in front of me, middle-aged and rail-thin with curly hair that may have once been that color red on its own, but is now definitely chemically enhanced. She's wearing heavy eye makeup and dark lipstick, and her mouth is a mile wide.

I hate her immediately.

"You're the bathroom baby, right? From right over there?" She points over my shoulder toward the short hallway that leads to the bathrooms, and I see that her nails are long and sharp, painted blood red. She's blinking at me with that enormous smile, waiting for my confirmation.

"Yes, ma'am," I mutter, trying to maintain good customer service even though I wish the sticky floor of Hot 'N Crusty would open up and swallow this woman whole.

"I knew it! It's so amazing that you work here now!" She grins even wider, and I open my mouth to ask her what she wants to eat, when she charges on. "Your poor mama. I swear, I had my babies in the nicest hospital in the state with an epidural and a doula and I *still* hated every second of it. Do you know how *disgusting* childbirth is? You hear about those women who have home births, and I think after something like that happening in my living room I'd have to burn the whole dang house down. Just torch it up! It's like a *crime scene*, am I right?"

I take a long, slow, deep breath in through my nose and out of my mouth, but it does nothing to ease my tension. I can't believe it's not radiating off me like the aftershocks of an earthquake.

"I wouldn't know, not having a whole lot of memories of my birth," I say with more acidity than I mean. Or maybe I do mean it. Regardless, it bounces right off her.

"Can I get a picture?" she asks, pulling her phone out of her enormous designer handbag.

"Excuse me?"

"Just a quick selfie! I can post it on Facebook and show everyone what a good girl you turned out to be. My friend went into labor real fast, and she ended up having her baby at the *county* hospital where she didn't even get a private room, and she's always worried that something happened to her sweet little Payton after a start like that," she says with her nose wrinkled up, like her friend was forced to give birth at the town dump. "Seeing how you turned out okay after being born in a *bathroom* will give her some peace of mind."

I can feel the creeping tingle of rage starting to make its way through my body, like a fuse that's been lit and is winding its way toward a major explosion. My mom raised me to be polite, but this, as she herself would say, is a bridge too far. If I don't get away from this woman, and *soon*, things are going to get messy. And woe unto her if she manages to snap that selfie.

"Julianne!" I shout back into the kitchen, where I know she's finishing up her break. My voice is shrill and screechy, and it bounces off all the stainless steel. The swinging door comes flying open, and Julianne practically trips over herself getting to the register.

"What's going on?" she asks, glancing from me to the woman wielding her iPhone, and back again. I don't say anything in return, just whip off my Hot 'N Crusty ball cap and clench it in my fist as I stomp back toward the kitchen, trying to put as much real estate between me and her as I possibly can. I stalk through the kitchen, past the prep table and the ovens and the industrial dishwasher, past Del's office and toward the metal door that leads to the dumpsters. I throw my shoulder into it *hard*, and as it flies open I hear a grunt and a shuffle.

"Watch it!" comes the muffled voice of the person I've nearly pancaked between the door and the brick wall of the restaurant.

Tristan.

Of course.

The door closes with a loud clang, and I'm left standing

next to the dumpster with Tristan. He's wearing his usual denim jacket, only now there's a zip hoodie beneath it, the red hood poking out over the collar of his jacket. There's a knit cap on his head to keep out the late October chill, his curly hair poking out in wild directions beneath it. And his left hand has a white bandage wrapped around his palm, secured on the back of his hand with medical tape.

"What happened to you?" I ask, nodding toward his hand.

"What happened to *you*?" he asks, gesturing to my entire being.

"Awful customer trying to get a selfie with the bathroom baby to show that despite my filthy birth, I turned out okay. Though I'm not sure she still thinks so after the way I bolted."

"That's quite a synopsis."

I drop down onto the curb and try not to breathe in the smell of rancid garlic that's wafting out of the dumpster. I drop my head into my hands and take a deep breath, trying to steady my heart rate and bring myself down from wanting to absolutely deck that woman.

"Why do you even care about the bathroom baby thing, anyway?"

"I don't know, because it's embarrassing?"

"More embarrassing than wearing this T-shirt?" he says, pulling his jacket open to reveal the catchphrase.

I let out a bitter chuckle. "You forget I'm the reason for the T-shirt."

"Ah yes, I'll add that to your cosmic tab," he says. "But really, it's not like Del singles you out or anything. And I'm pretty sure that crazy lady is the first person to give you shit about it since you started. Well, and that reporter. And let's not forget the trauma of the free popcorn. So what's the big deal?"

"I don't know. It just . . . it made me a thing before I even got to decide what thing I wanted to be." I sigh. "She meant well," I say, more to myself than to Tristan, who I'm not even sure is still standing there. If the last week has been any indication, he should have bolted by now. We haven't said two words to each other since his bus pulled away from my house.

"Who cares how she meant it? She made you feel like shit."

I glance up in surprise. Yup, he's still there, leaning against the brick wall, arms crossed over his chest, feet crossed at his ankles. Julianne was definitely right about his James Dean act. I don't know what to say to him.

"You don't have to be so *tolerant*, Brix. It's okay to, like, unclench."

"Unclench?"

"Yeah. Relax your jaw. Tongue out of the roof of your mouth. Shoulders out of your ears." He lists the directions like a recipe, and I follow them to the letter. I do what he says, one at a time, and it feels good. I didn't realize I was actually so annoyed that it was causing me physical pain.

"I thought you were just being metaphorical," I say as I roll out the tension in my neck.

"Well, that, too."

"I'll take those tips as well," I say.

He pauses, glancing at his phone, then back at the door. "You closing tonight?" he asks.

I shake my head and pull my phone out of my back pocket, hitting the button to illuminate the screen. "Fifteen more minutes," I tell him.

"Screw that. Let's get out of here."

"Don't you have more deliveries?"

"Not at the moment. They'll text me if something comes in, but it's been ridiculously slow tonight. I won't even make the gas money back in tips." He pushes off the wall and pulls his keys from his pocket. "Come on. I'll give you a ride."

"I need to clock out," I say.

"Email Del and tell him you forgot. He'll fix it."

"And Julianne. I can't just ditch her."

He sighs, then pulls the back door open, shouting into the kitchen, "Hey, Jules! You care if Beck cuts out a few minutes early?"

Her voice comes echoing back through the kitchen. "Sure."

"Cool. Later." Then the door slams and he's walking around the side of the building toward the bus. "You coming?"

"Lemme grab my jacket," I say, suddenly realizing that it's kind of chilly out here, and I'm only wearing my Hot 'N Crusty T-shirt. Apparently my simmering rage was quite the insulator. I duck back into the kitchen and take my jacket off the hook, grabbing my purse, and then start to head out. But I pause to clock out, because I'm not going to lie to Del. Tristan may play Rebel Without a Cause, but I always follow the rules. I can only unclench so much.

Outside, the bus's engine is already rumbling. Tristan's behind the wheel getting it warmed up. I climb into the passenger seat.

"Where to?" he asks.

"I thought you had some kind of plan," I tell him.

A silence falls between us, like we're both just remembering the last time we were here together.

"I've got to stop by the house and let my dog out before anything else," he says, like that's an answer. "You mind?"

I shrug. "Fine with me."

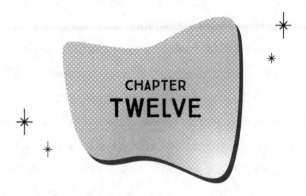

CHAPTER
TWELVE

Tristan lives on the edge of downtown in one of the little neighborhoods that was built in the fifties. In middle school social studies we learned about the identical little brick houses that were built for soldiers returning from World War II, ready to start their lives with their children that they were often meeting for the first time in perfect little homes built just for them. You can drive down the street and imagine what it must have looked like back then, with little squares of manicured green grass and window boxes of flowers, all the brick and driveways brand-new, the doors freshly painted, the shiny glass in the windows. But the neighborhood has since grown old and weary, and as more people have moved farther out of town into the newly developed subdivisions, the houses have begun to look shabby, the driveways cracked and the grass overgrown, with a few faded American flags waving from rusty poles and shutters hanging at odd angles.

Tristan's house, though, is immaculate. But not fancy. There are no flower boxes, but the grass is trimmed with military precision, like someone got out there with a ruler. The paint on the front door is black with nary a chip to be found, and there are no crooked blinds in the windows. Tristan pulls into the driveway and cuts the engine. I climb out and follow.

Inside, it's dark and sort of musty, but still neat. The living room is like a museum, as if it's been staged to show what life was like when the houses were built. There's a floral living room set and a coffee table with curlicues on the legs and gold etching. The books on the shelves all have faded spines, and there's an actual grandfather clock the size of a coffin in the corner. There are honest-to-god doilies on the backs of the couch and the wingback chair. The only thing that looks like it's from this century is the flat-screen TV hanging on the wall above the brick fireplace.

A floppy-eared, brown-and-white oaf of a dog comes bounding through the living room and jumps up on Tristan, who catches his enormous paws with a practiced ease. The dog gives him a big lick on the chin, then drops down to the floor and looks at me with big, watery eyes.

"This is Bandit," Tristan says. "Bandit, meet Beck. You okay with dogs?"

"Yeah, I hate to tell you this," I say, "but I think that's a pony." I hold my hand out, and Bandit wanders over to give it a sniff. He must determine I'm okay, because he takes a few steps forward and leans into my thighs. He's so big and heavy that he nearly takes me to the ground.

"C'mon, Bandit. Let's go outside." Tristan disappears through the doorway with the dog hot on his heels. I hear a door open, and I assume Bandit's out doing his business. Then Tristan is back in the living room, where I'm standing awkwardly, trying not to disturb anything.

"You can come on back," he says, though he doesn't say back *where*, just heads down a hallway. I follow him, but immediately get hung up by the framed photos that line the wall. There are black-and-white ones of people in stiff clothing, the men in ties and the women in dresses with buttons down the front and cinched waists. I realize right away that they're standing in front of this very same house. The color photos, with their orangish tints, show guys in jeans and tight T-shirts, hair long, the women in maxi skirts and long ponytails. The photos get newer, and I spot Cecilia, her pea-soup-green paint job looking new even in the old photo. A white guy who must be Tristan's dad leans against the door. He has the same flyaway hair and freckles, only he's blond and pale to Tristan's tan skin and dark hair. And then I see the same guy in a wedding photo with a beautiful black woman, her hair long and curly with a delicate tiara atop her head. Her dress is bright white and beaded, with thin straps, little pearls in her ears. She's grinning at the photographer, but Tristan's dad is grinning at her.

"Is that your mom?" I ask, pointing at the photo.

He pauses, glancing at the photo, then quickly looks away.

"Yeah."

"What does she do?"

"She was a real estate agent, but she died when I was a freshman." He says it sort of fast, his voice never wavering, like he hopes maybe I won't pick up on the meaning of the words. That his mom died. That she's been gone nearly four years. I get the same selfish flare of panic I always get when I hear about parents dying. That fear that it could be catching. That *my* parents could die. Just the thought makes me want to lie down on the floor and cry. The reality would be so much worse.

"Oh. I'm so sorry, I didn't know."

He shrugs, like I'm apologizing for spilling a drink on

the carpet. "She had cancer. They said she only had a few months, but she lived another four years." And then he disappears into the room at the end of the hall.

Conversation over. Textbook Tristan.

I move to follow him, but stop at another set of photos, because there's a tiny Tristan, perched atop a tricycle, grinning, followed by one of him climbing inside Cecilia with his front teeth missing. And there's a whole set of photos of tiny baseball players, their pants bright white and their ball caps too big for their heads, so that they're slipping down over their eyes. There's a professional team photo, the front row of kids sitting cross-legged in the dirt while the second row stands behind, their arms crossed behind their backs, all glaring at the camera like serious athletes.

I squint at the photo, looking for Tristan's dark, floppy hair, but I don't find him.

"Which one are you?" I call to him, tapping the glass in the frame.

He pokes his head out of the room and grimaces, then steps out and jams his finger down on a kid sitting cross-legged in the front row. I missed him, because tiny Tristan is missing the impressive hair. Tiny Tristan looks like he's sporting a buzz cut underneath his maroon baseball cap. The kid next to him has pretty impressive hair, though the kid is blond, and—

"Oh my god, is that Mac?" I ask, pointing to the kid sitting next to him.

He doesn't even have to look up. "Yup."

And then I see the next frame, one of those collage ones with holes in varying shapes for different snapshots. There's one of Tristan batting, the ball just leaving his bat, and one of him on the pitcher's mound looking like he's ready for the World Series. And in the center, in an oval mat, is Tiny Tristan and Baby Mac, gloves in hand, arms thrown around each other as they grin at the camera.

"You and Mac were friends?"

"Yup."

"Do you know any other words?"

He pauses. Then, "Yup."

"So *that's* how you knew all about the *Golden Girls* theme song and the Boy Scout camp incident."

"It wasn't Boy Scout camp. And let's not forget his indifference to the Beatles."

"Why didn't you say anything?"

"Why would I?"

"Because you guys were friends! Good friends, from the looks of it."

"Because we're not anymore."

"Why not?"

"I don't know, because we grew up? We went our

separate ways? You're welcome to ask him that question." Then Tristan turns to walk back into his room.

I follow him, ready to grill him some more about his friendship with Mac and his illustrious Little League career, but as soon as I step inside I'm distracted by his room. It's *tiny*. Partially because it's not a particularly big room, but also because it's positively overflowing with stuff. It's like for every word he's saved by being silent, he's acquired something to store in here. There's a tall set of shelves in one corner stuffed full of books, with stacks going every which way and two deep. Another bookcase is packed full of records, some in fraying sleeves, some encased in plastic. There's a record player in a suitcase sitting atop an enormous speaker next to it. Next to that is a small wooden desk with a surface covered in stacks of papers, some rumpled and some rolled up with rubber bands, stray pencils and little block erasers littering the space. His closet looks like it's attempting to eject its contents, with piles of clothes—maybe clean, maybe dirty, I doubt even *he* knows—strewn about. There are posters on the wall of album covers and long-haired guys playing guitar or singing into an old-fashioned microphone in front of enormous crowds.

But what really draws my attention is a wooden chair pushed back from the desk. It's got a dark stain on it and carved spindle legs, the back and elegantly curved frame with more carved spindles. The seat looks like it's been sanded so it perfectly fits your butt. I have to go over and test it out. And yup, not only is it pretty, it's comfortable, too. It seems like it should be an antique, one of those fancy pieces of furniture you're supposed to look at, but not sit in. But what I love about this chair is that it's clearly well used and well loved. As I run my hands over the arms, I feel ridges and dings, and see places where the stain has been rubbed away.

I lean back into the wood and put my feet up on the edge of his desk, careful not to disturb the mountain of papers. "I like this chair," I say.

"Thanks. I made it." It's the first time he's volunteered information, and I don't miss the note of pride in his voice.

"You made this?" I sit up and glance back at the workmanship, the curved back and delicately tapered spindles.

"My dad and I took a class at the community center over in Dakota Hills. This guy came in and taught us how to bend and shape the wood. It was cool."

"That's awesome. Have you made anything else?"

He pauses, like he's considering saying no, but then he heads for the door and cocks his head for me to follow. He leads me back through the house, through a delightfully vintage and preserved kitchen with gold linoleum and avocado green appliances I know my mom would love, and to a door that leads into the backyard. There's a square of patio and more expertly trimmed grass, which Bandit is currently rolling in like it's the greatest day of his life, his long legs and enormous paws flying in crazy directions, looking like they're in danger of getting tangled. At the back corner of the yard is a detached garage, also brick, with a garage door painted the same shiny black as the front door. Tristan walks over and bends down to grab the handle and slings it open with a practiced motion; the smell of sawdust comes rushing out. It's dark inside, but he steps in and reaches for a string, tugging to illuminate the space.

I can't tell if the space is small or if it just seems that way because it's crammed with stuff. But it's not filled with junk like our garage is (my mom keeps promising to go through the Rubbermaid bins of my childhood memorabilia, but usually ends up in tears after opening the first one and the whole project just goes to hell). There are workbenches around the perimeter of the room, with one enormous table in the middle atop which sits a saw that looks like it could fully cut a human in half. There are several other monstrous-looking power tools strewn about, and I'm honestly afraid to step inside for fear I'll lose a limb.

"Everything's turned off," he says as he takes in my transfixed gaze on the sharp blades that seem to be everywhere. "You're safe, I promise."

So I step inside and inhale the woody smell and start to look around. Suspended between two metal things is what looks like a table leg in the process of being shaped. And there's an intricately carved picture frame held together with vise grips. On the back table is a small collection of wooden boxes, similar to the one he made for Julianne to give to her mom. The walls are plastered with blueprints drawn in pencil and showing tables and chairs and bookshelves.

"This is all yours?" I ask.

"I share it with my dad, but he doesn't really do furniture. That's all me."

"This is so cool."

"It's all right," he says. A smile tugs at the corner of his mouth. He leans back against one of the worktables, crossing his arms over his chest as he gazes around. "There's a lot of stuff I don't have, but luckily Coach Driskill is really cool about letting me use the woodshop at school."

"We have a woodshop at school?"

"Uh, yeah. There's a whole class and everything."

"Oh. Wait, is that where you go during lunch? When

you skip out the back door?" There I go again, letting my mouth operate independent of my brain.

His eyebrows shoot up. "You keeping tabs on me?"

I blush. "I thought maybe you went to smoke under the bleachers with the bad kids," I say, trying to make a joke out of it.

"Smoking kills," he replies.

"So does that," I say, pointing at a metal table with an enormous, circular jagged blade rising out of the middle.

"Only if you're careless."

"And what happened to your hand?" I point to the white bandage wrapped around his palm.

"I got a little careless," he says, raising his eyebrow.

"Seriously?"

"It wasn't the table saw. I was actually doing some whittling and lost control of the knife. Just needed a few stitches."

"I'm sorry, Old Man River, did you say you were *whittling*?"

He picks up a little piece of wood that's halfway to being what looks like a chess piece. "I'm making a whole set," he says.

"You play chess?"

"No, but I've never had a chess set before, so maybe that was my problem."

On a bulletin board over one of the workbenches, where it looks like mostly old, rumpled plans are tacked up, is a red pennant for State.

"You a Panthers fan?" I ask him, nodding at the pennant with its blocky white letters. Dad's got one in his garage, too. It's where he and Mom met while they were undergrads.

"Nah. Not really a big sports guy."

"Really? Mr. Little League?"

"You a fan of every sport you stumbled into when you were a kid?"

"No. But I played exactly one season of youth soccer when I was five, and it took me a full *three games* to understand why we had to share our ball with the other team," I say. I run my finger through a pile of sawdust on one of the tables, drawing swirls and cursive letters. "Is that where you're going next year? State?"

"Nope," he says.

"Still waiting to hear back?"

"Nope. Didn't apply anywhere."

"Why not?"

"I'm not going to college."

I pause, practically stumble. I don't think I've ever heard anyone say those words. Not going to college? Really?

"Why not?" I practically sputter.

"I'm going to do this after I graduate," he says, pointing to what looks like the start of another chair on a workbench in the back of the garage.

"Make chairs?"

"Furniture. And other woodworking stuff. Picture frames, maybe some wall hangings. Art, but that sounds pretentious. I'll work with my dad at first to supplement my income while I get started, but I don't think it'll take too long before I can focus all my attention on my own projects. I'm already working on a couple of commissions. If those go well, they could lead to more work with some good, high-paying clients."

He pulls out his phone and taps at the screen a few times before slipping it around to show me. It's a SocialSquare page. *His* SocialSquare page, for his burgeoning business. It's called Wreck & Salvage Designs. I guess that's why I couldn't find him when I searched his name. Because his focus is here.

"I thought you said you don't do social media," I say.

"Not socially," he replies. "This is for work."

He doesn't hand me the phone to scroll, so I can only get a quick glance of the first few photos on the feed. I see a coffee table and a bookcase, and an elaborate picture frame that looks like it was made with vintage wood. Is that a thing?

"These look really good," I say.

"Thanks."

"You're seriously not going to college? Not even community college?"

He shrugs. "Why would I?"

"I don't know. A business major could be valuable if you want to start your own business."

"I've been working with my dad, and he's owned his own business for twenty years. Anything else I need to know I just look up online or head to the library. And I already *have* started my business. It seems dumb to waste all that money and four years of time when I can go ahead and get started doing what I want to do."

"But, I mean, aren't you worried about missing out on that experience?"

"No."

"Seriously?"

"No. College isn't something I need or want. I'm not going to do it just because it's what everyone does. It's not thirteenth grade, Beck."

That stings a little bit. Maybe it's because he's so sure of what he wants to do, and here I am playing college counselor when I've got no idea what my future holds. All

I've been concentrating on is leaving Brook Park. Beyond that, I have no idea. When I binge *Law & Order* with my mom, I think maybe I could be a lawyer. And when I watch *The West Wing* with my dad, I think maybe I can do political stuff. And sometimes, during epic *Apex Galaxy* binges, I think maybe I'd want to actually work on a show like that. Write or direct or something. There's just so much out there. I always figured college was the place where I'd sift through and discover where I belong. Both my parents are teachers, so that's probably in my blood, at least. But, honestly, I just want to be a college student who doesn't live here. Because once I'm out of Brook Park, the probability of someone calling me the bathroom baby or trying to get a selfie with me or hurling a pizza pun my way will plummet exponentially.

And yet I still can't help but feel like it's my job to convince *him* that he's making the wrong choice. Me, who has no plans for the future, trying to change the plans of the guy who knows exactly what he wants to do. Who's already *doing* it.

"Okay, but if you're so ready to start your business, why don't you go ahead and do that? It's not like you need biology or geography or literature to build beautiful furniture. Why not just drop out?"

"I promised my mom I'd finish high school," he says.

Oh.

"See? The dead-mom card usually ends all conversations you don't want to have."

"Yeah, that'll do it," I tell him. "I can't imagine my parents' reactions if I told them I wasn't going to college."

"I think if they saw that you had another path, one that truly made you happy, they'd be pretty jazzed to help you get there. And glad that you saved them tens of thousands of dollars."

"Oh, my parents don't have tens of thousands of dollars. Wherever I end up, it's going to be a place that offers me a hefty helping of financial aid."

"I thought you were one of those Legacy Park Princesses," he says. I try not to feel stung by the accusation. I know he thinks I must be spoiled rotten after seeing me with Mac and Tamsin. The Range Rovers and the designer bags and the ski trips. Unfortunately, none of that stuff rubs off. Still, I try to brush it off. I don't want to start a thing with him.

"Uh, excuse me, I'm the Pizza Princess, and don't you forget it."

He bows deeply. "My apologies, Your Majesty."

"That's more like it."

His phone buzzes, and he swipes away from SocialSquare to check his texts.

"Damn, a delivery. Looks like a big one. You wanna help out?"

"Do I get tips?"

"Here's a tip: Don't step on that power strip, especially not with your hand so close to the band saw," he says. I practically leap six feet in the air and bolt away from the table, Tristan doubled over with laughter.

Back at Hot 'N Crusty, I help Tristan load fifteen pizzas, a dozen salads, and several small boxes of garlic knots into the back of the bus. It's enough to actually overpower the smell of gasoline that wafts ambiently through Cecilia at all times. It's a powerful scent, one that not even a tub of movie theater popcorn could hide, but apparently a few hundred dollars' worth of Hot 'N Crusty will do the trick.

I don't pay attention to the address Tristan punches into his phone's GPS, but it doesn't take long for me to realize where we're headed. The stone and iron gates of Legacy Park welcome us, as does a guard in a little stone hut, who waves us in when he spots Cecilia.

"Anton knows me by now," Tristan says as the gates

slide open and we cruise on through without stopping. "Perk of driving a distinctive car."

"I'm impressed by your connections," I say. I add a laugh, but it's completely forced. It feels weird to be cruising through Legacy Park in Cecilia like some kind of social Trojan horse.

Tristan steers the bus onto the bigger neighborhood loop, then makes an immediate left. The sign for the Legacy Park town green greets us as we cruise past a tennis complex and the pool, now closed for fall. He finally comes to a stop in a parking spot in front of the pavilion, which is lit up with twinkle lights. It looks like some kind of party is happening. I scan the crowd quickly, but don't see anyone I know.

I climb out and help Tristan with the towers of pizzas, then follow him toward the pavilion. I can't look to see if there's anyone else I know, because the half-dozen pizza boxes in my arms block my view. But then I hear a voice I recognize from TV. "Don't pay dealer fees!" It's usually shouted as the very tan, very handsome Mr. MacArthur draws the crowds into MacArthur Toyota.

"Tristan Porter! Good to see you, son," Mr. MacArthur's voice booms with authority. He takes a stack of pizza boxes from Tristan's arms and sets them on a nearby picnic table.

"Tristan! Oh my gosh, how long has it been?" Mac's mom comes hustling over. As soon as Tristan is relieved of the pizzas, she pulls him into a hug. "How are you? How's your dad?"

"Good," Tristan replies with a tight smile, looking more uncomfortable than I've ever seen him. "We're both good."

"Mac, Tristan is here!" Mrs. MacArthur calls to her son, who emerges from the crowd. I spot Eli and Colin back there with Tamsin, but none of them makes a move to follow Mac, even though I think they can see me standing right there. Mac sort of ambles over, tripping over his own shoelace on the way.

"Hey, man," he says, offering his hand for one of those complicated handshake-slash-slap situations dudes do. Only Tristan just sort of nods at him, leaving Mac's palm waving in the wind until he drops it to his side and turns to me, shifting back and forth on his sneakers. "Hey, Beck."

"Hi," I say, the word coming out small and quiet.

"So how's school going? Are you ready for graduation? What are your college plans?" Mrs. MacArthur is one of those moms who just peppers people with questions, hoping eventually one of them will stick. And that last one makes me wince. I know how into college the

MacArthurs are. Their entire basement looks like the University of Michigan barfed in there. Just yellow and blue everywhere. They go for homecoming every year and spend lord-knows-how-much money on a fancy tailgate. I've seen the photos framed above their wet bar. Mac and his brothers are all pretty much expected to follow in their parents' footsteps and move to Ann Arbor as soon as they graduate.

Tristan's got to know it, too, if he spent any amount of time there in elementary or middle school.

"Uh, I'm actually—" Tristan fumbled.

"He's doing an apprenticeship," I tell her. "In woodworking."

"Oh, well, that sounds interesting," Mrs. MacArthur says, her eyes darting back and forth between Tristan and me, apparently his newly appointed spokesperson.

Mr. MacArthur pulls out a wad of cash and passes it to Tristan. "Oh, you already paid for the pizzas," Tristan tells him, looking at what appears to be several twenty-dollar bills in his hand.

"That's a tip, son," Mr. MacArthur says with a wink.

Tristan stares at the money, and for one brief, horrifying second I worry he's going to drop it on the ground. Or simply refuse it. But he eventually folds it up and shoves it deep into his pocket.

"Okay, well, we should probably get back. Lots of deliveries tonight," I say, giving Mac and the MacArthurs a little wave.

"Oh yes, we're about to start our neighborhood association meeting; otherwise I'd ask you both to stay. I'm afraid it wouldn't be very fun for you," Mrs. MacArthur says.

"Then why am I here again?" Mac mutters, and his father shoots him a stern look.

"Don't be a stranger, Tristan," Mrs. MacArthur says. "We miss you around the house."

Mac looks stricken, while Tristan looks like he just swallowed a bug. So I put a merciful end to the awkwardness and give everyone a wave goodbye, then drag Tristan by the arm back to Cecilia.

When we're both back in our seats, Tristan lets out a long breath and grips the wheel.

"So that was weird," he says.

"Tell me about it," I reply. "Mrs. MacArthur is awfully chatty."

"No, I mean you. *You* were being weird." He shifts Cecilia into gear and stomps on the gas. I jerk back against my seat.

"No I wasn't! I was trying to save you," I say.

"From what? A hundred-dollar tip and a hug? I don't need saving."

"Well, it seemed like you did." I lean back and cross my arms over my chest. "I just thought I was returning the favor. Sorry."

"But something *is* going on with your friends, right? I mean, you didn't even say hi to them."

"They didn't say hi to me, either."

"My point exactly."

I stare out the passenger side window as the brick and iron gates of Legacy Park roll past. I feel myself relax the farther we get from them. I even do Tristan's unclench thingy. Soon we're back out on the main road, and I feel calm again. "I guess things are kind of weird with them right now."

"Why? Still not over MacArthur?"

"No!" I cry, and realize that for the first time that's actually 100 percent true. I really *don't* have any feelings for Mac anymore. I'm totally and completely over him. Hell, it would be easier if that *was* the problem. "I just . . . think maybe . . . we're growing apart?" I feel a catch in my throat, like maybe I might cry. "I don't know, we haven't really talked about it."

"Maybe you should."

"Why did you and Mac stop being friends?" I ask, eager to change the subject. "And don't tell me to ask him. I'm asking you."

"Oh," he says, the word whooshing out on a long breath. "Well, I guess because my mom died."

"Are you playing the dead-mom card again?"

"No," he says, and for a minute I think he's not going to explain. I watch his knuckles turn white as he grips the steering wheel, worrying it in his hands. He presses the accelerator a little harder, Cecilia jumping forward on the empty, straight two-lane road. And then he begins to speak.

"My mom was diagnosed right at the end of fifth grade. Breast cancer. Metastatic, which is bad, and they told us she wouldn't live for very long. We all thought that would be our last summer with her, so I quit baseball and my dad put all his jobs on hold and my mom handed off all her listings, and we piled in this van and we just took off. Mom wanted to see things, and so we took these crazy road trips between treatments. We saw Graceland and the Alamo and the Saint Louis Arch. We even drove out to the Grand Canyon. And then the summer ended, and she was still doing okay. Not great. She was basically always between chemo treatments. She looked sick, but she was still her. But there was always this, I don't know, threat? It was just hanging over our heads at all times. The breast cancer was definitely going to kill her, we just didn't know when. And I was only ten, and terrified, like if I went back to baseball or spent too much time at Mac's house, I'd miss something huge. Or I'd come home from practice and find her gone."

He's quiet for a moment. I look over to see his lips pressed together in a firm line, and I realize he's holding back tears. He blinks hard a few times, and lets out another long breath, seeming to have beat them back. I think he might have had a lot of practice at it.

"So I stopped hanging out, and hell, we were just little. Like Mac knew what to do in that situation. I had no fucking clue, and it was *my* mom who was dying. So I guess we just grew apart. I started spending all my time at home, which is when I started working in the shed with my dad. My mom would pick a project, and we'd work on it, and it was almost like if I could keep presenting her with birdhouses or shadow boxes or a new end table, she would stay. She could keep fighting." His voice shakes, and I know that he can't hold back the tears anymore. But I do him the kindness of keeping my eyes forward. I let him cry in peace. "And then at the beginning of freshman year, she died. We thought she had pneumonia, but it turns out that the cancer had spread to her lungs and heart when we weren't looking. It happened really fast. Four whole years of waiting, and then she was gone in one weekend."

"I'm so sorry," I say, but the words feel hollow, and anyway I don't think he even hears them. They barely rise above a whisper, because now I'm crying, too. I never even knew her, but I know him, and I know what she was to him. And so I cry.

Tristan sniffles, wipes his nose with the back of his hand, and then grips the steering wheel again. He shakes his head and rolls his shoulders, the whole thing looking practiced, like a ritual that he completes to pull him away from the sadness. To close the door and say "enough now." He's unclenching.

"Mac and the rest of the team came to the funeral. And afterward they asked me to come back to practice. I mean *immediately* afterward. Like, I'm standing there on the lawn of the fucking church wearing a suit my dad bought and a tie that made me feel like I was choking, and Mac was all 'Hey, dude, you should come to practice on Monday. We miss you.' And all I could think was *fuck you*. My mom just *died*, and you think that *baseball practice* is going to make me feel better?"

"Did you say that?"

"No. I just walked away and never looked back. I think at that point we'd all grown up and moved on, which, honestly, was fine with me."

"I don't think it was fine," I say.

He's silent for a moment. "No, it wasn't."

"I don't think it was his fault, though."

He glances over at me, his eyes narrowed. "What do you mean?"

"He was fourteen. What fourteen-year-old knows how to cope with that kind of grief? I sure as hell wouldn't have known what to do. What to say."

"He was my best friend. He should have been there."

"Do you think you would have been?"

He's quiet.

"It sucks that that happened. And maybe he could have done a better job. But maybe he did the best he could. Just like you were doing the best you could. I don't think either of you were to blame. I think you were both trapped in an unimaginably terrible situation, and you were *fourteen*," I say. "You should talk to him. It's never too late."

We drive a whole block before he speaks again.

"Maybe you should take your own advice," he says. And I don't ask him what he means by that, because I don't think I want to know. He was brave in telling me all that, but I'm still just a coward.

We ride in silence. I can barely see out the window my eyes are so clouded with the tears I'm holding back. Until suddenly, the bus shudders to a stop and I realize we're back at my house. I let out a long, shaky breath, and then I feel steady. I turn to Tristan, who is still staring out the front windshield. But after a beat, he turns and gives me sort of an anemic smile.

"Thanks for saving me," I say. "You know, from the selfie lady."

Tristan laughs softly. "Anytime, Brix."

There's more to say, but that feels like enough for now. I climb out of the bus, the metal door creaking open and shut. I hoist my purse up on my shoulder and start up the driveway, and then I hear a sound behind me.

"Hey, Beck," Tristan calls as he rolls down the window.

I turn. "Yeah?"

"Thanks," he says. "See ya later?"

I smile. "Yeah. Later."

CHAPTER
THIRTEEN

I think Tristan and I have become friends. Friends who kissed that one time, though we never, *ever* talk about that. It just sort of lives between us, this unsayable thing that rears its head anytime we get too close. Or maybe that's just me, and he's thoroughly forgotten about it all by now.

"Yo, I brought you something," Tristan says as he breezes in through the back door of Hot 'N Crusty, an empty warming bag hooked over his forearm. He drops it on the floor in the middle of the kitchen and reaches into the pocket of his denim jacket. He pulls out a square envelope and passes it to me. It crinkles in my hand, and when I flip it over I see a clear window showing off a shiny silver CD.

"What's this?" I ask.

"It's a compact disc, Beck. It's used to play music."

"I know what it *is*," I say, matching his snark, as has become our game. "What am I supposed to play this on?"

"Are you telling me you don't have a CD player?"

"No, because it's not 2002."

"Well, I guarantee your dad's car has one."

"Oh, you guarantee? And how can you know that?"

"Because your dad's car predates the Obama Administration, so I'm pretty sure there's a CD player in there."

"Who knew driving an old clunker would come with such perks."

"Me. I did. Have you met Cecilia?" He bends down to pick up the warming bag. His shirt rises slightly, and I have to drag my gaze away from the strip of tan skin over the waistband of his jeans and *oh my god* am I staring at his ass?

"Order up," Joey calls, slinging two pizza boxes onto the table toward Tristan. He deposits a clamshell full of salad and a bag of garlic knots on top.

"Duty calls," Tristan says, sliding everything but the salad into the warming bag. We've come a long way from slinking in and out the back door, avoiding eye contact and all verbal interaction. He nods at the CD, still in my hand. "Listen to that. Don't neglect your musical education, Beck."

"I'll fire up my time machine," I reply, waving the disc at him. He's just disappeared out the back door when it flings back open so hard it slams into the wall with a loud clang (that door truly is a menace). Julianne comes bolting in, her eyes wide and watery. Her hair is pushed back from her face like she's been worrying her hands through it for a while. I've seen her withdrawn, and carefully detached. I've seen her snarky, and even happy. But I've never seen her like this, and it takes me aback before she's even said a word.

"Beck, I'm in trouble," she says, her chest heaving. Her hands are knotted in front of her, the nails of her right hand working steadily at the cuticles on the left. She's seconds away from drawing blood. My first thought is that she's going to ask me to help her hide a body.

"What's wrong?" I ask.

She pulls in a deep breath, like she's trying to suck air through a flannel blanket. Her eyes dart around the kitchen, then she leans in, her voice dropping low. "Mrs. Russo pulled me aside before lunch and told me that I have to crown the homecoming queen."

"Oh," I say, my true-crime-podcast images dissipating, but Julianne still looks revved up. "Yeah, okay. That sounds . . . not great."

"Did you not hear me?" Her voice rises higher. Even Joey, who usually tries hard to ignore whatever conversations are happening around him, glances over his shoulder from the pizza he's working on, banana peppers paused in his hand. "I have to crown the homecoming queen. At the game. In front of hundreds of people *on the fifty-yard line.*"

"Why?"

"Because apparently the previous year's queen, who is usually a senior, but not when your school is full of bullying asshats, comes back to do it. So since I 'won,'" she says, hooking her fingers into the most hostile air quotes I've ever seen, the word sitting in her mouth like a bad piece of fish, "*I* have to do it."

"Can't you say no?"

"I tried. But Mrs. Russo can't fathom why anyone wouldn't be out-of-their-mind fucking *honored* to be homecoming queen. Trying to explain to her why that sounds like my worst goddamn nightmare was about as effective as saying it in Cantonese. I swear, I watched her brain turn into smoldering glitter as I was telling her."

I've never heard Julianne swear like this before. Even that one time she dropped an entire extra large, extra cheese pizza on a customer, she managed to keep it to a very emphatic "*shoot!*" This is a five-alarm Julianne freak-out.

"I'm sure it won't be as bad as you think," I say, trying to channel one of my mother's famous pep talks. "It'll be really quick, and, honestly, I doubt anyone will be paying attention to you. It's all about the new queen, right?"

"Are you kidding? *Everyone* will be paying attention to me. I'm the girl that got elected homecoming queen as a *joke*. They're all going to be getting second helpings of their act of petty high school sadism, half of them hoping I'll pull a *Carrie* while the other half will be waiting for me to burst into tears in front of the whole school. Anything for another tragic yearbook photo. In the meantime, I have to find a damn dress and relive the most humiliating moment of my entire life." And then she chokes out a sob, her anger and terror turning to pure misery as tears start to roll down her cheeks.

"I'm sorry," I say, pulling her into a hug. She cries quietly on my shoulder as I rub her back in big circles, another classic Mom move. "What can I do to help?"

236

Julianne pulls back and swipes at her cheeks. She sucks in a big breath to try to calm down, but it kind of just makes her look like she's hyperventilating. She shudders as she lets it out, then takes a second, this one slightly smoother.

"In through your nose, out through your mouth," I prompt her, miming the act. "Shoulders out of your ears. Tongue out of the roof of your mouth. Just . . . unclench."

And she does it. On her next deep breath, she outs with her request. "If I'm going to do this, I'm going to really do it. So I need someone to do my hair and makeup," she says. "Last year I did it myself and ended up just looking like a toddler let loose in a Sephora. This year, I at least want the pictures to look decent."

I nod, but already I know I'm not the droid she's looking for. "I want to help you, really, I do. But I don't think I'm the right person."

"Why not?"

"Do I look like someone who knows a lot about hair and makeup?" I ask, pointing at my bare face. The last time I bothered to apply any makeup was when I did an AP History presentation on women's suffrage. And even that was just some lip gloss and mascara.

"You look like someone who knows more than me," she says, and then we stare at each other, both realizing what absolutely basement level bars we've just set for each other.

"Julianne, I haven't worn makeup since I started working here, and that wasn't a new trend for me. If your goal is to look nice in pictures, you're barking up the wrong tree."

"But you're pretty . . . ," she whispers, picking at her cuticles once again.

"Julianne, *you're* pretty."

"No, I'm not," she shoots back, like a reflex.

But she is. And not in a "just let me remove your glasses and have you descend a staircase while a pop ballad plays" kind of way. She's got striking green eyes, though she's always hiding them—and the rest of her face—behind a curtain of dark hair. And her hair would be pretty, too, if she ever decided to stop copping Cousin It's style. Plus, she's curvy as hell, sort of like an Old Hollywood pinup. With the right hair, makeup, and dress, she'd blow all those other bitchy mean girls right off the field. She's already halfway to being a knockout.

But she needs more help than I can give, since my

beauty routine involves brushing my teeth and a healthy application of cherry ChapStick.

And I know just who to call.

As instructed, Julianne meets me at her car four minutes after the final bell rings. She has to be at the stadium in her full regalia an hour before kickoff for all the pictures, which only gives us a few hours to work with. She brought a garment bag in the back of her car, which I assume has her dress inside.

When we arrive home, Mom is in the kitchen working on her petits fours. She's been getting more and more requests for them for things like bridal and baby showers, and while her decorating is always on point, she claims the recipe she's been using makes them taste too much like sugar bombs.

"Don't people expect sugar in a tiny, frosted cake?" I'd asked.

"Yes, but they don't want their teeth to hurt when they eat dessert," she had replied, and she wasn't wrong. "Plus, they eat more when they're not too sweet, which means they'll order more."

"Wow, my mom, the capitalist."

"Hush, you."

As a result, we've had batches of petits fours hanging around the house for the last two weeks as she tries to perfect her recipe.

"I think I'm getting close," she says as Julianne and I hustle into the kitchen. She's putting the finishing touches on a dozen little pink cakes, topping them with delicate white flowers of frosting. "I'm only a couple batches away from perfection. Taste?"

Julianne and I both help ourselves. Beneath the sheath of pink frosting are delicate layers of white cake alternating with buttercream and what I think is some kind of strawberry jam.

"Oh my god, this is heaven in a bite," Julianne says, and my mom beams.

"Are there any petits fours? I've had a *day*," Dad calls as he breezes into the kitchen, the front door slamming hard behind him. "Every year I pray the eighth graders will have moved past boob and fart jokes, and every year I am sorely disappointed."

"Hi, Mr. Brix," Julianne says. "You probably don't remember me, but I was in your seventh grade social studies class. Your Civil War lessons totally got me hooked on history. I'm thinking of minoring in college."

My dad beams, and I swear, if I'd brought Julianne home as a date, my parents would be trying to marry me off to her right about now. She's sweet and charming, without a whiff of suck-up about her. Soon I think they just might like her more than they like me. I'm reminded yet again of the ways in which Julianne hides herself when she's at school. I always just assumed she was shy. That that was why she never talked to anyone and avoided eye contact and sat alone at lunch. But that's not it at all. Although it took her a minute to warm up to *me*, to everyone else at Hot 'N Crusty, she was outgoing. She's been cool since my first day there, when she pulled that stuffed crust pizza out from under the counter. I don't blame her for hiding her real personality, of course. It's only natural to retreat once you become synonymous with weirdness at your high school. And after the home-coming queen fiasco last year, I'm surprised she didn't try to transfer, or even drop out. If I were in her shoes, I think I would have lobbied my parents hard to be home-schooled. Julianne is just surviving, doing what she has to do to get through the day.

It sounds kind of familiar, honestly. After all, even though I'm still sitting at Tamsin's table every day at lunch, I have the most fun when I'm hanging out with the HnC crew. Yet I've never made any attempt to sit with

Julianne at lunch. Or talk to Tristan in the halls. I don't partner with Greg for biology lab or go out of my way to say hi to Frank or Jason. What does that say about me? Nothing good, I think.

The petit four suddenly feels like a brick in my stomach, and when I try to swallow the remaining crumbs, they stick in my throat.

"*Mmmmmm*, this is excellent, honey," Dad says.

"I think there's a better way to meld the strawberry compote with the buttercream," she says, making a note in a spiral-bound notebook resting on the kitchen island.

"I'm so jealous. My mom leaves the baking to Betty Crocker," Julianne says.

"Hey, Betty knows her stuff," Mom says. "I love a good boxed yellow cake with chocolate frosting from a can. Those flavors are *legit*."

"Mom, don't say *legit*," I tell her.

She rolls her eyes, a mischievous smile on her face. "Oh, I'm sorry, let me try again." She clears her throat and squares her shoulders, a twinkle in her eye. "Those flavors are *the bomb*."

"Ugh," I groan as Julianne giggles beside me.

The doorbell rings, and Dad shuffles off to answer it.

"You expecting someone?" Mom asks.

"Reinforcements," I say, turning to follow Dad. I find

him standing at the front door greeting Natalie. And behind her, she's got Tamsin and Cora in tow. I freeze. I'd called Natalie for backup, but I didn't mention Tamsin or Cora. I would never subject Julianne to that. She's already a bundle of nerves and terror. The last thing she needs is a metric ton of Tamsin snark dumped on her shoulders. But I guess I should have known that Natalie, Tamsin, and Cora are a package deal now. A trio. They're the best friends. I'm just the great pretender.

Cora holds up what looks like a bright pink tackle box that I hope is filled with makeup, and Tamsin is carrying an overstuffed garment bag over one shoulder.

"Why are they here?" I ask Natalie, trying to keep my voice low, but not succeeding.

"Gee, thanks for the warm welcome, Beck," Tamsin snaps as she breezes past me into the house. Cora smiles and shrugs, following close behind.

Natalie gives me a sharp look. "Tamsin has a good eye, so I figured she could help. And I've got hair, but Cora is much better at makeup than I am."

"That's not true."

"It is and you know it. What's the problem? We're all friends." She arches an eyebrow at me, a classic Natalie challenge, but I don't take the bait. Instead I just sigh away the conversation for later.

"Thanks for coming," I say, directing it to everyone. "Please be gentle, okay?"

"God, it's like you're talking to caged tigers," Tamsin says, rolling her eyes, which is a pretty apt description for the damage Tamsin could do.

We all convene in the kitchen, where my mom is still doling out petits fours and taking notes, even though there's a universal chorus of happy moans as people eat. Dad comes padding back into the kitchen in his after-school clothes, a pair of ratty jeans and bare feet, plus the *Apex Galaxy* T-shirt I got him for Christmas.

"Oh, my brother watches that show," Cora says. "He's always telling me I need to get into it, like I have time to binge another show."

"How's Jamar doing? He liking Howard?" Dad asks. In his personal hall of fame of favorite students, Cora's brother Jamar Jenkins ranks in the top ten for his nerdy love of history and photographic memory. Jamar's a freshman at Howard this year, majoring in political science, and Dad still talks about the time he named all the US presidents in alphabetical order in under a minute.

"Loves it," Cora replies. "Pretty sure he's already planning on law school after."

"Good to hear," Dad says. "Tell him I said he better be studying as much as he's watching sci-fi."

"Don't worry, he hears it from my parents every time he calls," she replies.

"Hey, so we should get started," I say, eyeing Julianne, who is standing in the corner of the kitchen suddenly looking terrified again.

"Yeah, we need all the time we can get," Tamsin says.

"Tamsin!" I hiss.

"What? I just meant that glam squad takes at least an hour. Honestly, they should really give us a half day on homecoming," she says.

"That's the scholarly dedication I remember," Dad says with a chuckle. Needless to say, Tamsin was *not* naming alphabetical presidents in any length of time in eighth grade.

"Someone's got to bring the fun to the classroom, Mr. Brix," Tamsin says with a grin.

"Oh, what fun it was, Tamsin," Dad replies.

"Okay, let's get this party started," I say before Dad can embarrass us with any more middle school memories. We all head back to my room. Once inside, I shut the door while Tamsin lays the garment bag she brought out on my bed. Cora deposits her tackle box on my desk and cracks it open, revealing three tiers of bins full of tubes, pots, and brushes. Natalie clears off my end table, plugs in two curling wands, and sets up an array of sprays and gels.

"It looks like you could make a whole new girl with all that stuff," Julianne says, her voice a little shaky, about two-thirds of a smile on her face.

"We're not making someone new. We're just making *you* turned up to eleven," Cora says with a smile, and I see Julianne warm a little from inside. "I'll start with makeup, then Natalie will do hair. Tamsin, you're on wardrobe."

"Got it," Tamsin says, moving to unzip the garment bag.

"I brought my dress from last year," Julianne says, pointing to the black dress still in its dry-cleaner's plastic.

Tamsin looks horrified. "No. No no no no. You *cannot* wear the same dress as last year. There are going to be pictures!"

Julianne shrugs. "Well, I don't have anything else, and I didn't have time to look."

"No worries, I brought options," Tamsin says. She starts to pull the sides of the garment bag open, revealing a pile of brightly colored satin and sequins.

"There's *no way* I'm going to fit into anything you brought," Julianne says. She doesn't sound embarrassed, just sure. And it's true, Tamsin and Julianne have figures from different decades. Tamsin is more of a Kate Moss type, tall and thin, with sharp angles. Julianne looks more like she stepped out of a Hollywood pinup calendar, all hips and boobs and curves.

"I know that," Tamsin says, pulling on the zipper. "That's why I raided Marin's closet."

Marin, Tamsin and Colin's older sister, is a junior at Wesleyan, though she's currently studying abroad in Italy. She wants to be a food critic, and she's literally spending the semester learning about wine and cheese. And though I've only ever seen her in pictures, she is shaped much more like Julianne.

Tamsin pulls out a selection of dresses, and Julianne at first gravitates toward something black. But Tamsin wordlessly pulls it out of her hand. "No," she says, all no-nonsense and borderline imperious. "Try again."

Julianne blinks at her, looking like she might protest, but instead she goes back to the pile of dresses. Her fingers linger on red chiffon, and Tamsin's eyes light up. "*Yes*," she says. She grabs the hanger and pulls it out, a floor-length red chiffon with a V-neck, the bodice crossed like a wrap dress.

"I don't know," Julianne says, her voice trailing off.

"Yes, you do. Your first instinct is always right. This is definitely the one."

"Isn't it kind of . . . loud?"

"And you don't deserve to be heard?" Tamsin asks.

And in that moment I want to hug her so hard her head pops off, because Julianne's eyes light up, her lips quirking up in a wicked grin. She reaches for the hanger and goes to my bathroom, shutting the door. She emerges in a matter of minutes, the dress hanging open in the back. She turns for Tamsin to zip her up, and when she faces the room again, we all gasp. The red pops against Julianne's pale skin and dark hair. The cut accentuates her waist and shows the perfect amount of cleavage, or as my mom likes to say, décolletage.

"Julianne, you look—" I break off, trying to find the words.

"You look *hot*," Cora says.

"Damn right. This is the one. Don't try anything else," Tamsin says, reaching to unzip. "Now go get changed so we can do your hair and makeup without making a mess."

Julianne puts her jeans and T-shirt back on, then sits down in my desk chair while the girls go to work. I play DJ and observe the action as the glam squad spends the next half hour putting about a dozen finishing touches on Julianne's look. Her hair is flat ironed and then curled with two different curling wands. Cora spends so long applying various shimmers to Julianne's eyes that I'm surprised they can't be seen from space.

"Close your eyes," Cora says as she shakes a can of something she plans to mist all over Julianne's face. Julianne squeezes her eyes tight. "So who's your escort?" Cora asks.

Julianne pauses, stock-still and racked with panic.

"I need an escort?" she asks.

"Well, yeah, it's homecoming," Cora says.

"But I thought that was just if you were in the running. I mean, I had one last year."

"Yeah, who was *that* guy?" Tamsin asks.

"A guy I met at a book festival last summer. He's in my fandom."

"He's in your *what* now?" Cora asks.

"Fandom. We both like *Crystal of Souls*." She looks at Cora and Tamsin, who are both blinking at her like she's speaking Sanskrit. "You know what? It doesn't matter. His name is Laramie, and he doesn't go here."

"He looked good in the pictures," Cora says with a gentle smile.

"Yeah, you couldn't see his braces at all," Tamsin says. "Anyway, everyone's supposed to have some arm candy. You know, to show you off to the crowd?"

I see Julianne go from zero to terrified in just a few seconds.

"I didn't know I needed an escort! I don't have one.

It's a two-hour drive from here to Barnesville; there's no way Laramie can get here in time, even if he was available, which he's not because he's spending this weekend at East Watkinsville Comic Con. He's probably already in his War Bringer costume!"

Cora is squinting like she's trying to figure out what a War Bringer is, and Tamsin just looks alarmed.

"Okay, you need to calm down before you shake all the curl out of your hair," Natalie says gently. "Just close your eyes and go somewhere peaceful." She sucks in a big gulp of air, her shoulders rising around her ears, gesturing for Julianne to join her. Then she blows it out.

"We can take care of it," Tamsin says, though I'm not sure what her plan is aside from blind confidence. Though blind confidence has managed to carry Tamsin through most of her life, so why knock it now?

"What about one of the guys? Eli? Or Colin?" I ask.

"They have a fall ball tournament this weekend. They all left right after school," Cora says.

Shit.

"Honestly, you're probably just fine without an escort. Everyone's going to be paying attention to the new queen," Natalie says, but she sort of looks like a nurse assuring her terminal patient that it'll be okay.

"It's true, everyone will be looking to see if one of the

losers is going to make a scene. No one will even notice if you don't have an escort," Tamsin says.

But I can see Julianne isn't buying it. And once again, I know who to call.

He answers on the first ring. "What's up?" Tristan asks.

"Julianne needs an escort for homecoming," I tell him.

"And?"

"And . . . ," I say, hoping he'll fill in the blanks, but he's either too slow or, more likely, too determined to force me to say it. "And I'm asking if you can do it. You're off tonight, right?"

"Since when do you keep track of my schedule?"

I blush, even though he's not here to see me. But the girls are, and they're watching me closely, trying to decipher who's on the other end of the call. Julianne smiles, because she already knows.

"Will you do it or not?"

There's silence on the other end of the line, and it goes on long enough that I'm almost positive that he's screwing with me. When I'm finally about to hang up out of frustration, he answers.

"I'll take care of it," he says.

"I have to be there early for pictures!" Julianne shouts from behind me.

"Pick her up at my house. Five o'clock." I bark the orders like a drill sergeant.

"Yup," he says, and then the line goes dead.

"Goodbye," I mutter to the darkened screen of my phone. I turn to Julianne. "It's taken care of."

Julianne heaves out a shuddery breath. "Thank you," she says. "God, this is such a nightmare."

"Why? You're going to look fucking fantastic," Tamsin says.

"Oh, come on, like you don't know," Julianne says, a bit of acid dripping into her words. It's the first time she's so much as hinted at what happened last year, and I can tell that it's making everyone a little tense. There's a thick silence over the room.

Finally, Tamsin speaks. "You know what? Fuck 'em."

"What?" Julianne says.

"Fuck 'em. Seriously. A bunch of trolls who are probably already flunking out of their freshman year," she says. She sees Julianne's puzzled face. "It was a group of stupid seniors with nothing better to do."

"Did you vote for me?" Julianne asks, and Tamsin doesn't hesitate.

"No, I did not. I don't have time for that petty shit. I voted for Amelia Brackin," Tamsin says. And I believe her. Sure, Tamsin can be *a lot*, and she's got one of the sharpest tongues I know, but I don't think she would do something that purposefully mean. "Now go get your dress on. It's almost time to go."

Julianne disappears into the bathroom, and when she emerges once again, the full look is a real knockout.

"You look *amazing*," Tamsin says, giving Julianne an up and down that I can tell is making her cringe. "And I'm not just saying that because you're my creation."

"She's not Frankenstein, my god, Tamsin," Natalie says.

I open my mouth to correct her, but Cora beats me to it. "Frankenstein was the doctor, not the monster, and Julianne is neither. She's lovely, so show some respect."

At that, Julianne blushes a deep cherry that matches her dress, but that only seems to make her look even more luminous.

The ringing of the doorbell pulls us all out of our reverie. Dad calls up the stairs.

"Ladies, your gentleman friend is here," he says. I'm surprised I didn't hear the familiar *chugga chugga* of Cecilia approaching. I hope the bus doesn't make Julianne smell too much like fossil fuels.

We all go running for the stairs, taking them two and three at a time before leaping the last four and landing with consecutive bangs on the wood floor.

But it's not Tristan at the door.

"Holy shit," I say. He's the same geeky Frank, tall and gangly, but the tuxedo he's wearing is unbelievably well fitted to his lanky frame, making him look a bit like a Secret Service agent. Nothing like a buser at a pizza parlor. The pants are a smidge too short, showing off red socks that may or may not have the quadratic equation on them, but he still looks very suave. Until he takes a step forward and trips over his own shiny shoes.

Frank rights himself, adjusting his tie so that it's somehow *more* askew. "Tristan sent me," he says. "I mean, I volunteered. I wanted to come. I heard Julianne needed someone, so, um, I'm, you know . . . here. For her."

Okay, maybe I wouldn't go *right* to suave.

"That's really nice of you, Frank," I tell him, and now it's his turn for his cheeks to turn red.

"I mean, it's not a big deal, I just wanted to, um—" And then he trails off as his eyes sweep up to the top of the stairs. His mouth drops open, and he stands there for a minute looking like a fish plucked straight out of Pearce Lake. Because Julianne's walking out to meet us, and if Frank's reaction is anything to go by, she's about to have an honest-to-god teen-movie moment.

"Isn't she *gorgeous*?" Tamsin squeals as Julianne

stops at the top of the stairs. Natalie swats at Tamsin to shush her.

Frank swallows hard, then steps forward as Julianne slowly descends the stairs. He watches her every step, but he doesn't give her any kind of up and down. Instead, his eyes appear to be locked onto hers, tracking her all the way down the stairs until she stops right in front of him. He's nearly a foot taller than she is, but in her heels, she doesn't have to look up much to meet his eyes.

"You look amazing," Frank says, his voice cracking only a little bit.

"Thanks," Julianne says, looking down at her shoes, loaners from Cora.

"I hope it's okay that I'm here. Tristan called and said you needed an escort."

"It's nice of you to volunteer," she says.

"Are you kidding? Getting to stand next to you all night is, like, an honor."

Tamsin lets out another tiny squeal before Natalie gives her an elbow.

Frank holds out his arm and grins. "You ready? My mom let me borrow her Lexus, as long as I promised to drive five miles under the speed limit."

A smile spreads across Julianne's face. It looks like

the last bit of fear has melted off her body. She's not thinking about mean girls or pig's blood or yearbook photos. It's just her and Frank wearing a pair of goofy, happy smiles.

We all pile out onto the lawn like proud parents (my actual parents included) and watch as Frank opens the door for Julianne, then slams his own finger in the door, then yanks his hand out before bolting around to the driver's side to climb in. We wave as they pull away from the curb and watch as the taillights disappear around the corner—which takes longer than it should, because Frank is, as promised to his mother, driving way under the speed limit.

"So you guys wanna grab a bite before the game?" Natalie asks.

"Can't. I've got to get to work," I say, turning back to head into the house. I need to change into my work shirt. I'm already late for my shift, but hopefully Del won't mind.

"You're not going to be there to see our girl do her thing?" Tamsin asks.

I pause, the words coming out before I can stop them. "*Our* girl?"

"What?"

"I didn't realize you and Julianne were friends."

"I didn't realize *you* and Julianne were friends," Tamsin says.

"What's that supposed to mean?"

"It means that you've barely been around, and it's because you're replacing us with your new pizza friends. And you're acting like that's somehow our fault," Tamsin says. And there's definite sass in her voice, but there's something else, too.

"I'm not! I still eat lunch with you guys every day."

"Sure, but you don't say anything. You're just, like, *there*. And apparently you've got this whole life that we're not a part of. I mean, who's that guy you called to get Julianne an escort? You managed to pull up his number pretty quickly, and you turned, like, six shades of red while talking to him."

"That's Tristan. He works at Hot 'N Crusty. He's a senior," I say, offering his stats like I'm reading off a baseball card. It takes all my effort not to betray any kind of emotion.

"Okay. Fine. But you don't get to act all high and mighty when you haven't been a very good friend lately," Tamsin snaps.

Her words are wounding, but I'm angry, too. *I* haven't been a very good friend? What does being a good friend to Tamsin even look like? Is it hanging around doing whatever she suggests and always following the group? Because that's what I've always done. And suddenly she's mad that I have new friends, one of whom she was calling weird just a few weeks ago? And I'm about to fire all this back at her when I notice Natalie, whose cheeks are blossoming into a patchwork of red that's also creeping up her neck. Her glossed lips are turned down, and she looks like she's barely holding in tears. And it's in that moment that I start to worry that maybe tonight didn't represent a joyful coming together of my friend groups. Maybe it's the moment they finally fracture in two.

And I have no idea what to do about it.

"I have to get going," I say, barely concealing the quiver in my voice. "Take lots of pictures, okay?"

Tamsin rolls her eyes, but seems to already be cooling down, and Cora nods with a smile, ready to defuse whatever situation is brewing. "You know we will," she says.

I hide in the bathroom while they gather their beauty arsenal, and they're gone before I emerge in my Hot 'N Crusty shirt, my hair in a ponytail through the back of my cap, ready for my other life.

CHAPTER
FOURTEEN

I stroll into work expecting most of the usual suspects to be gone. Julianne and Frank are at the game, and Tristan's off tonight. But when I walk into the kitchen to clock in at the office, I see Tristan standing at the prep counter slicing red onions next to Joey.

"I thought you weren't working tonight," I tell him, both shocked to see him and shocked to see him in the kitchen. When he's working he usually avoids the premises as much as possible unless he's picking up a delivery.

"Again with the keeping tabs on my schedule," he says with pure Tristan Porter snark, only this time his smirk seems to have morphed into an actual smile. Instead of just an upturned mouth, his genuine smile migrates all the way up to his eyes, which crinkle, and his nose, which wrinkles, making his freckles dance. Something feels like it's shifting between us. Something akin to the way Frank stared at Julianne when she walked down that staircase. The way Tristan smiles at me makes me forget I'm wearing an ill-fitting poly-cotton blend T-shirt and a baseball cap, the smell of garlic already seeping into my soul and sweating back out again under the heat of half a dozen pizza ovens.

"Okay, yeah, I know when you work," I say, starting off carefully before deciding *oh fuck it*. "I pay attention. Because I like the shifts when you work. They're more fun."

He grins as he works on the onions. "I knew it, Brix. You like me."

"Maybe I do, maybe I don't," I say, with a matching grin spreading across my face.

"Get a room," Joey mutters. "But not till you finish with those onions."

The air between us feels charged, because we're at work in an industrial kitchen. It's not like anything can happen, especially not with Joey standing between us tossing dough in the air.

Tristan smiles one last time before returning to his work.

"So why are you here?" I ask.

"Because someone had to fill in for Frank so he could take his dream girl to the big dance." He dices like a pro, another hidden talent, apparently.

"You knew he liked her? You big softie!"

"Yeah, yeah. I was just tired of watching Frank moon over her and never doing anything about it. He needed a push to finally make something happen."

"I can't believe Tristan Porter is a romantic. All this time, under that floppy hair and sarcasm lies a giant puppy dog."

"So did it?"

"What?"

"Did something happen?"

"Oh, you mean did he dip her right there on the front lawn and plant a kiss on her in front of my parents and everyone? No, that did not happen. But she certainly looked happy to see him. He cleans up pretty good, too. Where did he get a tuxedo on such short notice?"

"Apparently he keeps it for show choir," Tristan says, and we both burst out laughing at the thought of goofy, gangly Frank kick-ball-chaining across the Brook Park auditorium stage.

Del pops his head into the kitchen, a trickle of sweat already working its way down his temple. "Beck, have you clocked in yet? It's started to get busy out there, and we're down a cashier tonight."

"On it, boss," I say, and the honorific makes him beam. "It was nice of you to give Julianne the night off."

"She's more than earned it! I want that girl to have some fun," he calls before disappearing back out to the register. I quickly clock in and tie my apron around my waist, then head back out where, sure enough, there's a line starting to form at the register. Del is taking orders, but I elbow him aside so he can head back to the kitchen and help Joey with the orders that are starting to line up on the board. Soon, Tristan will have to stop chopping and start running food and busing tables. I glance at the schedule by the phone and see that Greg is due in an hour, which is when Friday nights usually pick up, but apparently homecoming's brought out the crowds, with alumni stopping in for dinner before the big game.

I throw myself into work, which mostly distracts me from the electric buzz I feel whenever Tristan pushes through the swinging door with a tray of food or a full bus tub on his shoulder. I try not to notice the bulge of his bicep when he's carrying a tray of sodas or a heavy stack of plates, but I fail miserably. I worry that I'm the walking, talking embodiment of the heart-eyes emoji, and the heavy eyeball I get from Greg when he arrives and takes one look at me tells me that yup, I'm not keeping the secret. Not at all. Greg is half an hour early, which earns him a bear hug from Del that looks like it's not appreciated. But when Del tells him to go ahead and clock in, Greg looks pleased to get the extra money, and all is right with the world again.

There's a lull right around seven when the game is set to start, but it doesn't last long. All the families taking advantage of the full stadium are out for dinner, and soon we're overrun with wild kids and their exhausted parents. Greg and Tristan spend way too much time on their hands and knees fetching stray silverware and pizza crusts that have been tossed to the floor beneath the tables.

And then when the game ends, the place really heats up. Hot 'N Crusty isn't the usual postgame hangout, but Margaritas across the street is mobbed with a line out the door, and we've ended up with the overflow. We're the "ugh, I don't want to wait, let's just go *there*" restaurant of choice. A few sweaty football players even show up, alight with the glow of gridiron victory. Apparently we won.

It's not until we're about to close that I even have a moment to pull out my phone and see the text from Natalie. It's just a picture, one she took on her phone that's zoomed in, so it's a little bit fuzzy. But I can see

Julianne in her red dress. She's wearing a tiara and holding another in her hands. The new nominees are lined up to her right, and to her left and just behind her is Frank.

And she's beaming.

"I have news," Tristan says, sliding into a booth across from me, where I'm wiping down menus. We closed about twenty minutes ago, and Del only just gently shooed out the last of the customers.

"You're selling Cecilia to finance your dream of being a pizza sous chef," I guess.

"Blasphemy," he declares, a twinkle in his eye. "This is better."

"Are you going to make me keep guessing, or are you going to cough it up?"

He gives me a wicked grin, then reaches into his lap and produces a paper plate, the same type of paper plate I remember from my first night at Hot 'N Crusty, topped with the very same kind of pizza that was definitely *not* made at Hot 'N Crusty, as evidenced by the congealing cheese leaking out of the edge of the crust. Unless Del

264

added stuffed crust to the menu this morning, this pizza definitely came from somewhere else.

"*Again?*" I cry, dropping the wet rag onto the menu so I can examine the pizza. Suddenly I feel like a detective on *Law & Order*, ready to interrogate the slice until it gives up its secrets.

"It gets better. Because I know where it came from."

"Shut up," I whisper. "Who?"

"You know the old couple that comes in and shares a single slice?" he asks, and I nod. Bert and Birdie (I swear to god those are their names; I asked twice just to be sure) have been coming in to Hot 'N Crusty since it opened all the way back in the late eighties. And according to them, they've always ordered the same thing (as Birdie told me with a sweet-old-lady smile and a wink that made her blue eye shadow sprinkle down onto her cheek). I always assumed they were just old and ate like, well, birds. Both of them look like a stiff breeze would send them into the next county. I swear, the heaviest thing about Bert is the dark brown toupee that hangs off his head at a jaunty angle.

I guess they were hungrier than I thought.

"I caught the old lady pulling a to-go box out of her purse," Tristan says, leaning back and crossing his arms over his chest.

"Birdie!" I cry, as if she can hear my chastisement. "What did you do?"

"I told Birdie that her secret was safe with me," he says. "You get that old, you can eat what you want, where you want. Did you know Bert served in Korea? He's got a huge-ass tattoo of his army unit on his bicep."

"Wow, I never would've pegged them for the ones."

"Everyone has the potential to surprise you," he says, his voice dropping slightly, getting husky in a way that makes my stomach fizzle like it's full of Pop Rocks. "So, when you're done with the menus, you wanna go somewhere?"

"Where?" I ask, as if it matters at all. Because the answer is obviously *yes yes yes oh yes*.

"I dunno, just out for a drive, maybe? We could listen to that CD if you haven't found a player yet," he says.

"Are you telling me *Cecilia* has a CD player?"

"Cecilia is full of secrets," he says, and then he slides out of the booth and heads for the swinging door to the kitchen. "Meet me in the back when you're done."

It takes me about point two seconds to wipe down the rest of the menus. I practically hurl them back into the milk crate beneath the counter where they'll wait for tomorrow's lunch shift. Then I bolt through the door so hard and so fast that Joey has to leap out of the way for fear of being flattened.

"Watch it!" he calls as I skid on my heel to turn into Del's office to clock out.

"Sorry!" I yell back over my shoulder, punching the time clock. I get it wrong three times before I finally succeed in ending my shift.

"Big plans?" Del asks from his spot at his computer, where he's peering over his reading glasses.

"The biggest," I say with a wide grin. And then I haul ass to the back door.

Cecilia is waiting by the dumpster, her engine chugging to warm up in the chilly evening. Tristan is in the front seat, and as soon as I climb into the passenger seat, I pass him the CD, which I've been carrying around in my purse since he gave it to me. I haven't been alone in Dad's car since that day, and I haven't wanted to explain to him why we're listening to . . . well, whatever Tristan put on it.

Tristan slips the CD from the sleeve and pops it into one of those old-school portable CD players that's attached to the car stereo with a cassette tape, and oh my god this is going to be a very old-fashioned car ride.

The music starts, Tristan adjusting the volume so it'll be heard over the roaring engine, and then we pull out of the parking lot. He doesn't say anything, so I think the plan here is to really listen to the music. And I do.

I recognize the first song. The Beatles version of "Twist and Shout." I bop along, mostly picturing the scene in *Ferris Bueller* during the parade, a movie I love. The second song is slower, and definitely still the Beatles, but I don't know it.

Here I stand, head in hand, the singer growls in this nasally tone.

"It's John Lennon. 'You've Got to Hide Your Love Away.' Iconic," Tristan calls over the engine, and I nod. By the third song, we're turning out onto one of the rural roads that'll lead us out to the hills of Monroe County. And that's when I realize the whole album is made up of Beatles songs. The fourth one has an old-fashioned big band sound. I assume it's called "Got to Get You Into My Life," since that's what the singer keeps belting. It's good.

We drive along with Tristan calling out song titles and glancing over at me sideways. I make sure to nod my head to the beat. Some of the songs I like ("Getting Better" and "Here, There, and Everywhere") and some I don't ("Revolution 9" sounds like punishment, I don't care how groundbreaking Tristan claims it was). But I don't offer up any opinions; I just listen.

Cecilia finally slows to a stop at the top of a windy

road, Tristan pulling the van into one of the overlooks at the top of the hill. I've been to Look Rock before, a big rock formation that rises over the county. But only during the daylight. Some people call it a mountain, but it's for sure not. I've heard it's where people come to drink or get it on, but I don't see any other cars. Just the twinkling lights of the entire town laid out before me.

"The stadium's over there, but it's harder to spot since the game ended and the bright lights are off," he says, pointing in the distance. Then he moves a few inches to the left. "And Hot 'N Crusty is over there."

Then Tristan hops out and trots around the front of the bus. He pulls open my door like a chauffeur, and I climb out. Then he hauls the sliding back door open and climbs in, inviting me after him.

"I know this is, like, the town make-out spot or whatever, but I promise I didn't invite you up here to paw you," Tristan says, his gaze out on the middle distance, beyond the lights of the town. "I just like to come up here and listen to music. It's quiet, and the smell of nature mitigates the smell of Cecilia."

I gasp. "You're saying Cecilia smells?"

"Only like nostalgia!" he replies. "Okay, and a little bit of gasoline."

I won't lie, my heart sinks for a moment as we stare

back out at the view. It's beautiful. And not that I want to be *pawed*, but I'd be lying if I said I wasn't thinking about our kiss behind the dumpster. And how much less smelly a repeat performance would be. The smell of nature would certainly help here, too.

"I would like to kiss you, though," Tristan says. And then he turns to look at me, a crooked smile crinkling his nose, his eyes twinkling in the full moon. And *my god* my stomach does one of those Olympic tumbling passes that involve six flips and a split at the end.

I want to be cool. I *so* want to be cool. But I am *not* cool. All I can do is open my mouth and squeak, "You do?"

He nods slowly, one arm up over his bent knees. "I do. But I don't want to surprise you. You know, like I did last time."

"You don't?"

He shakes his head, then turns back to me. "When I kiss you again, I want you to kiss me back."

I swallow hard, willing my body not to shiver, even though there's a cool breeze floating through the bus.

"I'd like that," I say.

He nods again, his gaze down at his sneakers. "Okay, then," he says, and right at that moment, I swear, the thudding drums and twangy guitar of "Something" kicks up—this one I know. The singer starts to croon, and just as George Harrison sings *something in the way she woos me*, Tristan turns and lifts his palm to my cheek and leans in. His lips brush mine, softly at first, then harder. Knowing it's coming is not the same as being *ready* for it, of course. And for a moment I'm sort of frozen, but as his tongue swipes at my bottom lip, I sink into it. I lift my hand to the back of his neck, letting my fingers weave into his hair. His skin is warm and smooth, and I sigh into his lips.

We kiss until the song is over. And then we kiss until the CD stops. And then we kiss into the silence of the night. We kiss until I lose feeling in my lips, and then we kiss some more.

I don't even know when we stop, or how, but eventually we climb back into the front seats of Cecilia and drive back down the winding road from Look Rock. Tristan holds my hand, except for when he has to let go to shift gears. And when he pulls up to the curb in front of my house, he turns and smiles at me.

"Thanks for, um . . ." I pause, because I almost thank him for all the making out. "Thank you for helping Julianne."

"Thank *you* for helping Julianne," he says. He shrugs. "I was just helping Frank."

"Well, either way, it worked out," I say. "I had fun tonight."

He doesn't say anything else, and I'm not totally sure how to play this. We just spent the better part of an hour making out in the moonlight, and it was honest to god the best hour of my entire life. And I want to know if there's going to be more. Please *god* let there be more. But I'm scared to say the wrong thing. To break the spell. To ruin it all.

And then Tristan saves me with a wink and smile. He leans over and plants a final kiss on my lips. "See you tomorrow, I hope?"

"Absolutely," I reply. I reach up and touch my bottom lip, feeling that last kiss like a promise. "I can't wait."

CHAPTER
FIFTEEN

We spend one glorious week just the two of us, stealing
kisses in Del's office/closet or by the dumpster between
deliveries. We go back to Look Rock twice, listening to
more of Tristan's vintage rock and making out. I spend
some time in his garage, parked on a stool a safe distance
from all the spinning blades, while he works on a hanging
shelf and explains all the steps. He even comes over to
watch a few episodes of *Apex Galaxy* and tolerates my
dad's inquisition about the safety of Cecilia. It takes a
demonstration of the seat belts, followed by letting Dad
take her for a spin around the block, before that awkward
interaction ends. But by the time Cecilia chugs back into

our driveway, Dad in the driver's seat next to Tristan, I think all is well. Dad is grinning like a kid riding Dumbo for the first time.

But by the end of that new, fizzy, crackly first week, I know I can't live in the cocoon forever. Natalie's face before homecoming keeps flashing in my vision. So when I text Natalie to see what's up and she asks if I want to come hang out at Tamsin and Colin's house for a cook-out, I call her instead.

"Did somebody die?" she asks by way of a hello.

"No, why?"

"Because you're *calling* me, which is, like, super dramatic."

"Can I bring Tristan?"

"The pizza delivery guy?"

"Yeah. We're sort of, um, dating? Maybe?" Saying it out loud feels weird, because we haven't named anything, not officially. And Tristan seems like the kind of guy who would roll his eyes at any kind of label. Still, I'm pretty sure that's what we're doing, even if I'm too chicken to officially ask.

On the other end of the line I hear a sharp intake of breath, and I brace myself. For her to say no. Or to finally spill all the hidden words behind that look the night of homecoming. For this to be the start of our breakup. The beginning of the end. My entire body tenses, and I realize I'm holding my breath.

"Oh my god, tell me everything. Have you kissed him?"

The breath whooshes out of me, and I laugh, the warm, protective, familiar feeling of our friendship rushing through me. "Oh my god, *so much*," I say. And then I proceed to narrate the last week of kissing and laughing and hanging out with him in Cecilia, and when I'm done, I can practically hear her smile through the phone.

"Bring his ass to Tamsin's so I can get to know him, would you, please?"

"Done."

I show up at Tamsin's with Tristan by my side. He seems remarkably calm, even though I know this wasn't his first choice of activity. I know that because he told me.

"Hanging out with Mac and those guys isn't my first choice," he'd said when I issued Natalie's invitation. "But I like you, so I guess it's time to get to know your friends for real."

Which is how I knew that this was more than just making out. We still hadn't named it. But this was important.

And things were pretty good. Mac and Tristan sort of hovered around each other at first, but it didn't take long before the old baseball bro code seemed to shine through. Soon Mac, Eli, Colin, and Tristan were reminiscing about Little League and talking about the World Series while Tamsin and Cora stole me away to the pool house to get all the details about our make-out-palooza, as Natalie called it.

"He's seriously cute," Tamsin says. "Well done, Beck."

I can feel my cheeks burning under Tamsin's compliment. It shouldn't matter what she thinks, but knowing she approves feels like maybe my worlds aren't going to split in two after all.

Back in the main area of the backyard, the boys are lighting up the firepit and stoking the grill. There's a tray of burgers and dogs ready to cook, and a tray of sides and snacks courtesy of the Roy family housekeeper.

"I'm going to grab a fizzy water," I say, heading toward the French doors that lead to the kitchen. "Anyone want anything?"

"Will you grab the other mustard? The gritty one?" Colin asks, and I nod, heading up to the kitchen. I've got my head deep in the Roy family's enormous stainless-steel fridge searching for the mustard in question (I've come across three different mustards, none of them gritty) when I hear steps behind me.

"So, you and Tristan, huh?"

I spin around and see Mac standing there, leaning against the kitchen island.

"Yeah," I reply. This is the first time we've been alone since before the whole Tamsin hookup. At first I avoided him because I was hurt. Then because I was mad. Then because I couldn't seem to come up with a reason why I wanted to hang out with him. It's weird to feel totally indifferent to him, after all that time I spent silently pining.

"For a while?" he asks.

"Not that long, actually," I say. He raises his eyebrows, and I know he's thinking about the dumpster kiss all those weeks ago. "What you saw was . . . confusing."

He shrugs. "It doesn't seem confusing now."

"Nope." I pause. "You never said anything. To Tamsin. About what you saw."

He shakes his head, his shaggy hair falling directly into his eyes.

My newfound indifference to the powers of Mac gives me confidence to ask what I've been wondering since that kiss he walked up on.

"Why not?"

He sighs. He screws up his face and ruffles his hair, a move I remember from back when I used to study him. It's the one he uses when he's unsure of himself, which isn't very often. I remember him doing it before he started his oral report in Spanish last year—which was never his best subject. "Look, I was a total dick to you. I knew you liked me, and I flirted with you because it was fun, but also because I was trying to get Tamsin's attention. It was so shitty. It felt shitty while I was doing it, but I just liked her a lot and I didn't know what to do and I was an idiot. Anyway, I figured if you wanted anyone to know about you and Tristan, you'd say something. I mean, I love Tamsin, but she's got a big mouth."

I laugh, despite myself. He knows her well.

"Anyway, I'm really sorry about the way I acted. That wasn't cool."

I blink at him, stunned at his confession.

"Thank you," I say. "For apologizing. And for the other thing."

He shrugs. "No problem." He reaches into the fridge, his hand going directly for the mustard Colin wanted. It was right in front of my face the whole time. He hands it to me, and we smile, then head back out to the patio. And as I close the door behind me, it feels like closing a chapter on a book that was fun to read, but that I have no desire to ever revisit. It's time for a new story, a story where Mac and I are just friends.

Tristan joins Mac at the grill, the rust succeeding in shaking off their old friendship a bit. Tristan remembers that Mac likes his dog badly burnt, just like when they were kids. Natalie shows me more photos of Julianne from homecoming. Cora and Tamsin look over our shoulders, oohing and aahing at the dress and the hair and the makeup. I'm a little sad that Julianne isn't here to be fawned over in person, and that sticks in me like a splinter in my foot. I'm not sure what to do about it. But I know I'm still a little too chicken to actually bring it up, and that feels even worse.

"Is there dessert?" Colin calls from an Adirondack chair, where I'm pretty sure he ate his weight in hot dogs.

"Please tell me you didn't bring kale cupcakes," Eli groans at Natalie.

Cora swats at him. "Be polite," she says.

"Actually, I brought dessert this time," I say, disappearing into the kitchen and coming back out with two boxes of petits fours. Mom finally perfected her recipe, but not until a punishing weekend when she made *thirteen dozen* of them. I can report that these are delicious, and that I never want to see another petit four ever again.

I swear, petits fours are going to haunt my dreams. She was more than happy to pile a few dozen into a box for our cookout.

"Thank Mrs. Brix for us," Cora says.

In a matter of minutes, there's nothing but crumbs left in the boxes. That's what happens when you pull out baked goods for a bunch of teenage boys. I swear, they eat like they need to store fuel for a long winter.

The sun sets, and Colin builds up the fire in the stone pit until it's crackling. We all settle into chairs, Tamsin draped over Mac's lap, Cora and Eli squeezed into one of those oversized Adirondack chairs together. I sit in another, with Tristan perched on the wide arm next to me, his arm thrown over the back of the chair. Everything feels right.

"Oh, Beck, I tried that *Galaxy* show. The one you watch?" Cora says from across the firepit. "I couldn't get into it, though. Too many characters. But I'm *super* into that *Roswell* reboot, if you're looking for another alien show."

"Babe, that's not sci-fi, that's a soap opera," Eli says, poking her in the ribs.

"You watch *Apex Galaxy*?" Colin asks. "Dude, my weird cousin is, like, Illuminati-level deep into that show."

"It's mostly my dad's thing," I say, the lie coming

out as easy as truth. The words taste sort of sour in my mouth, but I swallow them down. Tristan shifts next to me, and I glance up. "You okay?"

"Fine," he says, giving me a look I can't read in the dark.

"Hey, so I think we need to pay a visit to Hot 'N Crusty," Natalie says. "We still haven't been while you're working, Beck!"

"I *love* those garlic knots," Tamsin says, and groans like she hasn't just eaten her weight in sliders and petits fours.

"We totally need to come in and, like, harass you," Eli says, laughing.

"You will do no such thing," Cora says, swatting at him again. "But we should go in. It would be fun."

"Totally. Can you rustle up some free pizzas, Beck?" Colin asks.

"We're totally coming. When do you work next week?" Natalie asks.

"Ugh, please don't!" I say, covering my face with my hands. "That would be so embarrassing!"

Now Tristan fully stands up. "I'm going to grab a soda. Anyone want anything?" he asks, and Tamsin and Natalie both ask for fizzy waters. When he gets back, he hands them each a can, and I notice he didn't get anything for himself.

"So you're a senior, right?" Tamsin asks, though she doesn't need to. We all know. I'm just bracing for the inevitable next question.

"Yeah," he replies.

"What are you doing after you graduate?" she asks. The question is open, leaving room for an answer other than what college he plans to attend, even though she doesn't ask that directly.

"I'm going to work with my dad," he says.

"What does he do?" Colin asks.

"He's a carpenter. He has his own business doing residential stuff, some commercial. I'll apprentice with him for a bit, but ultimately I want to shift full-time into custom furniture. Stuff that's more about design and style than repairs."

"That's cool," Colin says. "I can barely put together an IKEA bookshelf."

"He's going to start his own business," I add, like I'm his PR rep or something. "Actually, he already has."

"So no college plans?" Tamsin asks, and this time the implication is clear, at least to me. I feel my spine wind up like a spring.

"Nope. Just gonna dive right in," Tristan replies.

"That sounds pretty boss," Eli says.

"You could do, like, classes, though. I mean, don't

count it out," I say. Why I reached into a bag of sentences and pulled out the absolute worst ones, I have no idea. But it just comes tumbling out like a reflex.

"I think I've got a solid plan," Tristan says, an edge in his voice. I know I should stop. Everything inside me tells me to stop, and yet as I glance around this landscaped backyard with the saltwater pool, the waterfall, and the hot tub, in this expensive subdivision surrounded by my friends who are all planning on fancy four-year degrees, I can't help myself.

"But getting a business degree could be a huge help," I say. "Even if you just went part-time."

Tristan levels me with an icy stare, and I shut my mouth. I glance around and see my friends all studiously trying to pretend they haven't noticed this exchange.

"Hey, did you see Mackenzie Morales's new car? Her dad made her get a *sedan*, and she's next-level pissed," Tamsin says. I glance over, see her cut her eyes away from me, and I beam her a silent thank-you for saving me from myself.

The night continues, and it's fine. Everyone gets along. I mostly forget our tense exchange.

Okay, that's a total lie. It keeps running through my head on repeat until we're walking down the lawn toward Cecilia, and the only thing that interrupts those thoughts is Tristan.

"What was that back there?" he asks.

"What?" I say, as if I don't know exactly what he's talking about. I've been waiting for this shoe to drop all night. Right on my head.

"You playing college counselor again. Why did you bring that up?"

I look down at my shoes and don't say anything. Maybe I'm hoping if I don't answer, it'll go away. And it almost does. But we're halfway home when I realize that it's not that it's going away, it's that Tristan is just going chillingly silent.

"I didn't mean—" I start, but he cuts me off.

"I don't want to talk about it right now."

I know it makes me a coward, but I'm thankful for the momentary reprieve. At least, I thought I was thankful. But three days later, when Tristan has been nothing but radio silent, I'm dying. I've texted, but he hasn't replied. And I'm terrified to call, for fear of having him end things on the phone. We're now on the schedule together for Thursday, so I plan to deal with it then. But it's the old Tristan who shows up at work on Thursday, the one who tries his level best to avoid all human contact—especially with me. At least back then there was some snark, a few dark looks. Now I don't even rate eye contact. Every time I try to get near him, he bolts for the back door like an Olympic sprinter.

Finally, I corner him with half an hour left of shift, just as he's dropping the empty warming bag on the prep table. I practically had to hide behind a trash can to get the drop on him.

"Why won't you talk to me?" I ask.

He stares at me hard, like he wants to keep the silent treatment going, even when directly confronted. But he finally turns toward the back door, beckoning me with his head to follow. Out on the pavement, he turns and looks me straight in the eye.

"Why were you giving me shit about college?" he asks.

"I wasn't giving you shit," I say, already trying to figure out a way to spin it in my head. But Tristan won't let me get away with that.

"You were. I've told you before. I have a plan. I know what I'm doing. And I'm not embarrassed about it. Why are you?"

"I'm not embarrassed!" I say. And that, at least, has the virtue of being true. I think his furniture is beautiful. I've spent the past week stalking his SocialSquare business page all the way to the beginning. I noticed how his likes grew with his skills, and how the comments started to flow in from all over. There were even a few video clips of him working on various pieces, his hair full of sawdust, his eyes focused on his work behind a pair of goggles. He takes his work seriously, and he's seriously good. And watching his passion for it only makes me like him more. And it only made me hate myself more for in any way minimizing it.

"You are! You looked around at your rich friends and thought they were going to judge me for not going to college, which meant they were going to judge you for being with me."

"Tristan, I'm not judging you."

"You're right about that. I spent all week thinking about it, and I finally figured it out. You weren't judging me. You were judging *you*," he says. I feel a prickle start up the back of my neck, like the cold tip of a knife point trailing across my skin. "I like you, Beck, but whatever fake personality you're dragging around is not going to work for me."

I pull back like I've been slapped. "Excuse me? Fake personality? What are you talking about?"

"I'm talking about how you brought me to hang out, but just me. Nobody else. Where's Julianne? Where's Frank? And how come she's still sitting alone in the cafeteria? Why, when Eli said he wanted to come in for pizza, why did you practically pull a muscle trying to tell him not to come? You even pretended you didn't like that sci-fi show you're obsessed with!"

"I'm not obsessed," I say, but the protest is weak. Even I can hear it.

"I heard you talk about it with everyone else. I've seen the way your face lights up when you're talking about ships and plots. I've never seen you more yourself than when you're duking it out with Jason over that show. What's wrong with admitting that?"

"I don't know," I whisper, the words coming out small and ragged. I can't look up from my shoes for fear that the tears that are welling there will spill down my cheeks.

"It's because you're so terrified of being yourself, and you're worried that isn't good enough. So instead, you're playing pretend with this made-up idea of what Beck should be. And the only person who even gives a shit is *you*."

"Stop it."

"*You* stop it. Stop trying to engineer your life. Just fucking live it. Just be *you* instead of who you think everyone else wants you to be."

"I don't know what that means."

He throws up his hands. "Then I can't help you."

The back door cracks, and Joey calls, "Order up." He holds the warming bag out the door, studiously avoiding the scene going on outside.

Tristan takes the bag, scooping it in his arms and heading for Cecilia, parked behind the dumpster.

"You're just going to leave?" I ask.

"I have a delivery," he says, his voice painfully distant. And then he's gone. In seconds, I hear the slam of the car door and the *chugga chugga* of Cecilia leaving the parking lot. I can't bear to look up and watch the taillights disappear, because then I'll be crying in earnest.

Before, I wasn't sure if we were dating. And now I'm not sure if we've just broken up.

I float through the rest of my shift like a zombie, barely remembering to plaster a smile on my face when I greet customers. More than once I tried to give change to people who paid with a debit card, and Del had to comp two orders because I rang them up wrong. I thought that vegetarian lady was going to fully pass out when I delivered a meat supreme to her table.

When closing comes around, I don't even bother to bring anything to the table game. Julianne hands me off to Joey to help him with the closing checklist, a job I've never done before because Joey usually does it himself.

But apparently he needs to leave early, thus his request for backup tonight.

"I'm meeting this guy about new rear sets for my motorcycle. He's over in Middlebury, and the guy refuses to meet me halfway. So let's do this," he says, handing me a clipboard that's splattered with what I suspect may be decades-old marinara.

I read things off the list as he bustles around the kitchen, me checking off each item and making notes where necessary. Joey calls out the temperatures on all the fridges and expiration dates on bags of shredded mozzarella. He covers and stores leftover metal tubs of toppings and replaces the rubber mats on the tile floor after mopping. He makes sure all the faucets are off and checks the ovens. I move through the list in a daze, my mind on Tristan and our conversation. He never came back after his last delivery.

When I get to the last item on the list, I pass the clipboard back to Joey and clock out for the night. Julianne asks if I want to go to Stefano's, but I wave her off. I've got Dad's car tonight, and I want to try to find Tristan. I drive by his house, but Cecilia isn't parked in the driveway. I even drive up to Look Rock, but he's not there. I text Julianne to make sure he didn't go to Stefano's, but she replies with a no and a sad face.

He's a prickly one, but he really likes you. Just wait him
out.

Which is why I'm worried that I really hurt him.
And now I have the added guilt of his accusation about
Julianne. Just as I hoped, she's warmed up to me. That
text proves it. But have I warmed up to her? Or have I
stayed cold?

I drive home boiling in a stew of misery, sadness, and
self-loathing. When I pull into the driveway, it's nearly
midnight, and I haven't heard a word from Tristan. I even
broke down earlier and tried to call him myself, but it just
went straight to voice mail. And, honestly, I was a little
bit relieved, because as I sat there listening to the ringing,
I realized I had no idea what I was going to say to him. I
have no explanation, not when it comes to myself. I think
that's going to take more than a few hours of introspec-
tion.

I'm walking into my house when my phone dings with
an incoming text. I've had my phone clutched in my fist
since I walked out of HnC an hour ago, willing it to ring,
and now that it has, I nearly drop it. But when I flip it over
to look at the illuminated screen, I see it's not Tristan. It's
Julianne.

There's a fire at HNC. It's bad.

"Oh my god!" I cry. My parents, who are in the kitchen sharing a tub of cookies-and-cream ice cream with two spoons, glance up.

"What's wrong?" Mom asks.

"There's a fire at work," I reply, holding up my phone screen so my parents can read it. My mom gasps, her hand going to her mouth. I turn and start for the door.

"Where are you going?" Dad asks.

"I have to go over there."

"I don't think that's a good idea."

"But, Dad!"

"It's a fire, Beck, and if it's as bad as Julianne says, it's not safe. And you'd just end up in the firemen's way. Besides, no one was inside, right?"

I shake my head. "We closed up. Joey usually leaves after us, but he had somewhere to be, so Julianne and I were the last ones out."

"Okay, then everyone is safe. That's the most important thing. You need to just stay here and wait to hear from Del."

But I've stopped listening to my dad, because now a new terror has set up residence in my brain. I was the last one out. I did the closing checklist with Joey, and I was supposed to confirm that the ovens were off. Did I call that out? Did I check the boxes? I rack my brain, but I can't remember. I close my eyes tight and try to picture the moment. I remember for sure seeing it on the list, but I have no memory of actually marking it off. If I didn't say it, Joey might not have checked. They might have stayed on. So did I do it? Or do I just not remember? All that I remember thinking is how worried I was that I'd fucked it up with Tristan. If Tristan was right about me, and I'm really nothing but a giant fraud.

Oh my god, did an oven get left on? Is the fire my fault? *Did I burn down Hot 'N Crusty?*

I open my eyes and see tears rolling down my mom's cheeks. She swipes at them with the heel of her hand.

"I'm sorry. This is so silly, crying over a pizza place. It's just . . . that's where our family started."

"It's probably fine, Jessie," Dad says, putting his arm around her and pulling her into his shoulder. "We're probably all thinking worst-case scenario here, but I'm sure it's not nearly that bad."

Then my parents are both staring at me in horror, and it takes me a few seconds to realize it's because I'm sobbing. Big, heaving, hiccuping sobs with tears streaming down my face

They rush around the counter and both scoop me up in their arms, a parent on either side. I feel my tears soaking into my dad's State U sweatshirt as my mom strokes the back of my head.

"It's okay, Beck. It's just a building," Mom says. "That's all."

But it's not just a building. Mom was right, it's part of my history. A part of me.

"I'm sure it's not that bad," Dad says again as I sob into his shoulder, not sure if I'll ever be able to stop.

CHAPTER
SIXTEEN

But it *was* that bad.

I texted with Julianne late into the night, but I didn't get any good information. The only reason she knew about the fire was because Del called her to make sure we closed up and no one was inside. Julianne reported that he sounded "like hell." We frantically googled Hot 'N Crusty all night, but the news didn't have any information. I finally drifted off close to three in the morning, my mind reeling at the thought of the fire.

And that I still hadn't heard from Tristan.

I'd texted him a bunch, but I couldn't tell if he'd gotten them because his read receipts were off. Which is so very Tristan. His whole persona screams turned-off read receipts. And when I tried to call him again, it went straight to voice mail. I must have heard his gruff voice saying, "This is Tristan, leave me a message," twenty or thirty times before I finally gave up and fell into a fitful sleep filled with dreams of Hot 'N Crusty up in flames. I didn't even know if he'd heard about the fire.

I wake up with a start to the sound of my phone, fumbling with it from its perch on my bedside table. It clatters to the floor, and I dive after it, landing in a pile of limbs and blankets. But it's not Tristan, it's another text from Julianne. I click on it and at first heave a sigh of relief, because it's a photo of Hot 'N Crusty, and it looks fine.

It's not until I zoom in that I see that it's not fine. Not at all. The glass on the front door is busted, as are several of the windows. The ones that aren't are dark with soot. The corner of the roof, right where the kitchen is, is blackened from flames or smoke. My stomach sours as I picture what the inside must look like, and of course my mind goes to the most apocalyptic scenarios imaginable. The register melted, the tiles cracked, all the tables charred with chairs tipped over, their vinyl seats burned away.

I text Julianne for more details, but she says this is as close as she can get. The fire department is still blocking people from even pulling into the parking lot. She's parked at Margaritas across the street. She saw a flash of Del talking to someone official-looking with the fire department, but she hasn't been able to talk to him yet, and he isn't answering his phone.

Downstairs, I pour myself a bowl of cereal, but I can't bring myself to eat a bite. Instead, I sit at the kitchen table and watch the Froot Loops get soft, their rainbow colors bleeding into the milk until the whole thing is a bowl of rainbow mush.

Dad shuffles in, his curly hair pointing at all angles. Mom is an early riser, probably already at the gym, but Dad is committed to what he calls "the weekend lie-in," bedhead and all.

"Any news?" he asks, pulling the box across the table to fill up his bowl.

"Julianne sent this." I hold out my phone. He squints at the grainy photo on the tiny screen.

"It might not be as bad as it looks," he says.

"Or it might be worse."

"The important thing is, nobody got hurt. That *you* didn't get hurt."

But I'm pretty sure that Del is hurt. And Julianne certainly seemed hurt when she was crying on the phone last night. I keep coming back to the realization that *I* feel hurt, too, and not just because the fire is probably my fault. The thought of Hot 'N Crusty being gone, of not clocking in for my next shift, of not cracking jokes with Jason or playing the table game with Julianne and the guys . . . it feels so much worse than I thought it would. When I started this job, all I could think about was how much I wanted Hot 'N Crusty out of my life. But now that it really might be, I feel like I've lost a member of my family. I flash back to my mother's tears last night. Maybe I actually have.

"Where's Mom?" I ask.

"She had some deliveries to make," he says. "A wedding cake and cupcakes for two different birthday parties. Then Michelle Obama arms." He's referring to Mom's commitment to weight lifting. She discovered it last year and is bound and determined to sculpt her biceps to FLOTUS levels.

"Can I borrow the car?" I ask.

"Where are you going?"

"Where do you think?"

Dad sighs, running his hands through his hair, which only makes him look even more like a mad (social) scientist.

"You have only yourself to blame," I tell him. "You raised me like this."

"Fair enough," he says. "But promise me you'll stay

out of the way. I don't want you charging into a danger zone."

"I promise," I tell him.

I hope he can't tell I'm lying.

I drive straight over to Hot 'N Crusty. The fire trucks are gone, but Del's car, an old red BMW that he loves like it's brand-new, is still there. I expect there to be barricades to the parking lot, or maybe crime scene tape, but to my surprise, I'm able to roll right up to the front door. I park and head for the door, now propped open, despite the metal frame being completely empty of glass. I step gingerly inside.

"Del?" I call, and immediately cough. The smell of fire is overpowering at first—way stronger than any firepit Colin has ever stoked—but I get used to it pretty quickly. The dark tile floor is shimmering with a number of puddles left over from what I'm guessing are fire hoses. My eyes burn with tears that I hold in. I force myself to look around, to take it in. It might be the last time I see it.

On instinct, my gaze travels over to the wall where my birthday photos hang, and the framed news stories.

Several of them are now lying cracked on the floor. The ones that remain on the wall are askew, and it looks like water leaked in, the edges curling, the photos wrinkled and blotchy. I have to bite the inside of my cheek hard to keep from crying out at the sight.

It looks like the dining room escaped the flames, though. Mostly it's just wet, which can't be good for the ceiling tiles or light fixtures. The tables are all upright, most of the chairs still upside down on the tabletops, though a few have fallen down and lie askew. The fire looks like it was mostly confined to the kitchen, which causes my stomach to clench. There are scorch marks that shoot out from the frame around the swinging door, which swings open when Del strides through it.

"Beck!" he cries, leaping at the sight of me. "What are you doing? You shouldn't be in here, it's not safe!"

He rushes toward me, his shoes crunching over broken glass and splashing through a big puddle right by the register. He waves me back through the door, stopping next to me on the sidewalk.

"Del, I'm so sorry," I say, and then I can't hold back the tears anymore. They come pouring out of me like someone's turned my emotional faucet on high and hot. Del frowns and steps forward, his arms open, but he stops short of wrapping me in a hug. I collapse against his big barrel chest anyway, crying into his polo, which smells like a campfire.

"It's okay, Beck," he says, patting me gently on the back. "Nobody got hurt."

"But it's my fault," I sob, the words catching in my chest. I didn't plan on confessing, but now it seems like there was no way I'd keep this to myself. Del's done so much for me. I can't lie to him.

"What do you mean?"

I sniffle and step back, swiping at the tears on my cheeks. I can't bring myself to look him in the eye.

"I did the closing checklist with Joey last night," I hiccup, trying to get the words out. "I can't remember if I actually checked all the ovens. I was . . . distracted."

He sighs. "That doesn't mean the fire was your fault. The fire department isn't even sure where it started yet. They suspect it was probably electrical, but, hell, it could have been arson. I know that Stefano's would love to put me out of business." He chuckles at his joke, but it's forced. His eyes look tired and strained, like he's trying to hold back his own tears.

Of course it wasn't arson. Who would want to burn down Hot 'N Crusty? Honestly, the only person I can even think of is me.

"Beck, don't beat yourself up. These things happen. It's just a building. All we can do now is move forward."

Move forward. I latch onto the notion like a touchstone. Suddenly it's all I want in the whole wide world. Like the sooner Hot 'N Crusty is back in action, the sooner my life will be normal again.

"When can you reopen?" I ask.

"Well, I've got to talk to the insurance company first. It's all going to be dependent on what they say. There's a lot of damage to the building *and* the equipment. It's going to be expensive, so I can't do anything until they figure out their end."

He doesn't sound optimistic, which is the most shocking of all of this. Because Del is *always* optimistic. The fact that this has him defeated already scares me. And it makes me sob some more.

"I wish I had more answers, but I think right now we're just going to have to wait."

CHAPTER
SEVENTEEN

My whole life feels like it's in a holding pattern. I spend the weekend wondering if I still have a job. Wondering if I still have Tristan, though that one seems to be increasingly clear. He's still not answering my texts, and my calls continue to go to voice mail.

Come Monday, I watch for him in the cafeteria, right by the back door. And sure enough, here he comes, a carton of milk and a bag of chips in his hand. I step right into his path before he can walk through the door.

"Can we talk?" I ask.

He gives me a look, like maybe he's just going to step

around me without saying a word. Or even plow me right over. But then a moment of something—resignation?—flickers across his face.

"Yeah, let's go outside," he says, and I follow him through the door. I follow him along his route until we end up in the woodshop. I vaguely knew it was here, but I've never been inside. It's empty except for Coach Driskill, who's sitting at his desk in the far corner, his feet up on his desk, headphones in, while he flips through a magazine.

"It's his planning period," Tristan explains. "So what do you want to talk about?"

"Come on, Tristan. I want to talk about the other night."

"You mean when you acted like you were embarrassed by me, and then just ended up embarrassing yourself?"

The words sting. "Yeah. That."

"Okay. So talk."

"I just . . . I'm sorry. You were right, I was way out of line. I knew as the words were coming out of my mouth that it was the wrong thing to say. I don't even agree with it! I think it's awesome that you've got your own business. Your furniture is amazing, and you're going to be wildly successful. There is no universe in which college will change any of that."

"Then why did you say it?"

I sigh. "I don't know. Maybe . . . maybe you were right?"

"Right about what?"

"Right about me being anxious around my friends."

"If your friends make you so anxious, then they're not your friends."

It would be easy to agree with him. It's the logical conclusion, after all. But even now, after everything, it doesn't feel right. They *are* my friends. Natalie's been by my side since forever. Cora is unfailingly encouraging and kind. And even Tamsin, Queen of Snark that she is, showed up for me at a moment's notice. They *are* my friends. Maybe I just haven't been theirs.

As if he can read my mind, he sighs, leaning forward on a workbench, his hands pressing into the wood.

"I just don't want to do this, Beck. I like you, but all this figuring out is exhausting. Can we just go back to the way it was before?"

"You mean when we didn't know each other and all you did was say snarky things to me?"

He cocks a third of a grin. "I'll be, like, fifty percent less snarky this time."

I guess we could do it. We've kissed and then become friends once before. It's not at all what I want, but I don't know how to fight for it. Or how to fix what's broken. I just know that I don't want to lose him, no matter what small piece of him I have.

"Hopefully we can get back to work soon," I say, because I don't know what else to say. "It's weird not being all together in the kitchen."

"Yeah, I wouldn't hold my breath," he says.

"What do you mean?"

"Beck, I need to find another job. I don't make enough money with the business yet to justify going full-time."

"But HnC is going to reopen," I say, but for the first time, saying it out loud doesn't feel completely true.

"Beck, even if they started the remodel tomorrow, it would still be a two-or three-month project. And Del hasn't even started dealing with the insurance. It could be a year before he reopens. I can't afford to sit around waiting. I need a paycheck."

It hadn't occurred to me that he'd find a job. That any-body would have to. Maybe that was me being naive, or even hopeful, but now the idea that we *wouldn't* all be back in the kitchen, that I wouldn't have that end point to fix everything—*everything*—really scares me.

I spend the rest of the day tracking down the others. I find Julianne first, finishing up her lunch period over a book.

"I already put in an application at Margaritas and the Deluxe Diner downtown," she says as she places a folded napkin in her book and slams it shut. "I have to save for college. My scholarship only covers tuition. I've still got to pay room and board and books. Do you know how much college textbooks cost?"

I find Jason next, slumped in front of his locker, poring over his chemistry book. He tells me he's already been accepted to Dartmouth with a full tuition scholarship, so he's not as worried about a job. But apparently Greg's cousin works at the movie theater and is trying to get them both jobs working the snack bar. Frank, of course, applied to the same places that Julianne applied. They've been dating officially since homecoming.

As for me, I start helping Mom with her baking. She officially applied for a business license, and Sweet Jessie's is up and running. She can't really pay me much, but my help is allowing her to take on some bigger catering jobs, and she throws that cash my way.

One Saturday I'm helping her with her second wedding. She was hired to do the cake, plus a whole dessert table and some cocktail snacks (her homemade cheese straws are a huge hit). I'm in a pair of black pants and a black shirt so that I won't show up if I happen to find myself in the background of any wedding photos. I'm helping Mom deliver and set up all the goodies, and then we'll be around for the reception to replenish trays and portion out the cake after the ceremonial cutting. The cake is *gorgeous*, a three-tiered masterpiece with a rustic finish on the frosting and hand-painted pink peonies on the layers. There are boxes and boxes of matching petits fours and sugar cookies, plus some mini gluten-free cupcakes and chocolate macaroons. Mom's acquired her own collection of silver trays and tiered displays from scouring estate and garage sales, and we start artfully arranging everything, with the florist filling in across the table.

"Mom, this looks really amazing," I say. "Make sure you get a picture."

"Ugh, I'm so bad with the social media stuff," she says. "I always forget until after everyone's telling me how good everything tastes, at which point it looks like the table's been attacked by rabid dogs."

I quickly whip out my phone and start snapping photos—wide shots and close-ups of the individual goodies. "There. Done," I say, stowing my phone back in my pocket.

"Excellent," she says. "Now make sure that thing's on silent. I don't want your texts blowing up during the father of the bride's toast."

"Mom, don't say 'blowing up.'"

She rolls her eyes at me, but she's grinning. I miss Hot 'N Crusty, but I am enjoying this time with Mom. It's cool to see her be a big boss lady outside of our house. I always knew she was—Dad says the reason our house isn't a smoldering pile of ashes with us standing hungry in the yard is because Mom is the best. And he's right. I'm just glad that now, other people know it, too.

With everything set up, we head back to the kitchen to wait for word that a tray is getting low or we need to rescue the cake from a drunken groomsman (as happened last weekend at her very first wedding gig—I thought Mom was going to have a straight-up heart attack). I scroll through SocialSquare, double tapping a photo of Tamsin, Cora, and Natalie at a dance competition in Hillsdale. Things are still weird between us, but I'm trying. Maybe liking a photo isn't much, but it's something.

Still, I miss my geek fests with Julianne and the guys, and I open my phone to text and ask when we can all get together. I can't let myself believe that without the actual HnC building, our friendship is toast.

"Petits fours are going like hotcakes," a cater waiter calls into the kitchen. "Time to refill."

"Can you get it, Beck? I need to start laying out the plates for the cake," Mom says, clearing off a giant prep table. Until I started working with her, I had no idea how involved it was to cut and portion out an entire wedding cake, but it's a job that needs to be planned with military-style efficiency. I try my best to stay out of the way and do only as I'm told.

"Yep," I say, shoving my phone back into my pocket. I grab a box of petits fours and head out the door to the dessert table, where I carefully replace everything that's been eaten—which is a lot. I'm just finishing up and closing the empty box when I turn and see a pair of familiar faces at a nearby banquet table. It's hard to miss tall, skinny Bert with the papery skin and tiny, hunched-over Birdie with her cotton ball nest of white, wispy curls.

I'm about to greet them like old friends when I remember that I don't actually know them—I just recognize them from their eating at HnC every week. And because they're the culprits of the great stuffed crust caper. But I doubt they recognize me at all. That is, until Birdie looks up and her face lights up brighter than the spotlights on the dance floor.

"Oh, look, Bert! It's that nice cashier from Hot 'N Crusty!" she says, her voice singsongy. "How are you, dear?"

I amble over, tucking the box under my arm, feeling warmed by their greeting. That they remember me, and that they didn't call me the bathroom baby.

"I'm good," I say. "How are you doing?"

"Oh well, we're just fine, which at our age is pretty durned spectacular." She winks, and I like her immediately. "Of course we're still so heartbroken over the fire! I just can't believe it. Do they know what caused it?"

"They think it was electrical," I reply, thankful Del delivered that news so I could finally sleep at night again. They haven't found the exact cause, but it definitely wasn't because I left an oven on.

"I do hope Del is about to reopen. We so miss our weekly visits. There's no better pizza in town, right, Bert?"

Bert grunts.

"Well, we won't keep you, dear. We just wanted to say hello," she says, patting my arm.

I smile and start to walk away, but then I pause. Because she said something that's niggling at me, and this may be my only chance to find out the answer. So I turn back and stoop down for a little private confab.

"I just have to ask, Birdie . . . What's with the stuffed crust pizza?"

Birdie flushes so red I actually worry for her health. Next to her, Bert wrinkles his nose in a little-boy grin. Something tells me he's the brains behind this operation. Birdie was just the wheelman.

"Well, that's all Bert," she says, confirming my suspicions. "He saw a commercial for Pizza Hut while we were watching Rachel Maddow, and he just had to have it. We tried going there, but that stuff is *awful* and the staff was just *rude*. But he really likes that stuffed crust, so I made him a deal. We can pick up a slice for him, but it has to be *to go*, and then we're going to Hot 'N Crusty. That's our *place*, and you don't mess with a good thing. Which makes it all the more heartbreaking that it's closed, because I don't care what those commercials say, that is *not* pizza over there at the Pizza Hut. It's a salty, over-cheesed mess!"

Bert shrugs, like *hey, the heart wants what the heart wants*, and I can respect that.

"Don't worry, I won't tell," I say, miming a lock and key over my lips.

"Oh, it wouldn't matter, dear. When you get to be as old as dirt, no one says boo to you. But I promise you this, if Hot 'N Crusty reopens, we will *only* eat there from now on! No more contraband pizza for us, you hear me, Bert?"

Bert nods, his loyalty to Hot 'N Crusty—or at least to his wife—trumping his love of the stuffed crust.

I head back into the kitchen just as the bride and groom are lining up to cut into Mom's beautiful cake with what looks like a Napoleonic sword. Mom's got fifty plates already laid out, with two more stacks of fifty on deck. It'll be my job to move plated cake to trays for the cater waiters to distribute, then replace the empty spots with fresh plates until all 150 slices are apportioned. Getting it all done requires you to sort of slip into an efficiency coma, only coming back to yourself when the job is done. And when it is, Mom and I hop up onto the now empty prep table and sigh.

"I met with Del the other day," she says.

"What about?"

"He's helping me with some logistics. I think I found a spot to open up a storefront," she says.

"Wow! Seriously? How did that happen?"

She shrugs. "It's time. I love this, but I can already tell it's getting too big for our kitchen at home. And I *want* it to get bigger."

"I didn't realize you were already at that point, though. Your own bakery? That's huge."

"Well, it's time for me to have a thing. You'll be off to college soon. And let's be honest, you haven't really needed me for a while."

"That's not true, Mom. I always need you." I just haven't been very good about showing it lately.

"I know, but the needs you have now require less of my actual day-to-day time. It's not like when I had to match your socks up for you or cut the crusts off your peanut butter sandwiches. Soon you'll just need me for a phone call or a load of laundry, if I'm lucky. And I'll always be here for you, of course, but I can't just sit around. I need to fill up my days." She brushes away a smear of frosting on her pant leg. "I thought about going back to teaching, but I think I've been out of it too long. And this makes me really happy."

"Well, you're really good at it. I'm pretty sure every petit four you brought is already gone, and I doubt that cake is going to last long, either," I say, and I watch her cheeks bloom under the compliment. "I hope you brought business cards, because I think you just wooed a bunch of new clients with tonight's treats."

She throws an arm around me, pulling me in. "I love you, kid. You're the best, you know that?"

"Well, you raised me like this," I tell her, leaning into the warmth of her hug.

The next day I call Del to check in, and he's finally got some news. And it's not good.

"The insurance company came through with the money that'll cover the building repairs, but I also have to replace all the kitchen equipment. All of it was old, and paid off, so the insurance company didn't offer much. The cost of buying that stuff new is astronomical these days."

"Can't you get a loan?"

"I'm having a hard time with the banks. HnC was profitable when everything was paid off, and I made a decent living. But when you factor in loan payments, it gets more dicey. And in this economy, banks are a little gun-shy about it."

It's the news I'd been dreading, but instead of falling apart, I feel oddly calm. I can fix this. I have to fix this. Hot 'N Crusty cannot close on my watch. It existed before me, and I need it to exist long after.

"Is there anything I can do to help?" I ask.

"Unless you've got an in with a loan officer, I think you'll just have to cross your fingers, Beck."

But that doesn't seem like a good enough strategy.

"I just can't believe Hot 'N Crusty would actually close for good. It's an institution!"

"Julianne was saying something about trying to get a show of community support, but I don't think that kind of thing holds much water with banks these days. We're not dealing with the Savings and Loan. Letters of recommendation don't go very far."

When I hang up, something Del said sticks in my mind. *A show of community support.* Like how Bert and Birdie are missing their weekly pizza night? And I'm missing all my friends? There's got to be more like us out there. Hot 'N Crusty was hardly a five-star restaurant, but we had our regulars who I'm sure miss us. All those houses Tristan would deliver to. Like Birdie said, Pizza Hut is no substitute. No, Del isn't George Bailey, and communities are a little different now, anyway. But I might know how to harness the power of this one.

I fumble around my room, finding a torn-off cover of a phone book with Ken Lunn's face on it, a donation to continue the Wall of Justice. And then, at the bottom of a pile, is the business card. I meant to throw it away, but it ended up on my desk in a pile of discarded receipts and scraps of paper that my mother is always pleading with me to *please for the love of god just throw it in the trash can, Beck, it's right there.* It's crumpled, but I can still read everything on it, including the email address.

CHAPTER
EIGHTEEN

Molly Landau didn't answer, so I had to leave a message. I have absolutely no idea what I said. I think it was mostly a rambling mess, but I must have gotten the point across, because it took her under three minutes to call me back. She seemed afraid I was going to change my mind, because by the end of our conversation, she'd bumped a segment on a local corgi race so that I could sit for the interview the very next night.

My next call was harder to make.

It's an hour and a half before I have to be at the studio when the doorbell rings. I bolt from my room and practically clothesline my dad to get to the door. "It's for me!"

I cry as I fling open the door. And there stands my glam squad, Natalie carrying a tote bag, Cora brandishing her tackle box, and Tamsin with a garment bag slung over her shoulder.

"Let's do this," Tamsin says, rushing past me toward my bedroom, Cora hot on her heels. Natalie pauses, though, still on the floral welcome mat that's been in front of my house my entire life. It's so old that the L has started to wear away, and now it just reads WE COME.

"Natalie, I'm so sorry," I say. "I've been a shitty friend."

"No, you haven't," Natalie says.

"I have. I haven't been myself, and I acted like that was everyone else's problem. And I ended up shutting you out because of it." As I say the words, I send out a silent thank-you to Tristan, because even though it hurt to be called on it, I think without knowing what I needed to say to Natalie, it really would have been the end of our friendship. And it might still be, if I've waited too long to fix the damage I caused.

"Beck, I just want you to be happy. And I didn't understand why you weren't."

"I don't think I did, either," I say. "But I do now. And I want to fix it. And most of all, I don't want to lose you. You're my best friend, Nat."

"Are you sure? Because I felt like I was doing all the

heavy lifting. I got tired of always having to be the one to call and make the plans."

"I know. I'm sorry. I'm going to stop just letting things happen to me, okay? I'm going to run this show from now on," I say, pointing two thumbs at myself. I'm done taking the path of least resistance. I'm done being the girl with no plan, just a label. It's time to take control, even if it means owning that label completely.

Natalie stands there, nudging at the newly fading C on the welcome mat. She hoists the tote bag up on her shoulder and sighs. "I hope so," she says, finally looking up. My words may have started the process, but I can tell I have a long way to go before we're actually back where we were—if we can ever get there. "I just thought you were so mad at me, and I didn't know why."

"I think I was mad at myself," I tell her.

"Well, cut that shit out," she says, looking back at her shoes. "That's my best friend you're talking about. You need to treat her nice."

She says it grudgingly, but it's a start. And I grin in spite of myself. She finally steps through the door. "Okay, well, let's go make you turned up to eleven, shall we?"

It's weird to be on the other side of the curling iron being fussed over, but I can see why it made Julianne so happy. As Cora gently brushes shimmer onto my eyelids and curls my lashes with what looks like a medieval torture device, she coos and tells me how gorgeous my cheekbones are. I try to pay attention to what she's doing, but I lose the plot sometime around the eyeliner, which she draws into a tiny wing. Natalie skips the straightener on my already stick-straight hair, and instead pulls out a salt spray and a curling wand, shaping my hair into pretty, gentle waves. And Tamsin dives into my closet before declaring my wardrobe a lost cause, instead pairing my own dark denim jeans with an emerald green V-neck with a little knot detail at the point of the V.

"Jewel tones look *great* on TV," she assures me.

"It's a *smidge* heavier than I'd normally do, but you'll be under bright lights, so I didn't want to screw around," Cora says, presenting me with a hand mirror. And when I glimpse my reflection, I see that, yeah, the eyeliner is dark, and the blush is a bit bright, but I still look like me. She didn't doll me up or turn me into a *Vogue* model. It's still me . . . just an amplified version.

Beck Brix, who loves *Apex Galaxy* and has never *ever* won the table game.

Beck Brix, who loves her friends, even if she doesn't always understand them.

Beck Brix, who was born on the bathroom floor of Hot 'N Crusty pizza.

"Thanks, you guys," I say, the words sounding watery in my throat.

"Don't you *dare* cry," Cora says, fanning her own face to beat back the tears. "I used waterproof everything, but that's still no guarantee."

"Okay, so let's skip the tears and just say this," Tamsin says, snapping the lid on Cora's tackle box. "Beck, we love you. And we're here for *whatever* you need, glam or otherwise. So stop acting like that's not true, okay?"

I glance over at Natalie, who nods and finally gives me a big smile. Leave it to Tamsin to finally broker the peace. I suck in a breath and nod, too, afraid of my voice and the tears that are welling in my eyes.

"Now get to that studio and show Molly Landau that you're just as much of a boss bitch as she is."

I nod again, and they file out of my room. I emerge into the living room, where my parents are waiting to drive me over to WCVB.

"Oh, Beck, you look beautiful!" Mom says. "I mean, you always look beautiful, but today you look TV beautiful."

"Well done, ladies," Dad says, nodding at Natalie, Tamsin, and Cora.

"Thank you, thank you," Tamsin says, dropping into a deep ballerina curtsy.

"Get up, you dork," Cora says, still sniffling.

"We should get going," Mom says, her voice suddenly wavering, too, and my god, I'm going to be in pieces before we even get in the car.

"Go save Hot 'N Crusty, Beck," Natalie says, stepping forward to wrap me in a final hug.

"Seriously, I *love* those garlic knots," Tamsin says, making me let out a much-needed laugh.

I tried to get Molly to pretape the interview, but she swore up and down that it would be better—and fine, *just fine*—to do it live. But as I sit in a gray armchair that is way less comfortable than it looks, an assistant clipping a microphone to Tamsin's shirt, I can't help thinking that nothing about this is fine.

In sixteen years of being the Hot 'N Crusty bathroom baby, I've *never* spoken on camera. That is, unless you count my righteous shrieking as a newborn. And with the lights bearing down on me, Molly sitting across from me getting brushed with all manner of things by a professional makeup artist (who took one look at me and nodded in approval—*well done, Cora*), I'm remembering why I made that policy to begin with.

"Okay, just like we talked about, there will be a short video package that'll play first, then they'll throw to us here in the studio. Just be yourself, and be honest. If you do those two things, you'll be just fine," Molly says, and for the first time I think she's being sincere. There's no polish, no shellac on her as she gives me that advice. She's really trying to help me.

The only problem is "myself" and "honest" are two things I haven't been very good at being lately. In fact, sitting here ready to talk to however many people watch the nightly news will be my first attempt at rectifying that.

"Are you ready?" she asks as everyone clears the stage and takes positions behind the massive cameras pointing at us.

"I think so," I say. My fingers tell a different story as they tap out a syncopated rhythm on the chair.

"Deep breath," she says, inhaling and gesturing me to do the same. I do, thinking of Tristan as I consciously pull my shoulders out of my ears, my tongue out of the roof of my mouth. *Unclench.* We blow out our breath together. We do it twice more, and I find my fingers settling, my heart pounding a little more gently. Then she hits me with a sweet smile, and I honestly cannot tell if it's fake or not. "You're going to be great."

Damn. Molly Landau is *good*.

And then my thoughts are swept away as the anchor at the desk across the studio launches into the intro, reminding everyone of my humble beginnings and promising a check-in. I watch on a monitor as bits from my original story appear under Molly's crisp, bright narration. I watch Del, slightly slimmer and with a whole lot less gray in his hair, talking excitedly about my birth, then presenting my parents with a comically large check (which they still have in the garage) promising them free pizza for life. There's an array of photos from my birthdays over the years. And then the camera cuts to a shot of Hot 'N Crusty, wet and smoldering shortly after the fire. Molly's voice gets serious as she talks about the destruction and the high cost of repairs. And there's Del again—Del *now*, gray hair and all—talking about the enormous expense of reopening, and how he's not sure if he's going to be able to secure a loan.

And then the monitor blinks out, and Molly takes a breath in. It's the reminder I need to smile and sit up straight.

It's time.

"Beck, thank you so much for being here today," she says.

"Thank you for having me," I reply.

"How does it feel to see those images of Hot 'N Crusty?" she asks, going straight for the kill. Which I guess she has to. This isn't *Oprah*; we don't have all night. There are at least a few people at home watching who want to hurry up and get to the sports highlights.

"It hurts," I tell her, the truth of it settling on my shoulders. "When my mom heard the news, she started crying. Because Hot 'N Crusty is where our family started. And since I started working there a few months ago, it's become a whole new family for me, too."

"So if the restaurant were to close, that would be devastating for you," she says. Not a question. More of a signal.

"It would. And I don't think I'm alone in that. We have so many regulars for whom coming to Hot 'N Crusty for pizza is a part of their lives. They've watched their kids grow up and go off to college there, had first dates and first loves. Del says more than one couple has gotten engaged there. Hot 'N Crusty is part of our community, and losing it would be devastating for *everyone*."

"Have you thought about what might be able to help Hot 'N Crusty survive?"

"Of course, but I'm only sixteen. How many bake sales can one girl hold? Although I do think we'd bring in a pretty penny with my mom's cakes from Sweet Jessie's," I add as Molly winks at me, because yeah, I just hustled for my mom on live television. "What Hot 'N Crusty really needs is an investment from the community. No, it's not some hot new start-up, but it has serious value, and we need someone to take a chance on that. Which is why I'm starting a FundUs campaign. You can donate any amount to help Del rebuild and reopen. We can help save this beloved institution."

Okay, maybe I'm laying it on a little thick. I don't think anyone has ever referred to Hot 'N Crusty as "beloved," except maybe Del. And if you'd have told me a few months ago that I would be sitting on live television calling it that, I would have tried to slap some sense into you. But I've got to pull out all the stops. I looked up how much a single pizza oven costs, and let's just say my dad is currently driving around in one.

And now it's time to go in for the kill.

"I had a customer once ask me how my unusual birth affected me," I say, putting a charitable spin on selfie-lady. "I'll be honest, for a long time I wanted to hide from it. I just wanted to be me, Beck Brix, not the Hot 'N Crusty Bathroom Baby. But then I realized that I can be all those things. That maybe being born in that bathroom stall was the best thing that ever happened to me. It brought me a whole other family, a second home—one that I don't want to lose."

I look into the camera, feeling the first tear crest my cheek. "It took losing it to realize just how much I cared about it," I say, and my mind flashes to Tristan, hoping he's watching. Despite saying we'd be friends, without Hot 'N Crusty, it hasn't meant much. Except now he gives me a smile and a nod as he breezes through the cafeteria. But I miss him. I miss Cecilia, and I miss listening to the Beatles with him even if I don't love them as much as he does. I even miss his snark. But if I can't have him, at least I can show him that he helped me find myself. And for that, I'll always be grateful. So I clear my throat and try for a smile. "And if you care about Hot 'N Crusty, too, then please donate. Every little bit helps."

Molly smiles and looks into the camera. "If you'd like to contribute to the FundUs campaign, you'll find the link to Beck's fund-raiser on our website," she says, then turns back to me. "Beck, it was wonderful to have you here. We wish you the best."

"Thank you, Molly."

And then the lights dim and the anchor starts chattering on about football scores before throwing to commercial.

I did it.

It's done.

My parents rush out from behind the cameras. I'd been so wrapped up in the interview that I forgot they were there. My dad is blinking hard and keeps clearing his throat, but my mom is just full-on crying, tears and mascara streaming down her cheeks.

"I'm so proud of you, Beck," she says, her voice muffled by my hair as she pulls me into a hug.

"You done good, kid," Dad says, wrapping his arms around both of us.

I sure hope so.

CHAPTER
NINETEEN

Unfortunately, my interview with WCVB isn't the end of my publicity tour. As I'd hoped, the video picked up some minor viral steam, and I end up doing a few radio interviews and a feature in the newspaper. Larry from the local paper even gets me to stand in the stall where I was born for a photo, which I have never *ever* in my life wanted to do. But at this point I'd reenact the whole thing if it meant helping Del.

And it does.

Because from the moment the interview aired, donations started rolling in. A lot of people gave small amounts, around twenty-five or fifty dollars. But a few gave a lot. Mac's dad contributed five thousand dollars from the dealership in exchange for a plaque by the door. An anonymous donor pledged ten thousand, which is absolutely bananas. And the more publicity we did, the more money that came in.

Two weeks later, Del shows up at our house as I'm icing a dozen stork cookies for a baby shower Mom's doing the next day.

"A guy from the credit union called," he says as he sits down on the couch, a plate of Peanut Blossoms my mom baked on the coffee table in front of him. "They're going to cover a loan for whatever the insurance won't cover, and the interest rate is incredible."

"Del, that's wonderful!" Mom cries—literally cries, which she's been doing a lot lately. But then again, so have I. It must run in the family.

"Beck, I don't know how to thank you."

"It was nothing, Del," I say.

"It wasn't nothing. I know you turned Molly down for interviews all those years."

I blink at him, my mouth agape. "How did you know that?"

"Because she always called me asking if I could intervene and try to convince you."

"But you never said anything to me about it," I say.

He shifts on the couch, looking down at his shoes. "No, I didn't."

"Why not?"

"Because I respect your decision. You're not our mascot," he says, and my eyes widen at the words, which seems to make him a little bit sad. "Beck, I appreciate you doing the annual birthday photo at Hot 'N Crusty every year, but if you ever said to me that you didn't want to do it anymore, ever came in and asked me to take down all the pictures and the news clippings and never mention your name again, I'd do it. Like you said in the interview, Beck—we're like family. And family doesn't put each other in positions that make them uncomfortable."

I feel like all the air has been sucked out of me. I spent so long hiding, from my friends and my parents and myself. I spent so long convinced everyone else was the villain, that I had to be someone else to shut it all down. But Del has seen me all along. He knew.

"So what happens now?" I ask, because if I don't change the subject, I really will blubber all over my lap.

"Well, I'm going to the bank tomorrow to sign all the paperwork. The insurance company has already sent the check, and the contractor is ready to go, so it looks like construction will start first thing tomorrow morning."

"So it's real? Hot 'N Crusty is really reopening?"

"It sure is. And I hope you know that there will be a job waiting for you there. If you want it, of course."

"I definitely do," I say, glancing over at my mom. "No offense."

"Oh, none taken. I think it's about time I hired a professional assistant anyway," she says. "I'm going to need a staff at the new place."

"You signed a lease?" Del asks, his eyes perking up.

"I sure did," she replies, the joy bursting out of her. "Downtown next to that salon."

"That's a great location!"

"Thank you so much for your help, Del."

I see a blush creep into his cheeks, running into his bushy mustache. "Well, I'd sure love Hot 'N Crusty to be your first customer. I think your brownies would be a great addition to our menu."

Construction is both ridiculously slow and incredibly fast. Slow, because I want it done yesterday, and fast because the fact that they can put the wreck of that building back together at all is shocking to me. But Del found a committed and enthusiastic contractor who had his crew working long hours, and the whole project was done in a matter of weeks. It was as unheard of as the donations that continued to roll in. The crew gutted the place practically down to the studs: new walls, new roof, new floor, brand-new kitchen. And by the beginning of Thanksgiving break, the new ovens are being delivered. Del set the grand reopening for the first week in December, but on Thanksgiving Eve, when we're all still giddy from the half day and the impending long holiday weekend, Del invites us for a friends-and-family soft opening. He's made all the pizzas and garlic knots and some actually gorgeous salads. And Mom has supplied an enormous cake with the (still very unfortunate) Hot 'N Crusty logo across the top and an OPEN FOR BUSINESS! sign underneath.

I walk into the new space giddy, both for the reopening and for seeing my friends. All of them. Because Del let me make the guest list, and I included a few extras. Let's just say I expanded the Hot 'N Crusty family a little bit.

And everyone comes. Greg quit his job at the movie theater, which paid terribly and never let him see the movies for free, a fact that he's still salty about and currently grumbling to Eli about.

"The smell of burnt popcorn is worse than the smell from cleaning the bathrooms here," he says, and Eli grimaces, since I don't think he's ever cleaned a bathroom a day in his life.

"I'll remember that the next time we're handing out jobs," I say.

"Like you ever handed out jobs," Jason says. "You *never* won the table game."

"What's the table game?" Colin asks, and Jason is more than happy to school him on the finer points of the rules while Julianne begins recounting some of the more colorful finds. Julianne quit her job at the diner as soon as Del called and offered to make her assistant manager. Which will work out great, since she'll be at the college this fall—a short commute with a good paycheck. And since Julianne is back, of course Frank followed.

And Jason? Well, he never got another job. He'll be leaving at the end of the summer for Dartmouth, but that's still a solid eight months of his dominating the table game and annoying everyone else.

I'm cutting the crust off a slice of pizza when the new bell on the door jingles. My gaze darts up, hoping for a familiar face, and I get one. Just not the one I was expecting.

Molly Landau strides in. She's wearing jeans, which I'm shocked to find out she even owns, and her hair is pulled up in a casual knot at the back of her head. I don't even think she's wearing mascara.

"Molly! I made the Mediterranean you love," Del booms, pulling out a chair. And she smiles—a genuine smile, not one for TV—and comes over. But before she drops into the chair, she leans over and plants a delicate peck on Del's lips. He blushes red, and then she sits beside him as he begins fussing over her plate.

I look over at the rest of the Hot 'N Crusty gang for confirmation that I didn't imagine that, and I see that they're all as shocked as I am.

"What in the sixth galaxy of the Luna Universe is that?" Frank asks.

"I'm sorry, did that just happen? Did Del just kiss a local celebrity? Like, with her *permission*?" Jason croaks.

"Oh, they've been dating for a couple of weeks now. Ever since she interviewed him for the package," Julianne says. The heads of the entire HnC crew swivel toward her, and she grins like she did that first night right before she pulled out the stuffed crust pizza. She's been keeping this one a secret for maximum effect.

"You didn't tell me?" Frank squeaks.

"Isn't it better as a surprise?" she asks, gesturing toward the new couple. Del has his arm around Molly. It looks like he's telling one of his abominable jokes, and she's actually *laughing*. I couldn't be more shocked if she sprouted wings and flew around the restaurant.

"I told you, Del just needed a strong woman," Lena says. She's nursing a Coke with a textbook in her lap. Her finals are the week after Thanksgiving, and Del is already planning her graduation and going-away party at the restaurant.

"And I guess Molly just needed a big cuddly dork to tell her knock-knock jokes so she could relax," Greg says with a shrug.

The whole gang's here, old and new. Well, almost. There's just one person I'm not sure about.

The bell jingles again, and there he is. I realize I've never seen Tristan come in through the front door before. He's wearing his denim jacket, his Hot 'N Crusty baseball cap actually on his head, curly hair poking out everywhere.

"Hey, man! Good to see you," Mac says, jumping up from where he's cuddled up next to Tamsin in front of a plate of garlic knots.

"You, too," Tristan says, and actually takes Mac's hand for one of those handshake-slap situations. Their friendly greeting is almost as much of a surprise as Molly and Del's kiss, but it feels worse, because it just serves to remind me that I haven't really talked to Tristan in weeks. I have no idea what's going on in his life. I guess we really did go back to the way things were before, where Tristan is a mystery to me.

But now here we are in the same room. From his SocialSquare page, I know he's been busy with orders. There's a couple of chairs and a beautiful custom dining table that he's added over the last month and a half. We've exchanged waves as he passed through the cafeteria, but that's it.

He ambles over to where I'm filling my cup at the shiny new soda dispenser, his hands deep in his pockets.

"Hey," he says.

"Hey," I reply.

And then we're in some kind of weird soda standoff, with Tristan staring at his shoes, me holding a quickly sweating cup of Coke.

"I've missed you," I say, the words tumbling out before I can slow them down.

He glances up from beneath the brim of his cap, a quirk of a smile on his lips. "Oh yeah?"

"Yeah," I say, trying to match his cool grin and failing *miserably*. Tristan always has seemed to have X-ray glasses for my personality. I couldn't hide anything from him. "You were right, by the way."

"I mean, about a lot of things, I'm sure. But what's this one?" he asks.

I roll my eyes at that trademark snark that I've missed so much. "I needed to figure myself out," I say.

"And did you?"

I pull open my cardigan to show off my T-shirt, a vintage *Apex Galaxy* tee depicting the ship from the original series. Dad gave it to me as a congratulatory gift after my TV triumph.

"Going full geek, I see," he says with an appraising nod.

I stick out my hand. "Beck Brix, Hot 'N Crusty Bathroom Baby, at your service," I say. He takes my hand, his warm and calloused, and gives it a shake.

"Nice to meet you, Beck Brix," he says.

"Also, there's one other thing you should know," I say, my heart pounding.

"Oh?" He cocks an eyebrow at me.

"The Beatles are *good*," I start, and he groans.

"I don't think I want to hear this," he says, covering his face with his hands.

"Look, I like the Beatles. Saying you don't like them is like saying you're not into puppies or chocolate or bacon. Everyone likes puppies and chocolate and bacon—"

"Except vegetarians," he says.

"I think even vegetarians like bacon, they just make the sacrifice for their beliefs."

"Fair."

"Anyway, what I'm saying is, I like the Beatles fine, but I think I'm more of a Motown girl."

A wide grin stretches across his face, then he reaches out and snakes an arm around my waist, pulling me in close. "I can work with that," he says, his minty breath tickling my nose. Then he tilts my chin up and brushes my lips with his.

"Oh thank god, *finally*," Greg shouts, and I hear Tamsin's squeal rise above the outbreak of applause, with some whistles joined in. Julianne *woo-hoo*s along with Frank. I hear my dad clearing his throat, his chair shifting around, and my mom laughs. And as much as I want to climb Tristan like a tree and kiss him until the sun rises, I'm not about to do it in front of my parents. *Gross.*

Still, I can't resist one more. And so as I inhale the smell of garlic and marinara, and my feet stick to the brand-spankin'-new floor (what is that?), I lean in and kiss him again.

ACKNOWLEDGMENTS

Thank you to Jackson Pearce, who sat in Jeni's Ice Cream with me and listened while I said, "I have this idea, but I don't know what to do with it." This book wouldn't exist without you. And thank you to Jeni's for making the best ice cream on the planet and being okay with two writers parking at your tables for hours talking about plots and characters.

I was incredibly lucky to have two champions working on this book. Thank you to Joy Peskin for the most encouraging phone calls that always get me back on track, and thank you to Trisha de Guzman for your sharp and thoughtful editorial eye. This book and I are so very lucky to have you both! Thank you to Cassie Gonzales and Agustina Gastaldi for the incredible cover. Thank you also to Starr Baer, Celeste Cass, Patricia McHugh, Hayley Jozwiak, Beth Clark, and the rest of the FSG fam.

Thank you to Stephen Barbara for keeping me sane and selling my books. You're the best agent ever. I love that whenever I come to you with new stuff, your answer is always, "Let's do this."

Thank you to Little Shop of Stories for always supporting my books and to Vania Stoyanova and the Not So YA Book Club for being, well, awesome. My book club can beat up your book club. Thank you also to The Mamas Book Club in Macon for reading my book one month, then inviting me to join the next! I love all my glorious book nerds. Thank you to the Cooler Moms. You ladies help me raise my children and lower my blood pressure, all while cheering me on. Your support means the world.

Thank you to my family for buying my books and gifting my books and telling *other* people to buy my books. Thank you to Freddie and Leo for learning to navigate Netflix on the iPad all by yourselves so Mama can get work done. And thanks to Adam for believing in me and giving me space to write. I love you I love you I love you.